By Jan Novak

THE WILLYS DREAM KIT

THE GRAND LIFE A NOVEL

by JAN NOVAK

POSEIDON PRESS
New York · London · Toronto · Sydney · Tokyo

This book is a work of fiction. Names, characters, places and incidents are either the product of the author's imagination or are used fictitiously. Any resemblance to actual events or locales or persons, living or dead, is entirely coincidental.

Published by Poseidon Press
A Division of Simon & Schuster, Inc.
Simon & Schuster Building
Rockefeller Center
1230 Avenue of the Americas
New York, NY 10020

POSEIDON PRESS is a registered trademark of Simon & Schuster, Inc.

Designed by Irving Perkins Associates
Manufactured in the United States of America

10   9   8   7   6   5   4   3   2   1

Library of Congress Cataloging-in-Publication Data
Novak, Jan, date.
  The grand life.

  I. Title.
PS3564.089G7 1987   813'.54   87-15165
ISBN 0-671-64354-1

Permission to reprint the following lyrics is gratefully acknowledged:
"Feel Like Making Love" by Eugene McDaniels, © 1974 by Skyforest Music Co., Inc. All rights reserved.

TO
ZDENA

THE GRAND LIFE

S. Q. CIGAR-STORE INDIAN

George Clifton ran a data-processing office of a large utility company in Chicago, where he got hired fresh out of the navy as a customer representative. He knew he had a job for life. He took the homicidal public on the chin for eleven years, ate his pile of aspirin, and the company rewarded him by kicking him upstairs. He was promoted to a first-level in computer operations. For the next eight years George held the fort, pushed the paper through, kept his desk clean, and spared his boss all surprises. When the Crusade of Mercy rolled around, George wrung fair share out of his troops, so that his fearless leaders got to see their big-picture mugs in the papers. He unloaded a lot of U.S. savings bonds that never reached maturity. He swallowed his pride and made sure that no users beefed about him to his boss. He made second-level in record time, and they put him in charge of a computer room.

After he became a deuce and got his modest empire, George made chamomile tea in his office and read his *Newsweek*. On occasion he had to listen. His first-levels would come in from the trenches of the computer room and ask for his help; they needed a deuce's leverage in dealing with their clerks or the union or other departments. They thought that it took a deuce to talk to a deuce.

They were wrong.

George put on a grim face and listened to the pleas of his young subordinates. Then he sucked on his teeth.

—Don't pass the buck, he said. You call the deuce of the department you're up to your ass in alligators with and you resolve this with him. Never mind the disadvantage and never mind the protocol. If you got a point, you got a point. And listen, keep me posted, okay?

George's first-levels learned fast, and they stopped taking their

problems to him. From then on George had it made, though there
still were the meetings a deuce had to go to.

George's strategy in meetings was to sit and smile. When
planning groups attempted to add a new computer to his operation,
George asked hard questions: Who's going to be the project
manager on this? We're just operations. Who do we turn to with
problems? Who's responsible? Who's going to load the generic?
We don't have the know-how. We just operate is all.

The corporate dynamos in George's meetings also learned fairly
quickly. Soon nothing was asked of Clifton or his empire. On
those rare occasions when some frustrated innovator or some
company-minded boy scout pressed George for his treated computer space anyway, George started firing off even harder questions:
What's your responsibility code? I'll have to add bookoo bodies, so
we're talking bookoo bucks. Give me your job-function and
responsibility codes and we're in business.

All the innovators, young Turks, guided missiles, and empire
builders in George's meetings would back off then and learn.
George was a great teacher, and over the years of his deucedom it
became understood that George was invited into meetings only for
scope and ambience. So George did not have to drag himself to so
many meetings anymore; when he strode into a conference room
he was suffered to sign the attendance sheet, sit, and smile.

But even as a meeting decoration George did not punch holes in
the memories of his fellow corporate dynamos. He looked handsome enough—he was six two and slim, had large kidney eyes,
wide cheekbones, and a full top of thick chestnut hair. His hair
was always meticulously combed, his smiling face smoothly
shaven, but he still dressed like front-line management. While
other deuces wore moderately priced three-piece suits, George
stuck to his dark, sharply creased polyester slacks, his light Sears
shirts, and his plastic-looking ties that never slipped their Windsor
knots. His trademark was a thick diver's watch. It showed the
barometric pressure and indicated where the North Pole was, and
it made a weather buff out of George: there were meetings where
he would check seven or eight times what the atmosphere was up
to, though the damn thing never changed enough to make

company time exciting. George never allowed himself any other diversions, never brought Styrofoam cups of coffee into meetings, didn't need ashtrays, hardly ever took notes. Nobody solicited his opinion. He volunteered none. He smiled. He looked at his watch discreetly. They sent him the minutes, and he filed them away in a cabinet and then went back to his *Newsweek*.

In the five years that George deuced around meetings he had only one unpleasant run-in. It featured Fred Foss, a fat slob, a cigar chomper, the only district man in the utility company who did not wear a tie. (Somehow Fred Foss made third-level even though he flouted protocol. This large fat man was suffered to wear a short-sleeved shirt, open at the massive neck, even in big-picture meetings: oh, Freddie Foss, they said, he's a real character, isn't he?)

Fred Foss always behaved like the antithesis of George Clifton, and George had hated his guts even before their incident, though he kept smiling at him same as at everybody else. Fred would show up late, storm into the conference room, his hands full of coffee cups, newspapers, and notepads, kick the door closed behind him, dump his load on the table, plop down on a chair, light up a fat cigar, grab someone's ashtray, grunting like a stuck pig as he leaned forward to pull it toward him, and then he would spear his piggy eyes into the speaker. The speaker's face would flush. You felt sorry for both the speaker and the chair because you knew what was coming: Fat Fred would soon cut off the presentation with a question. And his were good, hard commonsensical questions that terrified people: Which other vendors have you considered for the project? Do these jokers provide training in their package? No? So how much will the company have to fork over additional? So what else has been overlooked?

Everyone in the utility company agreed that it was good to have Fat Fred on your side in a meeting. Fat Fred usually came up with good guesses about costs. The son of a bitch was three hundred pounds of memory. With unfailing precision he could recall figures that had been laid out hours before, while the empire builder who had rattled them off scurried through his papers to check them again.

One day Fat Fred got impatient with a group of planners squeezing bits and pieces of treated computer space out of various departments for a new generation of word-processing minis. He sighed deeply, the speaker halted in mid-sentence, Fat Fred stabbed the ashtray with his cigar and turned to George.

—George, correct me if I'm wrong, but you've got all that space right there in one chunk, right?

George's heart took off like a fat pigeon, going straight up.

—Well, yes and no, he stammered, but—

He was about to pose one helluva question when Fat Fred had had enough of this full-haired, keep-smiling, do-nothing skeleton.

—No more "buts," George, do me a friggin' favor. I've been going to meetings with you for years, and all you ever do is sit there like a cigar-store Indian or else "but" people to death. You got the damn space. You got the bodies in place. So how about a little can-do for once in your illustrious career, George, huh?

All the eyes were squarely on George. He felt his cheeks light up. He didn't know what to say. He mumbled something about his room being slotted for expansion of his own minis.

—Gimme a break, George! Expansion of them dinosaurs you got? Fat Fred shot back. You tell that to the cleaning ladies, all right? He'll take it.

And all George could do was to shrug his shoulders and wait for the meeting to wind up. Then he staggered out to wash his face in the washroom. His pulse was sky-high. He felt as though someone had been watching him through a two-way mirror as he sat around his office, read, and made his chamomile tea. He had never had any idea that the fat slob knew so much about his quiet little empire—its obsolescence, its plots of unused space, the night shift snoozing in the lounge for a few hours every night. He splashed cold water on his face, wanting to gut the fat pig, to stick a gun in his briefcase and snap the next time Fat Fred said a word to him, whip it out, start pumping bullets through all that fat. Or get an Uzi and mow down all those meeting-happy bastards while he was at it. But instead he would have to smile at Fat Fred again and again. It made him sick.

In time the cold water went to work and George calmed down. But the nickname stuck. His first-levels were already calling him George S. Q. Clifton. "S. Q." stood for "status quo." And now he was George Cigar-store Indian Clifton to middle management.

George S. Q. Cigar-store Indian Clifton.

Good thing that no one in the utility company knew about his Mussolini epaulet.

CORPORATE DYNAMOS

Fat Fred was a big man. He smoked a big cigar, drove a big car, thought big, paid big bills, had a big mortgage and a young wife. Fred Foss had more kids than neckties. He had two little boys with his young wife, whom he had met in a utility-company meeting. There were also three daughters from his previous marriage. Fred's young wife loved him in a big way, and they had a big house with an oceanic yard. It was there that the fourth dimension came through loud and clear, there that George Clifton, after a big meal, would vomit all over the rose bushes and tomato plants.

George Clifton lived in a modest bungalow. He thought small, had a small mortgage, a small lawn, and no credit-card bills at all. George had no kids. His body was slim, and he carefully maintained it that way. He did sit-ups at night and he rode an old, heavy bicycle to his commuter train station. His wife was younger than he was, but she was the one and only lover of his life.

Fred Foss's life had a different scope from George Clifton's. His inner person was huge and boisterous. George's inner person was tiny and shell-shocked. The two corporate dynamos had one thing in common: their careers had plateaued on them. They had gone as far as they were going to go in the utilities.

Fred was district and George was a deuce, but neither of them was big-picture. Big-picture was a matter of style not substance. You had to dress and talk and pause and nod big-picture to rise higher in the corporation. Fat Fred had a lot of utility substance. He knew the company from top to bottom. He kept tabs on which deuces ran tight ships. He regularly stitched together better arguments than his fearless leaders, and his ideas often carried the day. But he wore no ties, smoked cigars in the meetings, spoke out of turn. He was fat, and when the coffee cart arrived, he pinched the doughnuts through their cellophane wrappers.

George looked anorectic enough to make the big picture, but he had little else to offer. He never had anything to say. This was big-picture-compatible, but George refused to open his mouth and put it in words. And he was too cheap in the way he dressed and carried himself.

Both George and Fred had come up through the ranks and they were corpo lifers. They had had no college, though Fat Fred wrote a mean memo. The corporate dynamos Foss and Clifton were staying put unless they blew themselves out of the water somehow. This was highly unlikely, but in time George would manage to beat the odds.

MUSSOLINI

The seminal experience of George Clifton's life took place on a muggy summer morning in Newport, Rhode Island, shortly after the Korean War. George had joined the navy, and the navy was training him to be a corpsman.

It was eight o'clock, and heat devils were dancing over the parking lot in front of the wooden barracks with classrooms. George's uniform clung to his skin like a huge, soggy heat compress. His skin was molting inside it. He was just sitting at his desk, feeling droplets of sweat slide down his spinal trough when a short, stocky captain strode briskly into the class. He carried a massive bald head right on top of his shoulders and wore a pressed uniform. Saying nothing, he strutted directly to the blackboard and started drawing horizontal lines across it. George thought the guy looked like Mussolini.

The corpsmen watched Mussolini in weary silence as he marked one side of his lines "Birth" and the other "Death." George always distinctly remembered thinking, Gimme a break, Uncle Sam. Now you're going to bust my brain with palm readers too or what?

Mussolini introduced himself as doctor Somebody or Other. His topic was "Prevention as the Best Medicine." He wanted everyone to step up to the blackboard and write his name above one of his lines. Then he went to work on the chalk lines with his dry, yellow brain-shaped sponge: as the corpsmen rose one by one and moseyed to the blackboard, Mussolini barked personal questions at them: Did they smoke? Any bum tickers in their immediate families? Did they like hard liquor? Play football? Did they collect speeding tickets? Party with party girls?

His macho questions got him macho answers: hell, yes, they drank and smoked; you bet there were high school football stars and weekend race-car drivers and Lotharios in this unit.

Mussolini nodded his immense bald head, his sponge flicking like a lizard's tongue, wiping off bits and pieces of their life lines. The length of his careless strokes differed. A few of the lines ended up cut in half.

While bleached skeletons and flayed musclemen from Gray's *Anatomy* stared at him from the walls and Mussolini was killing his company, George had a disturbing sensation: he felt as though he were sitting in a spectral chamber surrounded by guffawing cadavers who still giggled and twitched (Mussolini's yellow sponge was one big hoot to George's companions in arms) while their purple livers were already crawling with thick white maggots. Their gnawing had just not got to them yet.

Suddenly, in one expansive stroke, Mussolini canceled two

thirds of all their lives. He left only their first names and little Doberman tails on the blackboard.

—But of course we may have a nuclear war tomorrow too, soldiers, he explained.

The maggoty young men around George burst out laughing. The stupid asses now felt vindicated in their smoking, drinking, carousing, speeding, risking crippling injuries. But in George's guts, in his ears and sockets, a writhing mass of thick white maggots went on gnawing, so he listened intently to what the spiffy little man with the fleshy bald head had to say. Mussolini explained that everyone had his own personal life expectancy. This was a genetic given. You had only so much candle to burn. The candle could never be made bigger. But you could burn it faster. You could maximize your life expectancy or you could minimize it. It all depended on how you ran your life. Every infection took a little steam out of you, so if you slept with a lot of friendly dames, you were probably minimizing. Ditto if you smoked or broke your bones on the football field. It took valuable energy to mend bones.

Said Mussolini, and George never saw him again.

But it all made sense to George, and for the next twenty-eight years rarely a day went by without George getting a glimpse of Dr. Mussolini's spectral show. For example, passing by a bar he would see only nostrils spewing forth carcinogenic cigarette smoke, cholesterol eyes leering at each other, mouths gulping poisons and hissing, Come on, fox, gimme a little of your infection, lemme show you how romantic it is to die young. . . .

For ten months after Mussolini had jolted him with maggots the navy battered George with horrible diseases, with viruses, parasites, shattered bones, hardened livers, torn ligaments, clogged arteries, cancers mushrooming in cellular voids. The body was so fragile; there were so many ways it could wind up maggot stew years before it was supposed to.

By the time the navy discharged him George was resolved to maximize his time. He had already taxed his body enough, could never again eat or drink or live in the careless, unself-conscious way of the previous year. He now had his priorities and no longer cared what people thought about him. All that mattered was that he squeeze every last hour out of Dr. Mussolini's squiggly chalk line.

George was going to die old.

From then on George did what he had to do, because his health was the only thing that counted. In the utility company his priorities paid off and got him a fast deucedom. So if people wanted to call him S. Q. Cigar-store Indian, it was fine by George. He had other things to worry about: Captain Mussolini now sat on his left shoulder day and night like a bird of ill omen.

INNER PERSON

The Cliftons shared one thing—a fascination with breasts. Mary Ellen had always wanted big boobs. She was a small woman, with a dancer's body, intelligent hazelnut eyes in a plain face, auburn hair, and breasts that were small, pert, pointy, and far apart. Mary Ellen liked her nipples. The problem was that their salmon areolas covered almost one third of her bosom.

Mary Ellen's breasts were twenty-five years old. They had not changed much since they slowly appeared on her bony chest. She was in college before she gave up on them, was crushed when she had to admit to herself that she would never need a bigger bra. In her mind she carried a large pair of lovely tits on her bony chest and turned men's heads everywhere she went. So she began to toy with the idea of silicone implants; implants seemed the most logical way to tailor her body to her personality, her unconscious, her libido, her soul, or whatever it was that her body did not match. Mary Ellen wanted to keep only her nipples; her large pink firmly bordered nipples were her.

She met George Clifton too soon, however, and never got her

breasts. She was working in a real estate office; George was looking for a house; Elvis was married; she no longer waited for a drop-dead handsome quarterback in a silver Corvette; her breasts were nine years old, had been ignored for long stretches of time. Mary Ellen sold George a modest bungalow on a quiet suburban block lined with sycamores, dated him for five months, and married him at the city hall one overcast Thursday.

She spent the next sixteen years in the bungalow trying not to think about silicone.

She could not do it.

Mary Ellen never had the guts to tell George how cramped her inner person felt in her lithe, flat-chested body. She wanted to explain that she needed a little more room around her chest to fit, but she knew George would never understand.

—What the hell kind of a nonsense is this? she could just hear George yell. ARE YOU INSANE?!

The one thing that George got off on was his health; he was in closer touch with his body than a pregnant woman. So he could never conceive of anyone risking infection and permanent injury in the hospital, minimizing her finite energy, and for what? To put a little addition on herself?

Come on! George was sure to holler.

Mary Ellen had missed her chance to get the breasts that were the real her, and now she was spending the rest of her life watching other women. She appraised and classified their boobs according to how pointed, firm, or far apart they were; she weighed their specific gravity with her eyes; she read them for imprints of baby gums. She imagined them freed of bras and sagging or bouncing or flowing, estimated how much pleasure they would yield in skilled hands.

When the Cliftons met, George had his own, coarse, masculine thing for breasts: the bigger, he thought, the better. But there was so much more to breasts than that, so Mary Ellen got tasteful pornography for George, brought it into their bedroom, and showed him things he would otherwise have overlooked about the magical tits in the pictures: the tiny warts, the imperceptible asymmetries, the swell and ebb of passion in them. George was an attentive student. The education gave a permanent charge to the Cliftons' sex life.

When a well-endowed braless young woman in a tank top, her shoulders thrown back to show off what she had, passed by their table in a restaurant, both Cliftons took in the breasts. And then they would look at each other. And sometimes Mary Ellen would blush. Or she would just stare George down, but always there was an electrifying intimacy to it. Because they both knew that they were going to talk about those pretty tits in bed. About how they were carried. About how they sloped. About how they'd feel. About what nipples crowned them. About what could be done to them and how.

There were not many other times when the Cliftons' inner persons connected.

By teaching George how to appreciate breasts Mary Ellen was hoping to warm him up to the idea of her silicone fix. In the meantime she stayed current on all the advances in cosmetic surgery, read up on gel bags, on the chances of hardening of the tissues. One year she even called several surgeons and shopped around for the best deal on silicone. She was quoted prices that George would never consider paying. That money was out of the question; the insurance did not cover implants. But it was all make-believe anyway, so she went on and researched the mechanics of gender-bending, the problems of transsexuality. She even bought a gay porno book called *The World's Most Beautiful Boys*. The soft-focus photographs showed lovely women with regal faces and full magical busts. Between their legs hung freaky little relics from their former lives.

One of the many things Mary Ellen and George did not share was alcohol. George refused to touch it. Mary Ellen loved a little sip. On quiet family evenings Mary Ellen liked to pull a bar cart to the Lazy Boy in the living room and mix herself cocktails. Now and then she might glance at the television. George usually parked himself on the sofa and counted her drinks. One night Mary Ellen sipped herself into such a state that she asked the sullen George for advice. One of the ladies in her bridge club was thinking about getting a silicone job. What would George tell her? It was a big step, and there was no going back. But maybe it was worth it. The woman had always wanted big boobs, simply wasn't herself without them.

George jumped up yelling that the goddam crazy bitch was better off blowing her brains out, and he slammed the door of the bedroom behind him. That was George all right. A real talent in closing cases by slamming the bedroom door. And that was also the end of Mary Ellen's implant fantasies. She would have to leave George to get the breasts her inner person had coming to her. She would have to go out, get some underpaid secretarial fanny-busting while moonlighting in real estate, wring blood out of radishes, save money like mad to get those tits that were her. But then what? Take her silicone bust to some over-the-hill singles' lounge and lay them on top of the bar? No, George was a good provider, and he loved her after his own fashion: Mary Ellen was more or less comfortable with her skinny, wiry, bony, maximizing, organized George.

Between her dream tits and her husband Mary Ellen had to go with George.

POLYESTER MISTER

—I don't own a single thing you gotta dry-clean, I'm not nuts, said George to the three younger men in the first-levels' office of his modest empire. Then he got up and stepped out of the room. In his mind he had concluded the tongue-flapping that passed for philosophy in his department. They had been discussing the outrageous cost of dry cleaning all morning.

—Polyester mister, said Walter, a young man with a walrus mustache, as soon as the door clicked shut behind George.

The three first-levels laughed. They did not hold their fearless leader in high esteem. George had been their boss for a year now. Before him they used to be able to get away for sojourns in various technical classes, order company-issue jackets and briefcases, throw the overtime around in the trenches. George had put a stop to all that. He got his kicks from holding the line on departmental costs. He would not let them go to classes anymore. They weren't programmers, merely ran computers, didn't have to know all that fancy stuff to do their jobs. He didn't care that it was just company funny money. He didn't care that other districts were treating money like the government was. His decision was final. George was tight all right. So his first-levels labeled him the S. Q. deuce, and they started talking about him behind his back.

—Now he be takin' his mornin' pleasure, said the big black man, and all three of them snickered again.

The black first-level knew his fearless leader.

It was nine o'clock, and one of the benefits of the life George S. Q. Cigar-store Indian Clifton was leading ever since Newport, Rhode Island, was well-regulated body rhythms. So on workdays at nine o'clock in the morning George would be sitting in the outsized stall of a roomy washroom and swinging his feet in the air: there was only one john on George's floor, and it housed a single toilet bowl—the tall crapper for the handicapped. It took a basketball center to reach the floor from this thing.

There was a poem scratched into the beige wall of the stall and, as he did every morning, George contemplated it. The jury was still out on whether it was true poetry or not. Soon it would be coffee time. George would fearlessly lead his three young subordinates into an elevator and up into the cafeteria. He would lift a small cup off a column of Styrofoam on the self-service line, pour it full of coffee from a chrome-plated machine, raise it to his nose, smell it, and smile at the ugly cashier.

The small cup of black coffee was George's only vice, and he indulged in it mostly for reasons of balance: a total absence of bad habits would amount to an even bigger vice.

TWO-WAY MIRROR

A year before, George had been transferred to the handicapped crapper from an empire with a standard-size toilet where he had been promoted to a deuce and where he had been happy. He did not want to go, but he had had no say in the matter. As usual at his level of management, his was to do or die. The reason for his imperial uprooting was that George had got too efficient for corporate culture.

Every year the utility company erected a pyramid of job appraisals: everyone in management had to evaluate the performance of his subordinates. The first-levels evaluated the hell out of the clerks, their emperor zapped them in turn, and so on. Then the office doors got closed for adrenalinated one-on-one meetings. The tense bosses solemnly read the appraisals. Their underlings listened, fidgeting tersely. Some puckered their lips and blew liters of carbon dioxide through them. A few stared their leaders down. The undercurrent of violence would not surface until the office Christmas party: when the ladle began showing in the punch bowl, the appraisees loudly recalled phrases from their job evaluations. The bosses smiled sourly and tried to stay mellow. And after Christmas the underlings worked harder. Nobody in the company was immune to this experience, except for the president, and he had to kiss stockholder ass.

George dreaded writing and giving the appraisals. They were a goddam pain. Nobody ever read the crap anyway. All they ever did was create bad blood. People never had any idea about how the world saw them. They had never watched themselves operate through two-way mirrors, so they all thought they were superstars. Which did not mesh with the departmental curve at all. In the utility company you could have Einstein, von Braun, and Johnny Carson working for you, and you would still have to come up with a curve at appraisal time. It was crazy.

George composed bland evaluations for his troops, trying to keep them in the gray middle of the district curve. This way he did not have to speak up at any meetings later. (Let other deuces whose empires were top-heavy with Einsteins and von Brauns slug it out for the piddling bonus money the district handed out.) George was not about to set himself up for any unnecessary questions from his leaders.

When he was supposed to bequeath them to posterity on a sheet of paper, words did not come easily to George. He sweated all his reports. He kept a large file cabinet in his office, and under lock in this olive-green metal box he kept all his bureaucratic tricks, his imperial working capital: he had copies of every appraisal, memo, report, chart, and ditty the company had ever squeezed out of him. Every time they squeezed him again now, George unlocked his cabinet and leafed through his old output. He lifted useful phrases and pasted together a bureaucratic collage that said as little as he could safely get away with in as many words as possible. He implemented, projected, absorbed, estimated, determined, found impossible, rejected as not feasible or cost-efficient, cost-loaded figures, suggested other venues to objectives, forever headed off corporate reportables. He spent hours on end perfecting his bureaucratese, killing the few fresh turns of phrase that ever seeped in, whispering the dry sentences back to himself over and over again until they became a utility-Latin office chant that issued from the door of his office as though from a monastery.

In the second year of George's deucedom, as the appraisal chant started to resound through the modest empire, a muse pecked George lightly on the cheek one breezy morning. He was pedaling his bicycle to the commuter station at the time. He realized in a flash of inspiration that he could modernize this imperial pain. Why not bring the appraisals into the machine age? Why couldn't he just manufacture the damn things? That morning, for the first time in his working life, the seven-fifteen seemed slow to George. He couldn't wait for it to pull into downtown Chicago. He felt like questioning the conductor about the crawling train. This was an awesome feeling. He jogged into his office. He arrived ten minutes before his usual time, feeling light-headed. So this was what people meant when they talked about divine inspiration.

I can deal with this, he thought, yes, sir.

The office was empty. His underlings were still in the cafeteria upstairs. They would not mosey down till just before George's usual arrival time. No doubt they did so every morning. This was good to know at appraisal time, though George preferred being alone this morning.

He unlocked his file cabinet, removed all the appraisals he had sweated out in his career, and began leafing through them. The phone started ringing. George did not bother to pick it up. He did not care if it was his fearless leader wanting George to hold his hand. The phone went on ringing. George liked it. It was giving his modest empire a beautiful sense of urgency. There had been very few days in his life when he had something important enough to do to override the bossy instrument.

The phone stopped ringing at some point. Later his first-levels descended from the cafeteria. The sight of their do-nothing S. Q. leader, in the imperial office before his usual time, shuffling old files and taking feverish notes, shocked them, so they quickly retreated into the computer room. George barely knew they had passed through the office. He was hard at work composing his master appraisal, rating the first-level John Doe average in job performance, somewhat lukewarm in attitude, solid if unspectacular in job knowledge, and supportive of company EEO/AA policies.

The next day George typed his master composition into a word-processor, then had the machine plug in the names of his underlings where applicable. One by one he called his first-levels into the imperial office and presented them with how their past year's job performance looked from where he was sitting. His heart was beating away as he watched them read their appraisals; he was committing the most criminal act of his career with the utility company.

As always, the trick was to get his subordinates to sign the evaluation while limiting the damage they could inflict in the

Employee Comments section. George's crybabies did not take their appraisals any easier than they had every other year. They got in their usual digs about how they thought that this appraisal did not do them justice, wasn't fair, adequate, complete, or some damn thing. One of them got so emotional that he brought up George's chamomile tea.

George listened to his underlings beef, thinking, Nobody appreciates a genius in his lifetime. He did not see what the big deal was; his arrogant first-levels were merely getting perfunctory glimpses of how they appeared to other people. This amounted to an intimation of insignificance to be sure, but who the hell did these people think they were? They were nothing but minor corporate dynamos. Same as George. They weren't going to get rich or famous or even notorious. They were corpo lifers who were going to retire from the utility company same as George did. One or two of them might make a deuce one day. All right, maybe even a district. None of them was a guided missile from the Harvard Business School, shooting through the ranks of management, routed for the big picture. The bottom line was: you had to accept two-way mirrors to attain corporate maturity.

George did not share any of these thoughts with his followers. He sat behind his desk, wore a serious face, nodded to their bellyaching, and listened to them till they ran out of steam.

—I'm sorry that you disagree with me, he finally said, but that's how I called it.

In the end, seeing that they were not going to change anything, George's geniuses all signed his master appraisal. In due time George wiped the smile off his face and forwarded the five copies of his composition to his fearless leader for his signature.

For the next few weeks George had problems sleeping. His Swiss-clock bowel movement even came close to mistiming. Gradually the suspense wound down. It became clear that George's appraising efficiency was paying off. He had been right: his boss did not read the damn things, and his underlings did not compare notes about them. They weren't too anxious to share their outrage over being rated solid lukewarm supportive. So George had come up with another brilliant way of saving himself a little energy. He was maximizing away.

The following year George's unassuming efficiency went unnoticed again. But the year after that, just as George, for the first time in his career, started sleeping soundly through the appraisal season, the efficiency backfired. George had to evaluate a recent promotee from the clerical ranks, a young black woman. He gave her her dose of the usual composition and she threw a fit. An hour later George's fearless leader was on the horn, icy and distant. He wanted a heart-to-heart ASAP. The bitch had got to the bottom of George's efficiency and she had gone right over his head with it, taking all the other first-levels with her. Their uproar had the air of a palace revolution.

George's district man said he was not amused at all. (He had already signed the five identical appraisals and sent them to his fearless leader, who had also signed them.) So George found himself propelled to a new work location in a speed-of-light lateral. His efficiency had bombed.

But after busting George, Murphy and his law let one get away: George's new fearless leader turned out to be a fellow S. Q. Cigar-store Indian. He hated surprises, and he soon learned that George was his best steady-as-you-go deuce. So George moved on to the tall crapper for the handicapped in one of the company's satellite buildings, and, when cornered on the subject of his unexpected transfer, he would say that he saw he was about to become surplus in his old job so he had started making phone calls. Being surplus was a pathetic admission, and no one asked George any more questions. They looked away, sipped their coffee, and talked baseball.

While George lucked out with his new boss, he also wound up with a real choice herd of followers. His new first-levels had all been hired off the streets straight into management. They all had college degrees and thought they knew everything. They were young, arrogant, and contemptuous. Their ambition in life was to minimize George's candle. They bled their new emperor with nonsensical projects and costly ideas for little improvements.

Starting with George's empire, they wanted to change the world. —My hands are tied, said George.

They wouldn't listen, so he laid down his first imperial edict: no more technical schools and no more classes. He had noticed that they always came back from these dizzy with ideas; they found all manner of things to streamline, simplify, speed up. And George did not want to volunteer their services or to soak up new responsibilities just because they could run some dinky job faster and easier. Neither he nor his fearless leader needed them going around upsetting the ways of the district. None of that do-gooder bullshit was part of the routine. And in corporate culture as in life, routine was everything. Or damn near that.

ROUTINE & REASON

All summer long George got on the fifth car of his commuter train. When the government started monkeying around with daylight in October, George transferred into the first car, where he stayed all winter. He had never set foot in any other car of his commuter line.

George's commuter seating reflected the geography of his suburban station: the municipal bicycle rack lay deep inside it, and from spring till fall George rode a bicycle to the train. So on a good day of no surprises on the commuter rails, the fifth car of the four thirty-three came to rest right by George's bicycle.

George always got on the fifth car, and he always rode his old Raleigh, a heavy, three-speed workhorse. This was his exercise, and he pedaled hard under any weather conditions. He kept a change of clothes in his office for poochy days, and he had once braved a tornado warning to punch his ancient bicycle through forty-mile-an-hour winds.

After they pushed back the clock and it got too dark and too cold for bike-riding, George drove to the station. At the same time he made his seasonal move from the fifth to the front car of his train; the first car of the four thirty-three always wound up closest to the municipal parking lot. This way he did not have to fight any blizzards to get to his car.

George had his routines carefully thought out: you considered everything you did and you nailed the most efficient way of accomplishing your objectives, and that was how you did things day in and day out. There was no better way to maximize your givens. For example, the Cliftons had a string of twelve Michigan vacations going. In the last two weeks of July they always went to a cottage George's cousin owned on a lake.

The cousin was a gruff, lonely man in his early sixties. He seemed to like their company, though he would never put such feelings into words.

The lake lay between steep hills covered with tall pines. It was deep and measured several hundred yards across. The cottage perched on a sloped clearing between two ravines. A few paces below it a sandy beach rimmed the blue-black lake. George's cousin owned a powerboat, a pair of beat-up water skis, and all the fishing rods and lures a once-a-year fisherman ever needed. The Cliftons always stayed for two weeks, because the price of their summer vacation was right too: George would help his cousin do some repairs around the place. He cut grass and felled a couple of dead trees on the wooded section of the lot and sawed them up for firewood.

There were other reasons why the Cliftons had no need to experiment with their summer routine. In the year-round house on the hill above the cottage lived a divorcée and her teenage daughter. The mother's breasts were large, pointed, full, though not too milky, firm, sitting far apart. They were pure poetry, and the woman spent a lot of time on the little beach below the cottage. Sometimes the daughter, in a tiny bikini, came down the steep path with her mother, and at fifteen the daughter's breasts were already considerably larger than Mary Ellen's. Those lovely tits were now the size that would have fit Mary Ellen's inner person perfectly, the size Mary Ellen would have rushed to get if, somehow, she became a widow.

George collected the rest of his vacation time on both sides of Christmas every winter: the Cliftons always drove down to a trailer park near Jacksonville to spend some time with Mary Ellen's retired parents.

There were routines within routines in George's life. For example, he always left the office early on the last Friday before Christmas. This was his day to give their ancient, comfy eight-cylinder Ford, their second family car, its once-a-year, need-it-or-not, do-it-yourself tune-up while Mary Ellen packed their things. Then he loaded it up with their beach gear and parked it in the driveway. The next morning, at three o'clock, the yawning Cliftons stumbled into their old car and headed for Florida.

Most of George's machines were old workhorses it was easy to get emotional about, but George really loved his Ford; it was a true-blue American car. Unlike the puny contraptions Detroit put out these days, it did not have a sewing-machine motor under its hood. Its body bore quite a few rust spots, so the Ford was getting hard on the eyes now, but it still ran like a dreamboat. Its big engine purred, its heating system put small hair dryers to shame, its ride was smooth as a baby's ass.

George cranked the heater up, and by four o'clock, leaving the dark, cold, windy Illinois, he would be down to his cotton T-shirt. The short sleeves hung around his bony upper arms; droplets of sweat were forming in the corners of his forehead; Mary Ellen was fast asleep in the back seat; the snowy fields were whizzing quietly by; and George was happy with his life.

Mary Ellen would not wake up till southern Indiana, where George had to get gas for the first time. The weak winter sun would be out now, the expressway crawling with semis. George always pulled into the same oasis, filled her up, and ordered the special in their home-cookin' restaurant. It offered two eggs any way you wanted 'em, three sausages, orange juice, and a bottomless cup. He always asked for his eggs over easy, and he drank only the first filling of the bottomless cup, black.

Now the gas and caffeine would be good till southern Tennessee,

where George had another place picked out. There George pecked
on the usual off-white cottage cheese bowl. The peaches were
usually dry on top. They looked as though they had been smeared
with glue. But George was a loyal customer—he swallowed them
and sipped his second cup of coffee, happy with his routines.

A familiar Holiday Inn restaurant in southern Georgia served
the Cliftons dinner. Here George had a friend at the corner gas
station. The name on his overalls said "Hank," and George felt as
if he was on a first-name basis with the guy. Hank ran a tight ship
for Texaco, wasn't above pumping a little gas with the masses, had
the air of a boot camp sergeant. You didn't have to worry about
any surprises with Hank.

—Been waitin' for ya, the carefully combed Hank would say
when George got out of his Ford to stretch a little.

—Well, here we are, George always said.

—Almost took me a day off this year, old buddy, Hank would
joke.

—You would of shot my vacation, was George's line.

—I know, and I couldn't do that to the little lady. Hello,
ma'am, said Hank now, bending down to the window and striking
his forefinger off his brow to salute Mary Ellen.

—Well, we'll see you next year, then, George would say. Hold
the fort, will ya?

—I'll be here, Hank would always say, but I'm not so sure about
you, partner. You look awful skinny to me. You sick?

—Don't worry about me, George always said.

—Well, I know the Ford's gonna make it anyway, said Hank.

—You betcha.

George always concluded the conversation with these words and
tipped his friend a buck. Buck was a lot of money, but what the
hell. It was worth it all the same. For the sake of the routine. Plus
the guy was some kidder too; made George think of his navy days.
Not to mention it being Christmastime and all that.

—Remember me to your dear mother-in-law, Hank always
quipped as George set the old workhorse into motion again for the
last leg of their trip.

Now George's head was full of memories of Newport and all those kids he'd met there who were now fat old men—or maggot stew, some of them—and of Dr. Mussolini and the flayed, raw-red bodies of Gray's *Anatomy* on the thin walls of the barracks classroom. And how he had gotten drunk for the last time in his life shortly after coming there (and how unreal it would have seemed if someone had told him then that this would be his last taste of whiskey—he would have roared with laughter—but sure enough that was how it turned out), and how he had puked his guts out, and how the company cocksman had screwed this floozy he'd dragged into their hotel room from some cheap dance hall while George and this other guy both watched through an open doorway from the kitchen. The lovers went at it like rabbits in the bedroom, and everybody, most certainly including the floozy, knew what the score was; what the hell, they were all young. And how none of the clothes the navy put on you ever fit except the boots—the boots fit you like a glove, because Uncle Sam wasn't quite as dumb as he seemed, those boots fit like a piston fits its housing. And how funny it all was, how long ago and how distant and how funny, and how it never was coming back, sure wasn't, not ever, and how bad he wanted that last lick of whiskey back, and that it all really was pretty goddam sad.

Now George didn't have to touch the ignition key till he parked the Ford in front of the trailer home of his in-laws, where there was a pitcher of cold, fresh-squeezed orange juice waiting for them on the kitchen table. (George drank nothing but fresh-squeezed orange juice for the two weeks around Christmas. It tasted so good, was so damn healthy, and didn't cost a left lung, like up north.) They were now only a hundred yards away from the beach, and Mary Ellen's father would be on the lookout in the window.

When they pulled up, the old man in the lighted window would lift his watch to his ear and pretend to check it. Then he would mimic winding it. Then he would race to the door. But unlike Hank, Mary Ellen's father could not be depended on to remember his lines.

—Mother, our clock's off again! It must be ten-thirty, the

Cliftons are here, he cried one Christmas. We must of been fifteen minutes off all year!

—Hey, you're early! What happened?! Somebody rear-ended you or something? he would shout the next year.

The old man's jokes gave George a glimpse of how his wife's family was talking about him behind his back. They had him pegged as a pretty odd bird, an eccentric, a real character maybe. He could tell. But the opinions of Mary Ellen's family got through to George about as much as the appraisals his fearless leader gave him every year did. He knew that he'd be on the beach the next morning, watching the boob parade with Mary Ellen, sipping cold orange juice from a thermos, smelling the sea air, tasting the dried salt on his lips, letting the warmth of the sun wash over his body in long, delicious waves, hoping a blizzard had Chicago tied up in knots. He was happy with his life. He knew all he needed to know. He was conserving his energy. He felt young for his age. His routines all had their good reasons, whether Mary Ellen's family realized it or not. His life had the efficient beauty of a wooden glider.

This was precisely why any little glitches in the routine upset him so much. George would have a fit whenever Mary Ellen asked for an unscheduled stop on their way to Florida. Out of the blue she wanted to stretch out a little. Or she wanted to watch the sunset from some goddam hill in Georgia. Or she needed to go to the washroom.

George acted as though he did not hear her. Then he would suddenly swerve onto the shoulder of the road and slam on the brakes. Then he would turn morose for hours. The whole thing just didn't make any sense to him. Why screw around with a perfect, rational, working system? Oh, them damn pissin', stretchin', sunset-watchin' women.

But unless people sideswiped his routine, their opinions did not matter to George one bit. Let his father-in-law yell as many of his laborious semifunny remarks as he could muster. Let his fearless leader go off on George's appraisal. Let Fat Fred call him names in a meeting. None of that amounted to a canceled check as long as George had his routine.

And George had always kept his body free of poisons and infections and injuries, and it was all paying off now. He had an iron health. He had thirteen years of unbroken perfect attendance going at work. He never as much as sneezed. He had never been overweight in his life. He had had a regular bowel movement for the last twenty years. His digestive tract ticked like a clock, coming through nearly always just before the morning coffee break. And whether George's shoes were swinging in the air or planted firmly on the floor, the product of that brief visit to the washroom had looked the same for years now too. Same length. Same thickness. Same color.

The bottom line was: George Clifton had been shitting the same shit for over twenty years now.

Life was grand.

THE GRAND LIFE

On the morning the cost of dry cleaning had outraged his office, George's bowel movement occurred on time, expelling the routine excrement from his body. The coffee upstairs was fresh and strong too. George had a meeting to go to, and he was going to smile warmly today.

The utility company owned buildings all over downtown. George's modest empire occupied half a floor in one of the windowless satellite towers on the southern edge of the Loop. A brisk walk to the company headquarters on the other end of the Loop took fifteen minutes, so George was provided with Yellow Cab coupon books for his trips there. He refused to use them, however. He always insisted on walking to his meetings. Even on rainy days George could not bring himself to flag down a cab. Cabs struck him as an insane waste of company money. And George certainly had never been a taker. Besides, a fifteen-minute stroll through midmorning downtown was not only pleasant, it was constitutional. And it moved him a little closer to the four thirty-three than a cab ride would.

Most meetings George had to attend were scheduled for late morning. They were artfully fitted around the arrivals of coffee carts, which circulated through the headquarters and paced the rhythms of its floors. Usually George had to leave his empire soon after his bowel movement, and that agreed with him. Having just unburdened his body, he would sometimes feel so light stepping through the busy streets that his feet barely touched the ground. He bounced off the sidewalks on his tiptoes, swinging his weight flamboyantly through each step. You didn't call this walking. You called it ballet.

George had his headquarters route mapped out of course. He always kept to the same sidewalks, so many of the faces he saw at this time of the morning were familiar. There were the habitual late sleepers and tardy secretaries rushing to work. There were the well-dressed executive types and the indifferently dressed city bureaucrats strolling leisurely to show off their clout. It gave George a buoyant, light-headed feeling to fly to headquarters on a late morning, through the village of downtown Chicago, where he was on glance-of-recognition terms with so many people.

The bad part about it was: once through the revolving door of headquarters, Peter Pan was converted into a cigar-store Indian. He stepped inside, and his soaring inner person (which only moments before had felt as though it were on a first-name basis with the city) had to contract again and kill time in a room choking with cigarette smoke, watching people yawn and pick their noses or drone on and on or bicker over meaningless decisions. Or even worse, when Fat Fred lorded it over the meeting, Peter Pan had to poison his lungs with secondhand cigar exhaust at twice-the-normal rate of breathing: you never knew when Fred Foss would come at you from way out in left field. What a way to crash. But that was life. And even grand lives had their downsides.

This morning George entered the conference room on the fourteenth floor and greeted the customary mugs there. There were a few strangers at the periphery of the large rectangular table, but most of these corporate dynamos he had known for years. They were the decision-making troopers who trekked from one conference room to another and waited for the coffee carts. In the meanwhile, they killed time planning, supporting, and running company computers. Week in and week out these corpo lifers put on the same playlets: purchasing, leasing, training, staffing, feasibility, responsibility, cost-benefits, recommendations, acquisitions, treated spaces, floor plans, organizational charts, security, real money, funny money, QWL, EEO/AA, performance reviews. The particulars faded in and out, but it was the same faces and the same words rearranging themselves in the same rooms.

George sat down, nodded to his fellow dynamos with whom yesterday afternoon, only hours ago, he had chewed feasibility. They looked fiercer now, he thought. This had to do with oxygen. Now, before lunch, they had less blood in their stomachs and more blood in their brains.

Sprinkled among the habitués were the wild cards, the users, the aliens from the field. They were the corporate pain. They always did their best to lob monkey wrenches into the well-oiled proceedings. They were sure to press their (irrelevant) needs, squabble about outage reports, try to drag out the tongue-flapping right into lunchtime. They never knew when to shut up, never sensed the moment when a consensus had emerged and it was time to start falling in line. But you had to have users to have computers, just as you had to have customers to have utilities. Users and customers were the unavoidable static of a corpo career. They were God's will.

Someone was talking, and George's head kept buzzing with theological binaries. He had gone on contributing his classic cigar-store Indian smile (a slight, wise, you-don't-know-what-you've-got-in-me grimace) for over half an hour when it began to dawn on him that something odd was happening here. This meeting concerned an acquisition of some ultramodern gizmo, some network concentrator—whatever the hell that was—and George realized that he had no way of connecting it to his empire.

He thought of all sorts of farfetched reasons why somebody might have wanted him here, but none of them made any sense. With a pang of dread George concluded that he must have wandered into the wrong meeting. He probably had the wrong room. This meant that he was missing his own explosion of corporate fireworks somewhere else.

God damn it, he thought.

But no one had noticed anything. Nobody thought it strange that George Clifton would sit here and smile. George's problem was that he had already signed the attendance sheet; when the chair went to mail out the minutes, it would be noticed that George had sat through the wrong meeting and had not even realized it.

Damn.

The question was, Would it be any less embarrassing to get up now, half an hour into somebody's else's gizmo, grab his notebook, and head for the door? People were going to stare at him, and he'd have to admit his mistake. He was damned if he did and damned if he didn't, and time was ticking away. The longer he sat there the more stupid he was going to wind up looking. Thank God, at least, that Fat Fred was chasing some other coffee cart this morning.

As he wrestled with his decision George realized with a start that he had even taken some incomprehensible notes on the goddam switcher. He flipped his notebook over, got up, stretching his arms, and, leaving his things on the table, walked out into the hall. Everyone assumed he was headed for the washroom, but he rushed to a phone and dialed his office.

Walter read off to him what it said on his calendar. He hung up, not bothering to explain anything to the puzzled young man, and hurried to the elevator shaft. The floor, the room number, even the time of the meeting all pointed back to the stupid gizmo. George was where his calendar said he was supposed to be—so his original meeting must have been rescheduled, and George had never gotten the revised invitation. This was a little better. He could live with this.

He strolled back into the conference room. No one paid any

attention to him till he started to collect his pen and his notebook. When he pushed his chair back to the table the speaker broke off and stared at him.

—Wrong meeting, George announced with conviction.

There were the predictable guffaws around the table, but they were rather muted: a wrong meeting was not an uncommon experience for corporate dynamos. The chairperson cheerfully scratched George's name off the list of participants. While he did, everyone else was helpful in establishing that a different meeting had been originally scheduled for this room; the people running it had obviously neglected to notify George about the switch. The old hands were almost eager to absolve George, and he did not end up looking nearly as stupid as he had feared.

All the same, though, on his way back to his modest empire, George no longer soared above the sidewalks. The ballet was over, the light-headed buoyancy gone. The faces ceased to be familiar: he never walked down his streets this late in the morning, and it was a different city he was negotiating now.

Returning to his building on a fine early-May day like today, George would normally linger in transit. He would not, of course, go as far as to change his route (not usually, not unless there was a good reason to, not unless he had some errands to do), but he would definitely take his sweet time. He never crossed a street if the DON'T WALK sign was about to start flashing. He stopped and waited for the pedestrian cross traffic on the corners to blitz over. He inspected display windows. He took in the ladies.

The previous night the weatherman had talked light overcoats, but the morning had turned out to be windbreaker material. The wispy breeze off the lake still had a chill edge, but the sun was pretty high up already and it shone brightly. The volumes of shadows below the downtown buildings were no longer coffee. They were mint tea now. The world was soon going to fill up with leaves and gather more mass. Girls were going to march out in their light summer dresses and give you a pain in the neck.

George was in no mood to look at pretty girls today. People passed by him, strolling as though they were going to turn the next corner, and it would be summer while he trudged grimly on. He prided himself on being organized. He might not talk anybody's ears off in a meeting, but he could be counted on to make the right conference room. He wasn't like Fred Foss. (That fat pig was legendary for sitting through the wrong meetings and ending up running them too.) George took this morning's mistake personally. It almost made him want to question his priorities, his values, his life.

THE EMPIRE & THE BIG PICTURE

The empire with the handicapped crapper, George's second deucedom, extended over a large computer room, a sizable tape library, a clerical lounge where the night shift took their beauty rests (the way the coarse back pillows lay across the sofas in the morning left no doubt about this), a crammed office shared by George's first-levels, and the imperial office. George's room lay behind the office of his underlings, so George had to pass through the territory of the first-levels to reach the seat of his modest empire.

George kept the door of his office open all day, whether he was in the building or not. He locked it only when he was leaving for the day. The open door was protocol: it showed that the deuce had nothing to hide. The open door was convenient: it allowed George to call his subordinates into the imperial office without getting out of his chair or dialing the intercom. It also permitted him to get in on the philosophical disputations that erupted in the larger office while sitting at his desk and talk Cubs or taxes or fixing dishwashers or hanging wallpaper. Or the outrageous cost of dry cleaning. Finally, the open door showed off George's sumptuous office.

George had inherited the place from his predecessor, a true empire builder, and it looked nothing like a deuce's den. For one thing, the company did not even give second-level people their own offices. At headquarters the deuces drowned in such amenities as their twice-a-day beeping-robot delivery of company mail, their restaurant with splendid views of the city, their lunchtime bridge tournaments, their barbershop, post office, library, check-cashing window, flower-and-magazine stand, not to mention their goddam coffee carts, but they sat in the same offices as their flocks. You had to make district to get your own space. For another thing, the little emperor before George had furnished his office in a heady, big-picture style.

There was, for example, the AVP desk. It was all wood, spread on and on, had a key for each drawer. Its top was so nicely finished you wanted to caress it. George had heard all the stories about this amazing piece of furniture from his subordinates. They all recalled George's predecessor with affection, calling him "the old man" or "boss." They were still in awe over how he had wheeled and dealed with acquaintances at the furniture stock to get it.

George's own fearless leader whiled away his days behind a lousy plastic-topped desk. You spread out your *Tribune* and the desk was gone. The district office also had no love seat with bright-green cushions, had nothing at all like George's wooden wardrobe that sported a large mirror inside the door. Its rounded corners gave it a flowing oval shape; the wardrobe was class. George's boss did possess a credenza, but it was no match for the slick dark wood affair in George's office. Then there were the two fancy blond wood chairs with wing armrests; George could make himself dizzy in minutes just running these comparisons through his mind. He had to keep his phenomenal chair out of it: if he threw in the chair, he would probably black out.

George's chair was all leather, had a headrest, swiveled, pitched, and yawed. No other utility company ass worked out of such a comfortable seat. George could lean far back, put his hands behind his head, kick his feet up on the desk, and be out like a light after lunch. (Even after what George misrepresented as lunch: an apple and a couple of graham crackers, washed down with an unsweetened cup of chamomile tea, brewed by George himself right there in the office in an electric pot.)

In the utility company it took a lifetime of favors to lay out an office with this much zip; George's predecessor had to have been quite a shaker. Fred Foss himself would not have been able to pull off an office like this. George had twenty-four years in the utilities, enough time to realize that you didn't screw around with perfection. So when his leaders yanked him to his second deucedom, George did not touch a single thing. He even kept the large framed picture of a huge orange sun where it had always been setting, on the half wall opposite the Kremlin desk. Its cold rays were slicing through bare oak trees, and white cows lay steaming in the foreground, chewing cud on a foggy pasture.

The handicapped crapper was the downside of George's second deucedom. The office was its upside. And George knew he was set for the rest of his career the moment his ass sank into that imperial seat.

Later on George wound up making an original addition to his chamber: he crammed a large filing cabinet between the green love seat and the dark credenza. The contraption was too bulky, too iron, too drab, and too beat up to fit in, but George took full responsibility for it. He had to have the thing. It contained every word he had penned over the course of his career. It housed his collected works.

This addition notwithstanding, George's office still looked so goddam luxurious that it made him nervous to show it to the big-picture dynamos who traipsed in from headquarters on infrequent occasions. That usually took a reshuffling of the corporate deck. When the organizational charts were redrawn, the dynamos suddenly came out of the woodwork in their tailored pinstripes, with their platinum Crusade of Mercy pins, to inspect the new frontiers of their segments. They always moved in groups. They walked around. They stared. They cocked their heads. They shook hands with clerks and penetrated them with funny questions. They had the big picture, while the craft had the small picture. The twain never met. The small picture was too small to make the big picture, but the clerks didn't care. They felt safe in their union. They did not have opulent offices.

Finishing the ten-cent tour, approaching the imperial office at the head of a herd of his distant fearless leaders, George would go into a slow sweat. He felt queasy. He hated the little emperor before him. He cursed his taste, his style, his ambition, his corpo prowess. But, as usual, he had to swallow his feelings and smile. However, he always made sure the big-picture crowd understood that George had inherited all this unspeakable luxury from the previous regime. He was very glad when the leaders of leaders finally took their cabs back to their big picture and got the hell out of his modest empire.

TWO-WAY MIRROR II

When George got back to his deucedom from the wrong meeting there was nobody in the large office. All his contemptuous young men had disappeared. Presumably they were on the floor of the computer room, wrestling with some software gremlins, or bird-dogging a hardware glitch, or overseeing the printing of some reports or labels. (More likely they would be playing Treasure Hunt from one of the terminals, or they were holed up in the tape library reading or shooting the breeze with their clerks or flirting on the phone.)

George passed through the empty office of his first-levels and through the open doorway walked into the seat of his empire. He stopped in front of the wardrobe and was pulling his overcoat off when two of his arrogant underlings entered the adjacent office from the computer room. Walter, the walrus mustache who had read the room number off the calendar for George earlier, was talking. That guy was always talking. And he knew it all too.

Neither of the two first-levels could see George, because the wardrobe stood in the near corner of his office. George instantly understood that the pair were talking about him, and he was going to slam the door of the wardrobe shut to alert them to his presence. Spying on people was deeply repulsive to him. But for some reason he hesitated for a fleeting moment, and then it was too late.

—George wound up in the wrong meeting this morning, can you believe that?

—He's pathetic.

—Not only ain't he got no balls, now he's wandering around like a senile aunt too.

—No shit.

—But at least he was doing *something*. He could of been jerking off in his office, reading his fucking *Newsweek* like every other day.

—Shootin' us down on everything: don't do this, don't try that. . .

—Known quantities only . . .

—Status quo, lay low . . .

—Stand pat . . .

—The man gonna be the death of this department, you watch.

—Shit! We're dead in the water here already, buddy.

George was standing in front of his wardrobe, frozen in place. He was holding a hanger in his left hand. His light black overcoat hung limply from his right hand. A shiver went through his body like an electric shock. He didn't know what to do. His first impulse was to step inside the wardrobe, carefully pull its door shut, wait till everyone had ambled out of the office again, then sneak back out and pretend he had just walked in.

He had never heard anybody talk about him like this before. He suspected that his wife's family probably regarded him as a mild kook. He knew that he was no heavyweight in the utility company. He realized Fred Foss did not think a whole lot about the job he was doing whipping his empire along. But he had no idea that anybody might see him as a pathetic, senile aunt. Nobody, but nobody had any right to feel such loathing toward him. He had never done anything to those two cocky bastards. They had it good under him in fact. He left them alone. And he couldn't help it that he was one of the few deuces left in the company who still remembered where the bottom line was. He was saying some of the most meaningful no's uttered in the utilities. He was holding down the costs. Everybody else in the corporation thought they were blowing funny money. But ultimately money was money, so somebody had to draw the line. George was needed in the utilities. He didn't expect anybody to kiss his feet for it, knew his was a thankless function, but he was getting frustrated. Somebody had to do what he was doing, damn it! These two malicious assholes had it all wrong!

They were collapsing into their chairs now, fifteen feet away from George, lighting up cigarettes, not suspecting a thing. There was no way to outwait them, he had to do something. One of them might walk into his office. They were probably snooping around it whenever he stepped out. He caught a glimpse of himself in the wardrobe mirror: his face looked singed, hot pink, leathered with the skin off a baboon's ass. And he was locked into this ridiculous pose, balancing a hanger and a coat, a Red-faced Bureaucrat Returning from a Meeting in Springtime. His heart was about to burst out of his chest. Wouldn't it be something if he dropped with a heart attack now? The two sons of bitches would investigate the strange noise coming out of his office and find George's unconscious body in the goddam wardrobe, his face a baboon's ass. They would probably just close the door again and wait till he croaked. Or worse still, they might try to give him artificial resuscitation. Fuck.

The screeching sound of an ashtray being dragged over a glass tabletop startled George. Minutes must have passed.

—Did you hear what he said this morning?

—Shiiit. He never do wear nothin' but polyester!

—I've never met anybody as cheap as him.

—Me neither. The boy so tight he squeak.

—But he sure keeps a clean desk. I've never seen a desk as clean as his.

—You right. I'll give 'im that. That and his mornin' shit. You can set yo' watch by George's trips to the john.

—Yeah, George sure can shit.

—No balls, but an asshole with a timer.

As he listened to the two stuck-up no-good assassins cackle, a flash of anger shot through his body. His pink face started draining of blood. He was really pissed now. His fury broke the spell that had held him suspended in this preposterous pose. He slapped his overcoat on the hanger and slammed it into the wardrobe. Then he kicked its door shut.

Now it was the turn of the two sons of bitches to choke on their cigarette smoke. George Clifton tore through their office like a hit-and-run truck. He was moving with a sense of power and purpose that he had never known before.

—I'm taking a shit, in case somebody calls, he barked as he ripped by them.

THE STUFF OF ETERNITY

Punching the elevator button, George realized that he had walked out of the office without his overcoat. He was not returning for the damn thing, that was for sure. The two arrogant assholes would stammer some two-faced, bullshit excuses, and he would puke on their shoes. Not professional from a boss.

He had never in his life talked about anybody with such wanton brutality. If that had not been a character assassination, then he didn't know what was. They all must have been talking about him that way. He was George S. Q. Cigar-store Indian Asshole-with-a-Timer Clifton to all of those lousy sons of bitches. Only now he knew it, and they knew that he knew it, and they would all take it from there.

The elevator doors spread open and George made a clean getaway, overcoat or no overcoat. The day had turned colder since he had Peter-Panned it to headquarters. As he stepped outside the building the wind puffed up the back of his shirt into a freezing balloon, so George headed for the leeway behind the windowless high-rise. He turned the corner; the cold fabric promptly flapped down on his back. This was a little better, though even on this sunny, wind-screened sidewalk you still needed a windbreaker.

George had on only his thin polyester slacks, a synthetic shirt, and a tie. Yet for the first time in memory it did not matter to him how cold he got. Let him catch flu and break his perfect attendance record. So what. Let him upgrade the flu to pneumonia while he was at it. So fucking what. Let Mussolini's yellow sponge wipe a few weeks off his life line. So who cared. By rights he already had the *Guinness Book of World Records* entry as the oldest living American sewn up anyway. So big fucking deal.

He was marching down a street that was completely unknown to him. He had merely walked around the windowless tower he had been working in for over a year, but the block was unfamiliar. He had never been here before. It hit him how little of downtown he was acquainted with. There were his routes—to headquarters, to the commuter station, to VanCura's Hardware. Then there was State Street and the Magnificent Mile at Christmastime. He never wandered anywhere else. He decided that this was going to change. He was going to explore this strange city today.

But adventurers always have it rough, and George soon felt goose bumps springing up where the cold fabric of his shirt kept slapping the skin on his back. Then his teeth began chattering. Then his whole body started shivering. Then the shivering got so bad that it became visible to passersby, and people started looking at him funny.

George trudged on.

He certainly was not used to people looking at him that way. He had always been careful to blend in, to dress as much or as little as other people, and now here he went, scandalously underdressed, stared at as if he were some kind of a nut—and the hell of it was, it flattered him. He figured that Columbus had been zapped by his share of funny looks too, and he found he enjoyed shocking these

folks in coats and windbreakers and shawls and hats and caps; these
people all noticed George S. Q. Clifton today. They wouldn't look
into his face (they weren't quite sure about him, the tie really
threw them off), but they were very conscious of him. They all
paid attention. He had the sidewalk intimidated, and he couldn't
believe it, and it warmed him up just enough to go on playing
Columbus and begging for pneumonia.

Every corner was a revelation. He had never before noticed the
dark-green El trains screech through the orange thighs of gigantic
cranes, their progress underlined with blue bursts of electricity.
The ocher sun swam shattered in the layered corner of a
copper-green high-rise. George was freezing, but he marched
stubbornly on, enduring the strange, cold, beautiful city. His
exploration was something Mary Ellen would have appreciated.
She was the Columbus in the Clifton family, she hated Mussolini,
she wanted to die pulling romantic crap like this.

Mary Ellen was an all-right gal.

Suddenly, out of the blue, it struck George that he was going to
bury Mary Ellen. She was eight years younger than he was, yet
there could be no doubt about this: Mary Ellen made it a project
to be as careless and irresponsible with her health as she could.
She felt she only lived once. So she gulped wine every night while
George sipped ice water with his dinner. She ignored George's
dirty looks. She refused to hear what Mussolini thought about
alcohol.

Several times a month Mary Ellen got so loaded with her wine
that she left the dishes on the dinner table, got a bucket of ice
cubes, pulled the bar cart within easy reach of the Lazy Boy,
punched the television on, and went to town mixing herself stiff
drinks.

George had no comment, but he was pissed. When his time to
hit the sack came, he jumped to his feet abruptly and left the
room. He did not bother to say good night or croak bitch, or
anything else. Mary Ellen was sure to be in a real contrary mood
now, so it wasn't worth the row. He brushed and flossed his teeth,
swallowed his vitamins, did his thirty sit-ups, set his alarm clock,

and turned out the lamp. Behind the wall, bottles went on clinking and clanging deep into the night; the late-night movie was coming on; Mary Ellen did not have to get up and go to work in the morning.

Mary Ellen had a problem all right—she was damn close to being a certified alcoholic. And it didn't stop with her boozing either. She disdained vitamins. She pigged out on junk food. (Because she didn't put on weight, she refused to pay any attention to her diet.) She was an all-American pill popper too—loved her Valium, tossed off Tylenols, Alka Seltzers, aspirins, sleeping pills, slugs of milk of magnesia, painkillers as though they were candy. And she winged everything, didn't have a single routine in her life.

Thinking about Mary Ellen, George forgot about his chattering teeth and goose bumps. He stopped paying mind to the looks he was getting. He and Mary Ellen were the oddest goddam odd couple ever to tie the knot. The flat Chicago sidewalk, running on and on into the distance, no longer seemed level under his shoes. It was sloping down, pushing him forward, speeding up everything, and George saw his future clearly: he was going to wind up a widower. He was going to bury Fat Fred too. He was going to get a chance to spit on the graves of the two cheap character assassins in his office. He was living a far better and healthier life than anybody else he knew, so he was going to see off his fearless leader and all the other corporate dynamos when they paid with lung cancer and clogged arteries for their thoughtless ways; he was going to lay out all his relatives, his neighbors, his clerks. It was a good thing that he and Mary Ellen could not have kids, because he would have wound up going to their funerals too, with his grandchildren.

A red light stopped him. Shivering in the fourth dimension on a windy street corner in the odd city where he was born, George faced himself as a toothless, nearsighted geezer, deaf as a doorknob, bald, impotent. There were purple veins and pouches of loose skin all over his body; thick glasses made his eyes loom bigger than his sunken mouth. He saw himself as he strained to drag the ton of his

wispy skeletal body from his smelly bed every morning a few
minutes before nine o'clock to do the thing he had always done
best—oblige his anus timer, still ticking away as though there were
no tomorrow. His taupe shriveled-up penis burning, he urinated
yellow stones the size of peas. His body expelled something, and
he peered at the thing, and it was the same goddam stuff as always.
The same length and the same thickness and the same color.

It was the familiar stuff of eternity.

THE CHAMOMILE TEA IS DEAD

George had had enough eternity and future and cold wind for the
day. There was a trendy-looking joint on the shaded side of the
street, so he crossed over and went in. It was better to gulp poisons
and wreck his lungs with secondhand cigarette smoke in the
spectral chamber of some bar than to go on thinking about what he
had done with his life.

The place had plants sprouting everywhere, poking out of the
walls, hanging down among the tables. And the frosted-glass
windows, the brass railings, and the bathtub aquarium sprawling at
the center of the square bar really packed in the lunch-hour
drinkers. They dressed big picture, smelled big picture, behaved
big picture. But it was warm here, so George grabbed a stunted
booth with a good view of the bubbles. One of two animated
bartenders, a young woman, rushed a hand-written work-of-art
menu to him. George waved her off.

—Chamomile tea is dead, he said, so lemme start off with a
beer and a shot.

The woman smiled at him warmly and jogged back to being
frantic behind the bar. You never saw anybody move so fast in the
utilities. George was not used to this farcical tempo. His world

flowed through its paces with the serenity of the fish in the aquarium. The farce struck him as distasteful, though he didn't mind its upside: the young woman was right back with his order. He lifted the shot glass and tipped it to her.

—To hell with Mussolini's goddam sponge.

He didn't know what made him say it, but he was on a roll now. The foxy bartender chuckled. She appreciated his non sequiturs, was used to the bizarre jokes of the big-picture crowd, did not think he was a character at all. Not any odder than they came here anyway. That was a nice warm feeling too, so George took a sip of his shot. The long-buried taste cut sharply into his tongue. He hadn't touched whiskey since his navy days, and he was coming to find out that the stuff still burned like a son of a bitch on the tongue. And it went straight to his head, making him feel the fittest, slimmest, healthiest, soberest man in the big-picture joint. He hated the feeling, so he quickly dumped the shot into his beer and downed it. This made him feel better right away, so he waved the empty stein at the fish foreground and got another beer. And while he was at it, he ordered a Reuben too.

Screw the graham crackers in his imperial desk.

Screw the funny bird Mussolini who had been bending the collarbone of his left shoulder for so long.

Screw his dry, dirty, yellow sponge.

And fuck the utility company and Uncle Sam and the U.S. Navy and every goddam body else.

If he was drunk already, it was fine by George Asshole-with-a-Timer Clifton: he had the future to deal with. There were all those goddam funerals.

George had always assumed that he and Mussolini would slug it out for the title of the oldest living American one day. But now he remembered Mussolini's crack about the nuclear war again and decided that the goddam navy was no place to maximize anything. The navy drove you to drink, sent you to wars. The wise son of a bitch was merely mocking them, making a living, and by now fat white maggots were probably stewing in his massive skull. Schools of cocky young men were passing through his morgue, but it had never occurred to him that, twenty-eight years later, in Chicago, hardly a day would go by without somebody thinking of his piggy eyes, his impervious manner, his lousy goddam sermon. He had had no idea that he could wind up costing somebody twenty-four wasted years.

Well, the Reuben smelled good anyway.

George picked it up from the dainty woven basket the woman had hurried it over in, sniffed it, his mouth filled with saliva, and he sank his teeth into it.

I may be drunk, he thought, but this tastes like Marilyn Monroe's pussy.

He split the sandwich apart and examined the ingredients: the corned beef was lean, the Swiss cheese aged, the bread a hearty pumpernickel. The sauerkraut had pounds of caraway in it. And the hell of it was, he could have had a sandwich like this every day for the past twenty-four years instead of crumbling his graham crackers and chasing them down with chamomile tea. For fucking twenty-goddam-four wasted asshole years.

That cocksucker Mussolini had cost him a district job. Had a few pounds of red meat been applied to his career in the utilities, George could have been a third-level. All he ever came up short on was Fat Fred's drive to maul people in meetings. So George waved at the bartender and asked for another Reuben. The young woman gave him a probing look.

—Fox, people have been looking at me funny all day, George told her.

She retreated in panic while George resumed munching on the remnants of the first pussy-Reuben and thought, I'll get another beer and a shot, then hit the bitch with a dessert and see how she handles that. I wonder if strawberry cheesecake is big-picture or not. There was only one way to find out.

THE BIRTHDAY PARTY

The cake is big and spongy yet barely large enough for all those candles to fit. Their pink wax is melting into the flaky chartreuse topping. There are a hundred and fifty candles jammed onto the cake, and it has taken three jittery white smocks to light them all up. The social room of the old people's home is packed with excited nurses, adrenalinated doctors feigning indifference, and elbow-swinging journalists. The director himself is standing next to George, looking dazed, holding a cordless telephone in his hands. The staff is waiting for a signal from him, but evidently he is too paralyzed with stage fright, so one of the nurses finally takes charge and starts singing, and everyone quickly joins in: happy birthday to yoooou, happy birthday, dear Jaw-orge, happy birthday to yooooooou.

None of the mugs in the room says anything to George. All the faces that had meant something once were gone generations and generations ago. His eyes hurt from the flashes that keep popping off constantly, building a wall of light around him, bleaching out the gloomy hospital room. George is glad he has borrowed this fancy pair of silk pajamas. With all the light they are throwing at him, if he had had his regular green hospital gown on they would have been liable to see right through him.

George is a frail, nutty, freaky old coot who has wound up where all the lives lived according to Dr. Mussolini end—in an airless room in a state-run old people's dumpster; the oldest living American; the hard worker who had sat around a utility company for thirty-eight years and then had sat around this old people's home for ninety more; the citizen who remembered funny presidents like Ford; the voter who voted for Kennedy against Nixon or for Nixon against Kennedy and who has forgotten which and it sure as hell doesn't matter now; the man who had actually watched the first primitive spidery spacecraft land on the

moon (these days of course the moon is connected with the good
old pedestal orb by continuous on-the-hour flights on which
cleanly shaven businessmen with briefcases full of computer gear
and eyes full of boredom gulp lousy airline coffee out of
Styrofoam cups personalized with their names and their titles,
check their watches, and run their offices tens of thousands of
miles away out of their beeping briefcases, every second of their
careers now productive to their companies); George S. Q.
Clifton, a celebrity this birthday morning as he attempts to blow
out the forest of tiny candles.

George is puffing his guts out and getting absolutely nowhere
with it. Not a single damn candle has gone out yet. His hundred-
and-fifty-year-old lungs ain't exactly what you'd call organ bellows.
They seem more like a busted accordion sack. They manage to
bend a few flames on the near edge of the cake, but that's it,
though George is pushing as much air as he can. The crowd of
people keeps staring at this pathetic sight, George's leathery face is
turning purple, and still nothing doing.

The first snickers are being choked off beyond the clicking wall
of light when it occurs to George that these goddam candles may
be the stuff of an old novelty trick. What if they are those trick
candles you could throw a bucket of water on and they would go
right on burning? (Perhaps the media is turning this whole event
into an obscure history lesson about barbaric novelties that had
been outlawed by the government decades ago—such atavistic
tools of wit as whoopee cushions and creepy crawlers and plastic
dog turds and horse manure packed like Godiva chocolates—
which the ancestors used to humiliate each other with in those
dark times that only this man, George Clifton, still remembers
firsthand, albeit dimly.) So George lifts the Styrofoam cup of
lukewarm champagne they have stuck in his trembling hand,
which he has almost dribbled out all over the silk pajamas, and
dumps whatever is left onto the damn candles. A few of them
sizzle and go out. So they aren't a novelty trick at all.

The photographers go crazy now and everyone behind the
explosion of light roars with laughter. They feel free to get all that

laughing they had been suppressing out of their guts now, because now they are hooting with George over his joke and not at him. They scream and gasp and shriek and howl so hard the IV bottles throughout the old people's dumpster start swinging like pendulums on their little hangers. The prettiest young nurse now bends down and begins blowing out the remaining candles. She has big tits and great pipes and a cool head, and she moves methodically around the cake, and it still takes her nearly a minute to finish playing the fireperson. Then she cuts the cake and hands George a slice; it's terrible—spongy and porous and sickly sugary.

Not only does the cake taste awful, the cordless phone in the director's arms begins to ring. George knows what's coming and hurriedly swallows a lump of the vile sponge. The director waits for the second ring, and, as he answers it, a hush descends on the social room.

Yes, it is, he says. Just a second.

The director hands the phone to George, who feels the lump of cake ooze down his esophagus. A youthful voice pours through the entire room (the telephone is just a prop) loud and clear and possessed of a fine diction.

George Clifton?

Yes.

Hello, George! This is the president.

Hi, Mr. President.

How are you this morning, George?

I'm fine, thank you, sir.

Well, George, I'm calling to congratulate you on this fine personal triumph. Hundred and fifty great years—how about that! I think that's marvelous! I think you're a heck of a guy, and I think you live in a heck of a country.

You're right, Mr. President.

And I am declaring this day George Clifton Day.

Thank you, sir.

I hope to congratulate you on your two-hundredth birthday!

Please, Mr. President. I've had enough.

Well . . . Happy birthday, George, and so long.

Mr. President, while I have you on the line here . . . Sir, I'm getting a runaround about my Social Security checks. I was wondering . . .

I'll certainly look into it, George.

They said their program doesn't have enough digits in the calendar for me. I haven't seen any money in three months.

I'll get to the bottom of this, George. You're getting your money.

Thank you, sir. Thank you kindly.

Happy birthday, George!

You bet.

The dial tone cuts on and George hands the phone back to the director. There is more laughter in the room. George resumes chewing the sugary sponge. The news conference begins, and the media hounds have given careful consideration to their off-the-cuff questions.

How is the cake?

No comment.

Does George still enjoy his food?

Not as much as sex anymore.

What is his favorite dish?

Graham crackers.

How is the kitchen here?

No comment.

How is his digestion?

Not as good as his sex life.

So is this party and this cake going to wreak havoc with it?

The hounds are all circling around the billion-dollar question of course. And George knows very well too what they are trying to get at. These media people all belong to the human-interest crowd. The *National Enquirer* and the *Washington Star* have sent three aces each, and it is one of these hotshots who finally spells out the billion-dollar question on all their minds.

Is it true?

Damn right it's true! Never missed a single day as far as I can remember.

And how long is that?

One hundred and twenty-one years. Maybe longer, because it ain't been much of an issue before then.

So this morning as well, then?

Hell, yeah, I dropped me a nice turd at nine-zero-nine this very goddam historical fucking morning, buddy.

Old coot George is annoyed on galaxial television, and all these media people just lap it up, because he has just given them a chance to bleep something out of his quote. And some things never change: you are still getting deep when you start to bleep. Their little bleeps signify REAL LIFE to media hounds, so George decides to give them more.

You try taking a good shit a hundred years from now, kid, and you're all right, I don't care what anybody else says about you.

From the corner of George's eye he could see two faces jerk away; his words had hit them like machine-gun volleys.

—Fuck, said George.

Two women, a white broad in a shiny-black raincoat and tennis shoes and a black matron with a bright-yellow shawl wound around her, stood at the sidewalk curb waiting for a bus. They had been watching George as he staggered toward them. He must have been talking to himself all along.

George stopped and stared them down; he was standing behind everything he did today.

The white broad quickly looked away. The older lady took her sweet time detaching her eyes from him. She acted as though she had been offended. Then she swung around to eyeball the traffic.

George circled around her to reestablish eye contact. Words flew out of him now, but he was speaking in his most managerial voice.

—You try taking a dump a hundred years from now, lady. You do that and you're all right too.

—Get away from me, you creep, shrieked the matron.

—As you wish, said George.

He bowed deeply and stumbled on.

—A rogue deuce on rampage, so shoot me, he said to a wispy,

lawyerly patrician, who hurried past him looking into the distance. The old big-picture son of a bitch was in good shape too. He was making time.

A green light sent a pack of pedestrians charging at George. Swaying, he waited till they'd got close enough for a conversational tone, then addressed them.

—I've kept my mouth shut in a million meetings, he confided to them.

His words were like the clean blow of an ax splitting a log of dry firewood: the crowd separated and surged around him.

—I gotta tell somebody, he said to the faces flashing by.

—Whatsa matter witchu, man? said a deep voice behind him.

George turned around to face a big, burly black guy. This man, at least, was unafraid of George. He looked as though he was waiting for a bus too. Finally somebody to talk to. And a captive audience at that.

—Not a thing, George told him. I've just realized that this one guy Mussolini's been laughing behind my back with the rest of them all these years. I can just hear him: right, kids, no balls but an asshole with a timer.

—You needchu some help, Jack. You havin' one of 'em nervous breakdowns.

—Are you a doctor? What the fuck do you know about nervous breakdowns? Huh?

—Dunno a goddam thing 'bout 'em, Jack. Cause we niggers ain't got 'em. But I be seein' you honkies freakin' out all the damn time.

—Shit! I'm okay. A little emotional, that's all.

—First getchu a coat or sweater or somethin', Jack. Then start freakin' out.

—I'll tell you what. I haven't talked to people in twenty-four years, thirteen of them of unbroken perfect attendance. But I like acting crazy today. I certainly don't think it's valid, you telling me I'm having a nervous breakdown.

—Hey, it don't make me no diff'rence, Jack. I do sees you be axin' fo' a scand'lous flu though.

Just then a bus pulled up and terminated the only conversation

George had been able to strike up on the endless chilly sloping streets of downtown Chicago.

—Nice rappin' witchu, Jack, said the large black man, stepping into the bus.

George ambled into the street and wove his way to the sunny sidewalk he had somehow left behind through cars that were stacked up halfway up the block, waiting for a green light.

—I drank my lunch today, he announced to a fat man in a little green Volkswagen who had his windows rolled all the way down.

—Been wantin' to do the same thing m'self, said the pudgy driver.

—You wanna join me? Come on, I'll buy you a beer, George proposed.

—Don't think I'm gonna find a parkin' space around here, said the fat man quickly and shot away with the traffic, stranding George in the middle of three lanes of go-getters. Or so he thought. His departure did not faze George one bit. He just walked right in front of a Yellow Cab racing a bus. The cab skidded, honked, the whole mass of cars behind it went through a violent contraction, but George made the sunny sidewalk again. And he did it with unsurpassable dignity.

These people did not care to talk to him. He understood. He too had been making detours around nuts who talked to themselves all his life. And who wanted to talk to a George S. Q. Clifton anyway? Not George. Clifton had nothing to say; George knew that better than anybody. So he saw their point. In fact, it made him feel real good to find out there existed folks like the tall black guy at the bus stop, folks who were good for a few words no matter how you looked or what you did.

Then it struck him that he wasn't sure that Mary Ellen would not have talked to rogue deuces too. She sure might. Mary Ellen was quite a gal. All of a sudden George started feeling real good about the world. Here he was, some fourteen, fifteen, sixteen years after he had met her, and he was still in love with his wife.

This had to be a record.

He had to get to a pay phone fast.

TACIT KNOWLEDGE

For a long time now George had perfectly understood Mary Ellen's innermost desire.

It had not been all that innermost.

Mary Ellen had never come into the open and spelled out the word "implants" of course, and she did not suspect that George knew about them. But George had guessed what she had so badly wanted long before Mary Ellen drank herself into a state one night and broached the subject.

Now there was a night that would be hard to forget.

It was close to George's bedtime. Mary Ellen lay in the Lazy Boy, the bar cart at her elbow, slurring her words, the works, when she suddenly went into a long soliloquy about implants. She spewed forth a lot of crazy nonsense—stuff about matching her person to her body or whatever the hell it was. Then she went into this pathetic song and dance about a girlfriend of a girlfriend who was thinking about getting the implants. Finally she asked what George's advice to her girlfriendz girlfriendz girlfriend would be. What did he think? What should she say to her girlfriendz girlfriendz girlfriendz girlfriend?

She was disgusting, couldn't stand up, was shaving months off her life expectancy in the course of one evening, was slaughtering her brain cells wholesale. George had got the point right away. (It didn't exactly take a genius, not with Mary Ellen skipping her bridge club to watch Donahue's "Silicone: Pro and Con," not with her underlining away in books on gender changes.) It all got George very hot. He jumped up, and he may have yelled. In any case, he went on record as being against implants. Then he slammed the door of the bedroom, whipped off his thirty sit-ups, and, tossing and turning deep into the night, listened to the bottle percussions in the living room. Clearly, if she could not get her tits, Mary Ellen was going to settle for cirrhosis of the liver.

George meant what he had yelled, of course: implants were bullshit. There were so many nerves in the breasts, and you would be taking such chances of infection, and even if everything were to work out, and the tits didn't harden (a big goddam if!), what about the mortifying social adjustments later?

Holy shit!

One morning George would wake up and find himself married to a wife with twice the tits of the day before. The Cliftons would just about have to move to a different part of the country. How was he supposed to explain that? He would die. Everybody would know what had happened anyway, and they would just wait and see what nonsense he came up with to cover it up. Everybody would be talking about the implants. Neighbors, friends, people who barely knew them would be calling each other on the phone: Did you see Mary Ellen yet? God, I can't wait to see her! At her age! Are they that much bigger, then? Oh, God! Are they really? Are you kidding? Jugs?! I don't believe it! So what is she wearing these days? Is she showing them off? Low-cut sweaters? That slut! She never did have a decent bone in her body. She said what? You're putting me on! She said George likes them? Then he has no shame either! He remodeled their bedroom?! No, he didn't! OH, MY GOD! No! No! Not mirrors! In their bedroom? Freaks! Jesus Christ! Friggin' freaks! And we always thought that he at least was normal! But boy, the body snatchers really did get the Cliftons! Did they ever!

That night George did not fall asleep for hours. The bottles clanged; breasts ballooned; the neighborhood whispered to him; time dragged on and on to the seven-fifteen.

In the morning George jumped on his bicycle, and the subject of implants was closed. In the six or seven years since, the Cliftons had not talked silicone again. A few times, in bed, Mary Ellen would ask George how he'd like it if she had full breasts, and George would say that he loved her tits the way they were. Mary Ellen would then say that he was a liar, and that was about as far as it would go. Mary Ellen had clearly reconciled herself to staying on the itty-bitty-titty committee all her life.

Except today was a day when all the rules were broken, and
George was reeling drunk and the Reuben sat in his stomach like
a rock and he had been cutting meetings and talking to passersby
and he had realized that he was madly in love with his wife and
when he had said that he didn't like big tits, it had been a tactical
lie anyway, so what the hell.

You only live once, he thought, Mary Ellen's got a point. And
what does it matter how long if you don't really live anyway?

Suddenly George wanted Mary Ellen to get her silicone
knockers and put on a bikini and go attack the dandelions on their
front lawn and cause accidents.

El trains roared overhead as he staggered down a narrow shady
street and looked for a pay phone. He finally found one in a small
vestibule of a drab corner diner. He dialed the operator and had
her call his house collect. The phone rang five times; the operator
said, I'm sorry, sir, but there's no answer.

—Hold it, please, said George. My wife should be at home.
Maybe she's outside.

—Okay, said the operator.

They listened to four more rings.

—Don't think she's there, sir, said the operator. She had her
quota of calls to think about.

—I gotta talk to her, said George. Gotta.

The phone rang three more times. George could hear the
operator breathing.

—I'm sorry, sir, but you'll just have to try later, sir, said the
operator and switched off.

—Jesus Christ! All right . . . All right, said George. He
slammed down the phone.

She is missing the chance of her marriage, he thought.

He stepped back out on the street with the El tracks. There was
no sun here. Plenty of wind though, filling up his shirt again,
making him feel like a hunchback.

He walked briskly down the street, swinging the doggie bag with
his reserve Reuben. He did not feel like talking anymore, had
nothing to say to anybody, was just too goddam cold in a shirt and

tie. But he wasn't going back to the office. That decision held. So he had to buy a sweater or something. That was his next order of business.

Then he could try calling Mary Ellen again.

U.S. ARMY JACKET

In the twenty-four years he had been earning a living, keeping his records, and paying the bills George Clifton had not missed a single payment. His credit rating had to be right up there with Saudi Arabia's, but George did not own any credit cards. Banks kept flooding his mailbox with offers; all he had to do to open a five-thousand-dollar line of credit was to mail back the pre-addressed, stamped envelope.

George never wavered. He always tore up the tenders. He was opposed to plastic money on principle—the principle being that he did not want to make it any easier for Mary Ellen to blow his dough. She was already going around spending his money like a drunken sailor, so she did not need to have the liquidation of George's paychecks made any more convenient.

But today, for the first time in George's memory, a credit card would have come in handy. He had just shelled out his incidental cash for whiskey, beer, and Reubens. All he had on him now was the fifty salted away in the deepest recesses of his wallet, his emergency fund, but fifty bucks was not going to get him very warm downtown. At Marshall Field's on State Street he would be lucky to get a decent pair of gloves out of his emergency fund. Then he remembered the seedy store a few doors down from VanCura's Hardware.

General Patton's sold everything from wooden limbs to army rations, cheap backpacks, flak jackets, plastic rain gear, old rubbers, and mosquito repellents with expired dates, but the store specialized in surplus clothes. The long underlit room had the musty smell of a warehouse. The merchandise lay in heaps as in a flea market. No salespeople pounced on him when he entered, so he would have to find his own way around the piles. But that was fine by George. He didn't exactly qualify as a survivalist on a mad shopping binge. And General Patton's prices were right.

George located the rack with infantry jackets and tried on three of them before he found one that came close to fitting him. He never took it off once he had it on. The jacket clearly had some mileage on it, but it was warm and gave off a clean, just-washed smell. It hung on his shoulders a little, which only brought back memories. The navy never put anything on you that fit, except the boots—the boots always fit perfectly.) The rough canvas was khaki. Above the left breast pocket, black generic letters said U.S. ARMY. And then there were all those pockets. The kangaroo-sized pouch above George's groin swallowed the doggie-bagged Reuben easily. He put his keys and his coins into separate compartments, then stuck his wallet into one of several inside breast pockets. Hell, the pockets alone made this jacket worth the money.

Strolling out of General Patton's in his awesome jacket, George felt gloriously warm, broke, and young. The city was his once more. The sun was shining; the early afternoon shadows remained stunted and tea; his wife was about to grow jugs. George was on a roll.

But the operator still could not make Mary Ellen answer his collect call. He thought of getting on an early train and telling her in person. He had promised Mary Ellen that he would redo the kitchen. He could have all the cabinets ripped out before the evening news. It sure seemed tempting.

Then he made his decision: fuck it—the kitchen, the cabinets, his work, his projects, all that shit could wait. It was so much better to roam around downtown and see what developed. That son of a bitch Mussolini was maggot stew, and for now George had a hell of a job on his hands just keeping his withered ass out of the nine o'clock dates with the john in an old people's dumpster. The sooner he got going on this the better.

He wasn't sure, however, about what exactly to do to make things develop, so he sauntered into VanCura's Hardware and bounced aimlessly from one shelf to another, picking up tools and putting them down again. Then he ambled out and drifted toward State Street. There were the display windows of peep shows, porno bookstores, record and shoe shops, and dill-pickle delis to look at along the way.

The lunch hour was long over and the early afternoon lull had settled over the streets. Fewer El trains rumbled overhead. They were shorter now too. Soon the rush hour would get under way and, in George's commuter station, a line of drawn men would form around a kiosk bar. The commuter specials of your choice went for a dollar. For the first time in his career it looked as though George would get into the line, buy a Bloody Mary or a can of cold beer, give one more jolt to his body clock, and knock a few more candles off that goddam spongy cake.

QWL

It was not until Fat Fred startled him that George remembered the afternoon meeting. Fat Fred, the district man, was sitting alone on a bench on the shaded side of State Street, staring at his shoes. George ducked through the nearest shop door. The bench stood across the street and half a block away, so he had been lucky: Fat Fred had not seen him yet. But it had been close.

He found himself on the ground floor of a department store. There were glittering batteries of lipsticks and perfume bottles and languid saleswomen with perfect makeup looking straight through him. They did not care that his heart was racing away for the third time today. But George had had enough. That was all he needed, to run into Fred Foss of all people when he was supposed to be smiling away in a QWL meeting. He made for the side exit door; he would navigate a wide detour around Fat Fred, cross State Street, and head for the train station before any more dynamos saw him. But then, leaning into another revolving door, George caught sight of himself in a large, sparkling mirror and froze. His face looked singed again. Even his ears were crimson.

The ears infuriated him.

He turned right around and briskly strode out onto State Street. To hell with Fat Fred. To hell with the company. And to hell with whoever saw him in the army jacket. He was through getting red ears.

He made straight for Fred's panorama. As he marched forward, it occurred to him that Fat Fred was probably supposed to be dozing off in the same goddam QWL session as he was. And self-incrimination had never been Fred Foss's style.

In a way it made perfect sense that Fat Fred should be sprawled over a wave-shaped bench on State Street Mall right now; these Quality of Work Life sessions were always a royal pain. Nobody ever knew what this QWL was actually supposed to be. It was corporate culture of course, and the big-picture leaders were real big on it. So the cleaning ladies' boss would complain that his crew bitched about the cigarette butts in the shells of men's washrooms and how these butts shot their QWL all to heck, because his ladies would always end up having to fish them out, and what a stinking job that was.

But the snotty-nosed guided missile, sent down from the big-picture floors of headquarters to chair the QWL meeting, didn't think that butts in urinals were corporate culture at all. He admonished the poor sucker from house services that this was no matter for a QWL quorum. And of course he didn't say what was. That left everybody confused. So they said what a wonderful thing QWL was and how vital and how long overdue and how everybody should bear down on QWL because it sure made bookoo difference in their department's WL, so much so that it knocked absenteeism way down. Then they dispersed, thinking that this company propaganda was getting out of hand.

It did not surprise George that Fred Foss had found something better to do than QWL. But there was something in the way the fat man sat on the bench that got to George: Fred Foss was wearing a white windbreaker with a stripe of company colors, black and red, running down the length of one arm, and he sat nothing like three hundred pounds of memory, nothing like the monstrosity of HQ meetings. The guy looked forlorn. His shoulders were hunched in, his hands shoved into his pockets, his eyes glued to his Hush Puppies. He had used two Quarter-pounder boxes and a milk shake to claim the entire bench for himself. But he wasn't eating anything. He rested on the bench, still as a hunter, making himself small.

George pressed his shoulders back, hoisted his chin up, and paraded right smack through Fred's panorama. Forty feet of air separated them. (State Street was closed to regular traffic, so there was nothing to screen George.) The infantry jacket took control of George and he marched straight-backed, his steps clipped and precise.

Fat Fred kept staring at his shoes.

Suddenly it hit George as pretty goddam sad: they were the two corporate dynamos who had had the balls to cut a QWL quorum; they were the avant-garde of utilities; they were like two trains passing in the night, had never really talked, never once connected.

Fuck it, he thought, if it takes a rogue deuce to announce himself to the rogue district man, so be it.

He headed straight for Fred's bench. He fitted his bony ass on the edge of the bench, nudging Fred's milk shake.

The fat man went on studying his scuffed-up shoes.

George unwrapped his Reuben and let out a loud sigh (because this wasn't easy, this was no second graham cracker, this was a second pussy rock).

Fat Fred contemplated his invisible toes.

So George pushed the milk shake all the way to Fred's side and spread himself out comfortably on the bench.

Now the rogue district man had to look up at the rogue deuce. George had expected to be shoved back, but Fat Fred started to eye him with a tired, imploring look that immediately changed into dilated astonishment.

—Nice jacket, Fred conceded after a while, reaching for a Quarter-pounder box.

—Just got it at General Patton's over on Dearborn, George announced proudly.

—General Patton's, no kidding, said Fred.

—Forty-one plus tax.

—That a steal or what, George.

They sat side by side, munching on their sandwiches. When it seemed that Fred had had enough time to digest George's shopping sophistication, George shifted his weight again.

—Ditching the fucking QWL too?

—Yeah, they'll just have to manage without my input today.

Fred sounded like a man starting to recover from major surgery that had turned out to be useless.

—Oh, well, said George, I hope they can do it without the cigar-store Indian sitting there, smiling.

He meant the remark to cheer Fat Fred up, but it came across sounding almost bitter.

—I'm sorry about that, sighed the district man, sinking back into his spleen. I'd been ad-libbing. I didn't mean it to stay with you for all those years.

—In one ear and out the other, George said, waving him off. And you were right about me too.

This time George got his recently acquired nonchalance across; he sensed that he and Fat Fred could talk. Really talk. Talk talk. It all seemed to be a part of the ease with which he had been gliding through the world since lunch. So he just started speaking his mind, and the words came out matter-of-fact.

—You look depressed, Fred.

—Shit, George, you're like a fucking stick. You don't know the first thing about life.

They gazed into space again. One wide sidewalk ran behind them; there was the narrow asphalt channel for the buses by their feet; then the opposite sidewalk; a row of witty shop windows in

which manikins clad in silk and pearls and tail coats swung
baseball bats at magnolia blossoms and plastic soap bubbles and
round purple telephones and crystal-ball vases and rolled-up socks.
They went on chewing their sandwiches. George ran his heavy-
duty zipper up and down. It worked like a Japanese-made charm.
The jacket was warm. He was hatching a premature load of
eternity from the rock in his stomach.

Though neither Fred nor he was saying anything, George knew
that for the first time in his career he was talking meaningfully with
somebody besides Mary Ellen.

—I damn near broke my back this morning, buddy, Fat Fred
opened up, and their inner persons suddenly took off.—I was late
for this meeting at 8G. Part of my image, right? I walk in, and I see
I didn't miss a thing. Some dizzy Lizzy's running her mouth, half
her purple lipstick licked off, all the ball-busters napping. So I start
sitting down, and my ass never stops. It just keeps on going, all the
way to the goddam floor. I mean the fucking chair busts right
under me. Oh, it was funny.

Fat Fred gave George a probing look, but George was not
laughing at all. He did not even have to suppress a chuckle. He
was watching the accident through Fred's eyes, and what George
was hearing underneath the story was breaking his heart. Here was
a guy who had it all; he could speak off the top of his head, didn't
have to wear a tie, was suffered to drift into meetings whenever he
got around to it and then to pollute the air with cigar smoke, could
expect someone else to sign his name on the attendance sheet for
him. Yet, if he had had a choice, he would have opted for being
a skinny cigar-store Indian.

This was bad.

—Can you picture me on my back, flapping my hands like an
overturned bug? But I got even. I had them lug me all the way up
to medical.

—You look all right now.

—It took five guys, buddy. Five guys, and they're all fat too.
They nearly dropped me twice. I bet their backs are in worse shape
than mine right now.

—Well, we're leaders, all we ever do for exercise is sit on our asses.

—My strongest point, George.

—How the hell much do you weigh anyway, Fred? I always wanted to ask you that.

—I don't weigh myself as a rule, buddy.

—I don't blame you.

—But they got this nickel-a-shot scale at my bank. This Saturday, with my shoes and my passbook under my arm, I clocked three hundred twenty-three. Call it three twenty.

—Okay, but did you ever seriously try to lose any of it?

—Shit, George, I tried it all. Even dropped ninety goddam pounds once. Had this apron of loose skin hanging down from my gut. I was gonna go and have it cut off, but something kept telling me to wait. I'm real glad I did too. One weekend I got sauced, and then I got hungry, and then I took Monday off, because I was still famished, and by Friday it was all back. And then some. I would of burst like a frankfurter you boil too damn long if they would of taken off my apron.

—Well, I know of a guy had his stomach stapled.

—And?

—He went from the big man's store right into the middle of the rack at K Mart.

—Nothing's gonna work for me, George.

—You don't know that.

—No, in about five, ten years my heart's gonna say Fuck this. And they're gonna have to get a special, reinforced coffin for me. My old lady's gonna have to rent a U-Haul to get me to the cemetery.

George started quietly laughing. Fred grinned back at him.

—Then it's gonna take about fifteen of my bereaved relatives to drag the damn thing to my double lot. And they'll probably drop me anyway. Oh, it's gonna be a riot. Fred went on, spinning his fantasies.

George did not laugh anymore.

—The worms will get so fat that they'll have to crane them over to other graves.

Fat Fred was funny, but it did not cross George's mind to laugh. Their bodies were sprawled on the wave-shaped bench. Fred started chewing another Quarter-pounder. People strolled up and down the sidewalk behind them. City buses spewed black diesel exhaust in their faces. Elegant manikins beyond held their witty tableaus. George now knew for a fact that Fat Fred would never stop eating. It was probably too late anyhow. He had minimized the hell out of his givens already.

They were both slipping into depression.

—So how the fuck do you keep so skinny, George? How do you do it?

This was a good question, and George had to really think about how to put it so that it made sense. They sat there for a long time.

—I guess I was always too goddam scared to unwind and eat like other people, was the way George finally phrased it.

—I wish to God I was such a chicken, said Fred wistfully.

—I've been taking such good care of myself, it makes me sick. For twenty-four years, every damn lunch, I've been eating an apple, a couple of graham crackers, and a cup of tea.

Fat Fred jerked his head up now and looked at George sharply.

—Chamomile tea—no sugar, explained George.

—You made me feel better already, gasped Fred. He looked horrified.

—Only thing I'd ever experiment with would be the apple. I'd go from Golden Delicious to Jonathan's to Granny Smith's to Roman Beauties to Red Delicious.

—You gotta be shitting me!

—Oh, I tried pears once, it's true, George confessed.

—Are you being serious, George?

—Oh, no, it's absolutely true.

—And?

—They tasted great. They were a nice change.

—So what happened, for God's sake?

—They knocked my body clock all out of whack.

—I don't get it, George.

—I take a shit between nine and nine-fifteen every day—when I stick to apples, that is. It's funny.

—I don't fucking believe it!

Horror and awe were slugging it out on Fred's face.

—Good as they tasted, George went on, the pears didn't do it for me. So the sucker I was, I went back to the goddam apples.

—Man, this has got to be the goofiest fucking story I ever heard, Fred moaned.

—Guess so. I hate apples with a passion by now.

—But I love it! Damn, and I had you pegged for a do-nothing pencil pusher.

—That's me all right, said George, George S. Q. Cigar-store Indian Clifton.

—Shit, I had no idea you were this complicated, buddy.

—Complicated, hell. I hear my subordinates go around calling me an asshole with a timer, George said, letting out a self-deprecating chuckle. Oh, it's funny.

But Fat Fred did not laugh: he saw everything through George's eyes. So they sat in silence for a while and watched the buses stir up dust and greasy papers.

—Well, I just had a pair of Reubens for lunch, George reported, thinking that it was time to cheer up again.

—Hey, great!

—I've been taking such wonderful care of myself that I saw myself having a birthday party in an old people's home.

Fat Fred burst out laughing. George watched the huge stomach that lay on his thighs quiver and palpitate, then indulged himself in a sour smile.

—Wait, he said, we're talking one hundred and fifty years. I even got a call from the president.

This got the rogue district man rolling around the bench, gasping for air. George went on smiling his sour little smile, waiting for Fred to tire himself out. It was news to him that he could make people laugh to tears.

—That's still not all, he finally said and had Fred going off again in anticipation. The *National Enquirer* had dug up all the dirt, and they asked me did I take a shit at nine o'clock that morning.

—Wait, please, wait!

—So I told them on national TV: look, I've been taking a nine o'clock shit for a hundred and twenty years, damn it! I'm not gonna stop today just because it's my birthday!

Fat Fred was slapping his massive thighs, choking.

—I didn't mention the pears, George confessed. I lied.

—Stop it, will you!

—On the news they bleeped out where I said "shit." Nothing had changed in America.

—Stop, George!

George waited and waited for Fat Fred to slurp in enough oxygen to speak again.

—God, George! Why the hell don't you ever speak up in meetings? You'd be division!

—Never got anything to say, said George.

He meant it seriously, but it came out deadpan, and Fred Foss started again. He whipped one of his huge arms over George's shoulder. George kept his hands folded on his knees.

—Let's go get a beer, said Fred.

—At that birthday party I couldn't blow out a single candle, George went on, and there were batteries of them.

—You should of blown them out with your ass, suggested Fred, and his body started rolling all over the bench again.

—That's when I decided to get a Reuben and a couple of beers. And to buy this jacket. I've been knocking those candles off by the minute.

—Listen, George, thanks. I was getting damn near suicidal there. Let's go get a beer.

—For me a Reuben's life in the fast lane.

—Let's go get a fucking beer!

George sprang to his feet while Fat Fred slowly heaved himself up, leaving the milk shake untouched. They walked in silence, staring at their shoes—a tieless, hard-breathing fat man in a company-issue windbreaker and a skinny guy in a used army jacket and a plastic-looking tie—striding side by side.

George watched his new buddy from the corner of his eye and thought, I could have been stuck across a conference table from him even now hating his goddam guts. This made him remember the meeting they were cutting, and George decided that now he finally had a working definition of QWL. QWL was right here. This was what QWL was all about. Then he turned it over in his mind a few more times and decided that no, this wasn't QWL. QWL was big tits.

QWL dictated that he get to a pay phone fast.

THE BODY & THE INNER PERSON

George put four beers and two shots into his liver today, made a new friend, wore grotesque clothes, ditched meetings, and hurried his Swiss-clock bowels, but deep down, appearances still mattered to him. He was reluctant to tell Fred that he wanted to call his old lady. He worried that grabbing for his wife's ear was not macho. And he certainly did not feel macho enough to confide in Fred that he was about to give Mary Ellen the go-ahead for new tits. So he decided to postpone the call and tagged along with the rogue district man to a bar. They were supposed to drink beer; he would call Mary Ellen when Fat Fred's bladder filled up.

George let Fred choose their watering hole (he sure as hell had no qualifications for this), and Fred picked out a classic gin mill: the dark room was little more than a long bar. Squeezed alongside it there were a few grab-bag tables with farm-style chairs. A silent jukebox stood by the door. No fish. No ferns poking out of the walls. There were only a couple of low-maintenance cacti in an opaque window and a few dusty plastic daisies sticking out from among mustard and ketchup bottles on the tables. The gardening bill of this gin mill was not going to drive their prices big-picture.

Five drinkers perched at the bar, two stools apart, minding their own glasses and cigarettes. They all looked like working people.

None of them would jump up and yell that stockbrokers were slimy buggers the way some big-picture dolly in tweeds had attacked a smiling guy with outsized, orange-framed glasses in the jungle bar at lunchtime.

—This joint's just like a regular corner bar in the old neighborhood, said George appreciatively.

—Just why I like it here, said Fred, sitting down at a table with a plastic daisy.

—Didn't even know they had 'em down here, said George.

—They got 'em all right, but you gotta look for 'em, said Fred.

A morose bartender took their order. He listened to what they wanted, said not a word, and shuffled off. He moved to the utility company tempo, and it took forever before he showed up again with their pitcher of Michelob. They didn't mind. The afternoon was young, their punch-drunk peers at headquarters still reeling in QWL. And the price of Michelob was right too. Fred was paying, because he intended to drink more beer than George needed to take a bath in.

George thought it polite to protest, though he no longer had any money on him.

Fred shot him down: he was paying and that was that. It wasn't just a matter of rank and protocol, it was noblesse fucking oblige; a third-level hauled home a bigger slice of bacon. Moreover, he needed George's total cooperation, because he was about to show him the best way to think about QWL. You could picture QWL as free beer.

Made sense to George. He couldn't find a thing wrong with Fat Fred's watering hole.

They drank beer and talked easily and freely. But their conversation began deteriorating to shop talk, so George decided to give their shrinking inner persons a boost: he started to relate what he, cornered into the seat of his modest empire, had overheard this morning.

The character assassination by the two punks genuinely upset Fat Fred. He had left his depression on State Street and became an observant companion: he made funny, cutting remarks, offered fat-boy-cynical insights into the nuts and bolts of the two assholes, spun out poetic images of revenge. They were on again, and Fat Fred kept waving at the bartender to bring more beer, and George could not stop marveling at the perfect fusion of personality that went on at their beer-splattered table with a dusty plastic daisy.

George had not given much thought to the concept of inner person before, never had much use for it. The notion was Mary Ellen's ball of wax. But now, for the first time in their marriage, George suddenly saw that Mary Ellen had struck a brilliant idea in her goddam inner person. He understood that while his body was dressed in a gray synthetic-fabric shirt and a flammable tie, his inner person was wearing an army jacket. Hot pink and khaki were the colors of the inner person, gray was the color of the body. The body ran on crackers and chamomile tea, vitamins and sit-ups, regular checkups and plenty of rest. The inner person required Reubens and QWL.

The problem was that George had been choking off his inner person ever since Mussolini had given him a bum steer in Newport. To maximize the longevity of his body, George had minimized his inner person. He hadn't gained much. His inner person revenged itself in meetings by shutting George up. It emptied him of ideas and left the triumphant body to sit and smile and look decorative and stupid. Because even at your average feasibility cliff-hanger, which peaked with the arrival of a coffee cart, inner-person business was transacted. It had been Fat Fred's inner person that dismissed George as a cigar-store Indian obstructionist a few years back.

As everything fell into place for George he began getting lovesick. He finally understood what Mary Ellen had meant when she said that she did not fit her body. All those months and years that she had had to compress herself into that skinny body were his fault. Why did he have to be such a rigid jerk? Why couldn't he let her talk about it at least?

Suddenly George no longer cared if Fred thought he was grabbing his wife's skirts, or any other crap. The only thing that counted now was Mary Ellen's silicone. Fred's bladder was turning out to be an awesome instrument anyway; they had been drinking beer for almost two hours and Fred was showing no signs of distress. The man had as much bladder as he had memory, so George got up.

—Gotta call my old lady.

—Good, I gotta go piss.

—Damn, I'm glad to hear that, Fred. I can't believe it took you this long.

—You're talking like a skinny shrimp again, George!

Fred headed to the back of the bar while George got change from the bartender, then made for the pay phone. It hung between the jukebox and the door. He stuffed coins into it so he would not have to haggle with the operator again. He was going to let the damn thing ring for a long time.

It took fourteen rings before Mary Ellen finally answered. George had dragged her out of her bubble bath, where she had been reading, and yes, she had heard the phone earlier, and yes, she had thought it was George, so she had not bothered. She didn't want to mess up the kitchen floor, but now there were puddles all over it anyway, so what was it?

George calmly shouldered the guilt. (It had been his decision not to put a telephone in the bathroom as Mary Ellen wanted. He was afraid that her life would turn into one interminable bubble bath.) Puddles on the kitchen floor did not rate the end of the world to George. He shifted straight into his new gear.

—Mary Ellen? I've been thinking about what I'm going to tell you now for years, he lied.

—Hurry up, I'm freezing my buns off.

—I've just decided: what the hell, have 'em.

—Have 'em?!

—Your damn implants.

—Oh, George, gasped Mary Ellen, her voice sounding shrunken and tiny, how long have you known?

While George thought about how long a time he was going to own up to, the door behind him opened, letting in the roar of the city street.

—George, where are you? What's going on?

—I'm in this bar.

—You?! How come?

—Oh, I couldn't eat another graham cracker for a million bucks.

There followed a delicious pause. George fed the phone a dime.

—Honey, you didn't get fired or anything, did you?

—Everything's fine.

—You've always been ready to kill for a graham cracker.

—So are you going through with it or are you going to chicken out?

—I can't believe you mean it, George. Are you sure there isn't anything wrong?

—I'm telling you I mean it. Go ahead.

Standing naked in a shiny puddle on the kitchen floor, Mary Ellen peered down at her dancer's breasts. She was tempted.

—I don't want it to screw up anything, she finally said. I'm afraid it might.

—I'm not going to twist your arm. I just thought it'd be something that'd make you happy.

—Oh, it would! It would!

—And like I said, I've thought about it a lot. I'm not saying this lightly.

—George, you know I'll go ahead and do it, George . . .

—I know.

—Have you been drinking?

—What's that got to do with anything?

—And you're not gonna regret it?

—Hey, aren't you freezing your fanny off standing there wet?

—It's not cheap either, George. I don't think our insurance will touch it.

—Oh, go ahead, for Christ's sake!

There was a brief silence on the twenty-five miles of telephone wire. George threw in his last quarter.

—George, I *am* going to have them. . . . Okay?

—Go ahead!

When George hung up he was relieved. He was getting burned out from all this inner-person business.

Fat Fred was back at their table already, presiding over the plastic daisy, checking his watch, wringing the last drops out of the last pitcher. He grunted that it was time to wrap up the QWL for the day, because his ship was about to pull into the North Western station.

Watching the rogue district man pay the bill, George thought, We're quite a goddam pair. The Laurel and Hardy of the utility company. But he didn't care. He was happy to have Fat Fred for a buddy. He would have settled for a lot less brilliant a friend. Three hours earlier this hundred and fifty pounds of memory and hundred and fifty pounds of bladder would have taxed his heart more than his morning bicycle sprints, but now here he was, the father confessor of the guy, and life was grand.

THE GRAND LIFE II

George and Fred left the bar and walked into the happy hour outside, shook hands on the crowded sidewalk, said they'd have to do it again soon, and headed for their commuter stations. Fat Fred was taking a train north. George strolled down flat streets to the Illinois Central station. He was criminally happy; Mary Ellen would have her new tits soon. He already had his army jacket. The army jacket and the silicone implants were as much as you could do for your inner person in this flat city: they were as close as you could get to the fountain of youth.

At the commuter station George got into a fast-moving line at the bar kiosk, and he picked up a Bloody Mary for a buck. The four thirty-three was waiting by the platform, and George got on the last car. He did not feel like walking any farther. The first and fifth cars of this train were full of nodding acquaintances, like the guy with the rain gauge who had kept George updated all summer long on how much rain they'd had overnight, but here he did not see a single familiar face. Many of the men shock-absorbed for Styrofoam cups from the kiosk. This seemed like the most relaxed car on the four thirty-three, and George immediately decided to become a regular. The atmosphere was definitely worth the few extra steps to the municipal bicycle rack.

When he got off the train George covered the additional distance to the rack and then kept right on marching. He had left his overcoat at work and he was leaving his bike chained to the iron ribs of the stand for the night. He wanted to give his neighbors a chance to admire his army jacket. He also wanted to clear his head. And today was a walking day anyway.

After she had hung up with George, Mary Ellen staggered to the living room to mix herself a stiff Southern Comfort highball. She collapsed on the sofa with it, water dripping off her and all. She didn't know what to do. Her practical side was telling her to run, track down a surgeon, and get her implants right now, this afternoon, before George got back. At the same time she was dying to see the George who would not touch another graham cracker for a million bucks.

George had clearly been drunk when he called. This was wonderful news, even though it scared her: the man had not touched a drink in twenty-four years. There was no telling what it would do to him.

In the end Mary Ellen reluctantly decided to wait and see with the implants. She had to live with whichever George walked in the door tonight, so it would not kill her to make sure: there would be plenty of time to make her appointment in the morning, assuming she was not dreaming this.

The old, dry, maximizing George would have been served some overcooked rice and a fatigued hamburger for dinner. It would have been fine by him. He perceived food in terms of calories. But hamburger would not do for the exciting new George. That boy had to be rewarded, even if his call was to turn out to be an isolated, drunken lapse of character. Mary Ellen had never even suspected that he was attuned to her silicone fantasies. So she got dressed, drove to the supermarket, bought two pounds of Orange

Roughie, a pound of large shrimp for hors d'oeuvres, cream, two tender heads of Boston lettuce, and half a gallon of black walnut ice cream for dessert. Then she went on a mad binge and got a dozen white roses. This was living dangerously; the way the old George saw it, only drunken sailors spent money on flowers. And while her neck was on the line, Mary Ellen stopped at the liquor store, where she got intoxicated just touching the bottles. It suddenly occurred to her that she was not obliged to wear underwear: she could be shameless. She could be a slut. She could break all the rules tonight.

Instead of a bottle of Gallo, trembling, she bought a case of German Riesling.

She felt light-headed putting three bottles of wine into the refrigerator. She pulled out her holiday dishes and set the table elaborately around the fragrant cloud of white roses. Dropping utensils, she baked the fish in the cream the way George liked it if he noticed what he was running past his taste buds. Then she headed toward her closet and rifled through her clothes. She wound up choosing the light-blue rayon dress with the short skirt. It was George's favorite. It showed off her nice legs. She put it on and started combing her hair.

Rules are made to be broken, she thought, staring at herself in the mirror.

She was not convinced.

—Rules are made to be broken, she said to the mirror.

She had to sit down to pull her panties off, however.

You could set your clock by George's arrivals. If daylight saving time had been revoked and George was not dismounting his bicycle and parking it in the garage by five twenty-five, there had been some problems with the train. In that case George would be a few minutes late and pissed.

At five forty-five Mary Ellen uncorked a bottle of Riesling, poured herself a glass, and downed it in one breath. She had a lavish dinner ready, and she was getting stood up. Incredible as it was, George was still boozing away somewhere. There were twenty-four years of pent-up drinking in George, so there was no telling when he would be home. Mary Ellen could not, however, rouse herself to feel disappointed. She liked the idea of George running the streets, wished that he would not show up till dawn, crawling on all fours, mopping the sidewalk with his tie.

Go for it, George, she thought, right on.

She began pecking at the shrimp cocktail, peering at the white roses, when George turned into the driveway. He was not riding his bicycle. George was walking. And he wasn't wearing his black overcoat. He had on some bulky khaki thing that wasn't his. George Clifton owned nothing even remotely resembling this rag.

Mary Ellen quickly poured herself another glass of wine and gulped it down, waiting for the door to open. When George entered, she saw that what he had on was a used army jacket. She refilled her glass again before she got up and went to the door to give him a tender kiss.

George was delighted to see white roses, an opened bottle of wine, the short blue dress that showed off Mary Ellen's fantastic legs. He pulled her toward him and gave her a long French kiss.

George's breath smelled of beer. He gripped her with unexpected strength. Her body was rubbing against rough canvas. And he had plunged his tongue into her mouth, slowly working it in and out.

It was as though Mary Ellen suddenly had a lover.

She drank in his boozy breath and felt herself getting very excited. The feeling was clearly mutual—George started running his hand under her dress and up her thigh. Mary Ellen grabbed it, stopping it before it reached her groin. She did not want George to know how excited he was making her. She definitely didn't want him to know that she wasn't wearing any underwear. She was too upset to start any erotic initiatives. Too much odd stuff was going on already: no overcoat, no bicycle, an army jacket, French kisses, a hand on her thigh as soon as he got in the door. . . . It threatened to overwhelm her. So while George washed his hands and brushed his chestnut mane Mary Ellen ran into the bedroom and slipped on a pair of panties.

When the Cliftons met again at the dining table Mary Ellen hastened to tell George that the roses had been on sale. She was lying: they had cost her eighteen dollars. It didn't matter; she could have saved herself the trouble. George merely waved her off, as though he was embarrassed that she would bring up something as vulgar as the price of roses. He didn't want to know about coarse things like money at all—another scary, exciting thing.

Mary Ellen served the dinner, and the new George noticed the food, praising it sincerely. The old George Clifton had never done that; the body snatchers had really got this man. They ended up eating in silence while they both struggled with George's metamorphosis. George was being everything Mary Ellen wanted in a husband, but the transformation scared her. She had a thousand questions (starting with the army jacket and taking off from there), but there was no way she could ask them. All she could do now was pump more wine into her body, try to relax, and wait till George got ready to bring up the implants. And it looked as though that might take a while.

George had briefly considered Mary Ellen's odd reaction to his stroking her thigh. He had expected that the idea of a new body would arouse Mary Ellen and they would spend the evening in bed. So when she stopped his hand and forced it away from her groin, George decided that she must have got her period or something, and he resumed the contemplation of this business of the inner person.

George was floating through the day on the wings of drunken elation. He had walked home wearing an army jacket and smelling of beer, but it didn't occur to him what a bizarre sight he presented to Mary Ellen. In his mind the old S. Q. Cigar-store Indian Asshole with a Timer was as dead as George Washington now; Mussolini amounted to an improbable memory. He never realized that Mary Ellen kept getting glimpses of the old time-wringing maximizer at the dinner table. For example, Mary Ellen had not given George a wineglass. As always, she had placed an ornate pitcher with George's favorite beverage, pure cold, delicious water of Lake Michigan, by his elbow. But tonight as soon as he sat down George asked her what was he supposed to drink his wine from.

—Oh, yeah, said Mary Ellen.

She got a second wineglass. Her tongue was burning with questions, but she swallowed them all, poured the Riesling, and watched George sip it obliviously, thinking, Boy, am I glad I managed to get some underwear on.

As George chewed the Orange Roughie and chased it with wine, he sensed odd vibrations and rumblings in his body. He was not used to eating a large dinner on top of a double lunch, much less drinking alcohol, and there were strange stirrings and hums echoing through his stomach. Was it his inner person, getting brave and invading the headquarters of the body? He saw this tiny, bearded humanoid raging, punching, kicking, and splashing up a storm in all that beer and wine in his rumbling stomach, getting even for all those years when the belly and its regular bowel movements had been calling the shots.

After George had thought of the rabid minnow-sized fucker, he couldn't get him out of his mind: the sluglike goddam little reject was stunted and withered and throwing a fit and condemned to keep doing this for another hundred years. He was making George sick.

He looked up at Mary Ellen, and she shot her eyes down: he had caught her studying him. She slowly raised her eyes again and gave him a smile full of pain, and he remembered her inner person now—this ogre, this goon, this monstrosity so constricted in her body that it was about to rip it apart.

The Cliftons were finishing their second bottle of Riesling, and Mary Ellen saw that George's eyes were glazed over. They peered at her from far way. George definitely was not counting her glasses today. She served the black walnut ice cream, and George attacked it as though he had not eaten in years.

The man was making her ill.

George's heart was overflowing with tenderness as he stared through Mary Ellen, picking at her ice cream, at her bruised inner person. This goon operated as a kind of a ventriloquist, using the body as its dummy. In Mary Ellen's case the dummy was smaller than the ventriloquist, but they were at least proportionate. How was George's tiny, feeble ventriloquist supposed to rein in a wiry, bossy, spoiled dummy that had been getting its way in everything for twenty-four fucking years?

Mary Ellen finished her dessert, got up, and started collecting dirty dishes. She was losing her mind, but she wasn't going to ask. There was no way she was going to bring up the implants.

—George, did I dream it? was the next thing she heard coming out of her mouth.

The question abruptly snapped George to. Mary Ellen looked so disturbed, so beautiful in her short blue skirt that George jumped up and embraced her.

—Oh, no, no. Go ahead and have 'em, please! he said.

He kissed her, lifted her slim body off the floor, and carried her to the sofa. She started to push him off, but there was no conviction in the attempt. He set her down on the sofa; it squeaked; he started pulling her moist underwear off. But when he tried to remove her dress she started fighting back with genuine conviction, whispering, Wait, wait, WAIT, GEORGE! till he let go of her. She slid from under him and ran toward the kitchen.

—What's the matter? he asked.

—Nothing's the matter. Don't move, I'll be right back.

—You forgot to turn off the stove or something?

She erupted into wild laughter and ran out of the room.

George undressed himself while he waited for her. He was completely naked when Mary Ellen returned with a huge pair of tits. They were the size that she was always talking about. She grabbed George by the hand and led him into the bathroom.

He lifted up the back of her skirt and took her from behind as she stared at herself in the large mirror above the vanity. She was hot and wet and he moved in and out of her with fierce urgency. She wouldn't let him grab her breasts however. They were the most intimate part of her and separate from her body; they were a pair of rolled-up woolen socks, one for each cup of her elastic bra. George had had his hundred and fiftieth birthday earlier—this was Mary Ellen's seminal flash-forward: for the first time since puberty she saw herself the way she had been meant to be, the way she was soon going to become. She looked at the hem of her dress that

George had bunched up around her waist, and she felt his flesh pumping behind her, and then she could no longer take her eyes off her new breasts. They looked so gorgeous. She had a body-ripping orgasm, shrieking at the top of her voice and keeping her eyes glued to her new tits, and soon after that George came too and collapsed on the bathmat. He couldn't remember it ever having been so good.

It never had been.

THE MORNING AFTER

The alarm clock went off like a dentist's drill, and George woke up. He was alone. He had a pounding headache. He lay in bed afraid to move a muscle; the inside of his head seemed bigger than his skull. He remembered that he did not have his bicycle. He had not moved the alarm up. He was going to have to drive to the station or else be late.

—Shit, he said.

But a phantasmagorical thought struck him as he said it: he was the boss, damn it. What if he tried acting like one?

The headache was making it hard to worry about anything else anyway. It started in his teeth, humming with dull pain, rose up, and got sharper and sharper. He groped his way to the bathroom and Mary Ellen's medicine cabinet. He had to find something that would reduce the size of his brain, so he could put it to yesterday. Yesterday seemed a dream. Could Mary Ellen really have stuffed her bra? Had he really got drunk? Could he now actually own an infantry jacket? It was all unreal, impossible, nuts.

But it had all really happened. Stepping out of the bathroom, George ran into Mary Ellen. She was setting two cups of coffee on the kitchen table, smiling at George—a little fearfully, he thought.

Mary Ellen had never before bothered to get up with George in the morning. He did not need her to. For sixteen years George would down a glass of two-percent milk, rinse it out, and call it breakfast. But here was Mary Ellen now, in her turquoise silk wraparound, beaming at him like a presidential candidate.

She certainly had George's vote sewn up. He lifted his cup and sucked in as much of its dizzying smell as he could. Then he started putting on the blue (synthetic) shirt and the maroon tie Mary Ellen had put out for him the night before as she always did.

—You're not going to wear your new jacket with that, are you? she asked as if she understood that the army jacket was the attire of his inner person.

He had to stop and think about it.

—Why the hell not, he decided.

—Then I'm going ahead and making my appointment, she said.

She was triple-checking, giving George one more chance to stop her.

—Right, he said and slipped his army jacket over his small-picture uniform.

After the hot coffee the jacket felt warm. Mary Ellen got up and pressed her soft body to him and to the rough khaki canvas.

—Wasn't last night fantastic?

—I'll say, said George.

Shortly after stepping out of the house George heard the seven fifteen rumble through town. He was marching through a golden morning of razor-edged shadows, past lime-colored lawns where excited dogs frolicked on wet paws. He wore his stunning infantry jacket, and he was marching like a conquering army until, all of a sudden, his stomach growled, contracted, and the conquering army had to rush to the station, fighting to control an unscheduled bowel movement.

At the station his bicycle still stood chained to the rack, its chrome tubes covered with silvery condensation. The conquering army kept moving. In the washroom of the little station house George carefully wiped off the toilet seat and took the weight off his feet almost two hours before his usual time. His feet did not swing in the air; a candle on the spongy cake flickered and went out; life was grand.

When the seven forty-seven pulled in George got on the last car, where the more muscular ventriloquists congregated. He was gradually working himself back into yesterday's frame of mind. Around him, grimly staring at their papers, red-eyed, hung over, were his brothers, the dynamos he wanted to nod to on this train from now on.

As George passed through the office of his first-levels he could sense the tension. All his arrogant young men had found something to busy themselves with in the office. They had been sitting there for a half hour now, getting very nervous; George was never late. But he had not come back at all yesterday afternoon, and he had not shown up on time this morning. Things were getting out of hand.

When George finally entered his empire his subordinates greeted him, keeping their chins on their ties.

—Hullo everybody, mumbled George.

Unlocking the seat of his deucedom, he distinctly recalled having left its door wide open yesterday. He kicked in the door stopper and strolled inside. He felt a tangible wave of shock pass through the first-level office behind his back: his underlings were responding to his army jacket. It was clearly knocking their studied apologies for a loop.

Yes, you jerks, this is war, he thought.

He dropped into his chair, checked to make sure none of the please-return-call messages on the imperial desk were from his fearless leader, then swept them all into the imperial circular file and looked around. There was nothing else to do: he had taken care of his bowel movement at the commuter station.

It was an odd sensation, to rest his body in his phenomenal chair, before the morning coffee, with an empty gut. Only yesterday, a mere twenty-four hours ago, he had still been maximizing his givens like crazy. But now Doctor Mussolini and his yellow sponge seemed too ridiculous and absurd to think about ever again. He pulled out the bottom drawer, kicked the imperial circular file beside it, and dumped into it all the graham crackers he had been storing in the drawer in a plastic bag. Next he fished out the fragrant bags of chamomile tea from the top drawer and filed them in same. What else? His desk was clean inside and out. His work for the day was done. He wished his underlings would hurry up with their apologies. He checked his calendar: there was some meeting at midmorning again. Good. Maybe he'd run into his buddy Fred there. They could have lunch. Or they could rip QWL wide open in some watering hole later.

The two young bastards moseyed into his office at last. George put on a stern face. He was through with both of them, though their little character assassination had shrunk to microscopic dimensions this morning. It now seemed an immensely trivial event. In a way George felt he should be grateful to the two little Judases: they had given him the first push, and now Mussolini was maggot stew.

He hated their guts anyway.

Walter, the cockier of the two sons of bitches, cleared his throat and spouted forth something about how what was said was said and could never be unsaid and how they didn't even remember anymore what they had been saying yesterday.

George cut him off and offered to repeat what he had heard verbatim, because he remembered it very well.

The walrus face flushed (George noted this with keen satisfaction) and stammered that that wasn't necessary. They did realize the drift of what they had been saying and they weren't trying to wiggle out of anything at all. They knew how unfair and stupid they had been—bad judgment all the way, no question about it. So now they were anxious to put it all behind them and go on kicking ass for George.

George blew up his cheeks, then slowly let the air out, stopping Walter dead in his tracks. There was a panicky silence. George lifted his arms, clasped the back of his head in his palms, and stared at the wilting assassins. They looked ready to run out of the office. At long last the black first-level blurted out that whatever the personal feelings here, he just hoped that they could be professional about it.

George shrugged his shoulders to imply that such a thing was not humanly possible. Then he hit them with the lead pipe of another long pause. When at last he spoke, his voice was coming out of his empty belly, which was just the way it sounded: it was the bark of a ventriloquist, using a deuce dummy to address the two big-mouthed, two-faced assholes in a way that they had never heard before. It said he was probably never going to forget what he had heard yesterday. He was just flabbergasted that somebody could talk about another individual that way. So business as usual was beyond him anymore. If they could arrange a lateral transfer for themselves, George would definitely okay their one-way tickets. (George of course was fully aware of what a corporate sweet spot his modest empire was.) Their one-way tickets would probably be the best way out of the royal mess for everybody.

Hanging their heads, the two sons of bitches dragged themselves out of the imperial office. Evidently they had imagined that it would be business as usual once they had apologized.

The skin on the bastards, thought George, pulling out his *Newsweek*.

He tried to immerse himself in the planetary griefs, but he found it tough going. He had forty-five minutes to kill before Peter-Panning it to his meeting. He knew that he could squeeze plenty more smiles out of the old cigar-store Indian. The problem was that the summer that had seemed to lie around the corner yesterday had taken a detour, and it was too cold to walk to headquarters in a shirt and tie. So George had a decision to make that had him pinned into the imperial chair: Did he have the balls to go to the meeting in his army jacket? Or was it better to default to the old overcoat?

He sat and stared at the same page for forty-five minutes. He was not able to string three words together. His stomach was empty, his concentration shot.

In the end George opened the imperial wardrobe and pulled out the black overcoat; he had shaken Mussolini off his left shoulder, and he figured he needed to slow down a little. It was more than enough for now that Mary Ellen was getting her silicone.

—Take messages, I don't know when I'll be back, he told his

subordinates as he passed through their office in the black overcoat—and left them for dead.

D-DAY

While George Peter-Panned it to headquarters through the mint-tea shadows of another sunny, chilly day, Mary Ellen was sitting down to the phone. Two years before, she had seen a cosmetic surgeon on Donahue, and his name had stayed hard-wired in her memory. She got the number of his office from the directory, called for an appointment, and was offered a slot for that very afternoon. She booked it and went to take her bubble bath.

In the bathtub Mary Ellen could not keep her mind on the contrived tempests in her book. Its romance now lagged so hopelessly behind her own life that she got out and started to clean the house from top to bottom.

That afternoon, at the surgeon's office, a crisp-talking nurse handed Mary Ellen several questionnaires. Mary Ellen filled in all the blanks they had dreamed up (though she could not fathom why they needed her mother's maiden name for this—she wasn't adopting the pair of silicone sacks, for Christ's sake) and stifled yawns while the nurse lectured her: the surgical alteration was potentially a very turbulent human event; all the candidates had to undergo an intense process of psychological screening.

Mary Ellen nodded, keeping her output ear wide open, and thought, Yes, yes, let's get on with it.

The nurse finally escorted her into the doctor's office, where a tanned, boyish, TV-compatible man glanced at her through tinted prescription glasses and asked simply, Why?

Mary Ellen said that the only reason she wanted the implants was to please herself. (He had listed this as a very good reason on Donahue.)

—That, my dear, said the TV surgeon, is a very good reason for breast augmentation.

The intense process of psychological screening was over.

Mary Ellen stripped, and the doctor touched her breasts with cold, clammy, clinical fingers, peering at them intently over the tops of his glasses. They had to settle on the scope of her cosmic cosmetic event.

—Let's shoot for the moon, requested Mary Ellen.

In the end they decided to go as far as the skin would take them. This was probably going to amount to around 250 cc's—whatever that meant—or to a better than threefold enlargement.

On the way out the nurse informed her that her D-day was Wednesday.

That evening, after dinner and two more bottles of German Riesling, George made Mary Ellen take off her blouse and her bra and stand by the potted palm in their living room. She had to turn and turn and turn till she showed him the profile of her dancer's titties. She was hunching her shoulders, and George had to shout in a goofy voice, Say cheese, Say cheese, Watch the birdie, Watch the cheese, Say birdie to coax a grim smile out of her. Then he snapped his Polaroid.

The photograph had all the elements of a "before" picture. George framed Mary Ellen's body to show from the waist up; a brushy bunch of palm leaves was balancing her upper torso in a symmetrical composition; she stood a foot away from the plant, smiling at it through her teeth. You could tell she wasn't comfortable at all. She wasn't showing anything off, didn't see how she could, didn't care to put the wrong body for her inner person on record.

On D-day at eight o'clock, when the bank opened, Mary Ellen carried out George's instructions: she transferred four and a half grand from their savings account into their checking account. Then she flagged down a cab.

The augmentation was a cab-in and cab-out job in a large hospital on the lakefront. Mary Ellen checked in, writing out the forty-five-hundred-dollar check. She had never before come close to giving away so much money, never even seen such a sum on a check before, so everything that came later proved anticlimactic. The most amazing part of this whole cosmic deal was that George had not batted an eyelid when she had told him how much money she intended to invest in her inner person. George Clifton, about whose tightness all the ladies in her bridge club cracked constant jokes (having been informed about it in brutal detail by her), shrugged his shoulders with the nonchalance of a demented heir: it cost whatever it cost. She had just better buy the best pair of hands in the business for it, that was all George had to say.

At H-hour an anesthesiologist gave Mary Ellen two shots in the back. Then she sat alone in a white room and looked through a streaky gray window. Seven stories below her lay a sunlit park. There were ashen paths crisscrossing the fresh green earth, and a silvery blue mass of water beyond that seemed to hang suspended above the lawns and the budding trees. On the edge of the land, under all that water, small bicyclists were weaving their way through tiny joggers weaving their way through mothers with minuscule kids weaving their way through teenagers with chip-sized ghetto blasters, while Mary Ellen slowly turned into a manikin behind the glass wall. There was no longer any connection between her fingers and her chest when she touched it. Under the blue hospital gown she stroked her cardboard nipple, then pinched it. Her flesh did not react. It felt like touching a duck in a supermarket.

She had absolutely no sensation from the incision. There was only a slight pressure against her entire body and the intent face of the TV-compatible surgeon, biting the tip of his tongue as he moved with the scalpel. A young black nurse brought in her new breasts on a shiny stainless-steel plate. They looked like small bags. Their surface seemed rough. They were full of silicone gel. Their polyurethane envelope would cut down on the scar tissue her body would form around them. This was the Même method, and silicone gel was what her inner person was made of. That was why it was so tough.

And tough it was. While her manikin body gaped open, while

the celebrity surgeon packed her new tit bags between the dancer's breasts and the pectoral muscles (as he pointed out so helpfully, doing a little PR, earning some of that money), and later, while he stitched her up, Mary Ellen kept on thinking about the amazing check she had just written to pay for her minor cosmic event.

Afterward, in the recovery room, under the sisterly grin of the young nurse, Mary Ellen examined the manikin's new bust. The surgeon had done a fine job. The thin lines of both incisions traced half moons at the lower border of the areolas of her nipples. They were closed with small precisely spaced sutures of even lengths. The nurse helped Mary Ellen into a special, postoperation bra, which she would have to keep on for six days, until the sutures were removed; they gave her a prescription for a pain-killer; and her silicone-gel chest was in business.

THE INVESTMENT

Two hours later Mary Ellen was standing in front of the large bathroom mirror wearing a low-cut sweater. For the first time in her life she saw herself the way she had been meant to look. She could not get enough of the sight. She studied her bust from every possible angle—twisting, turning, bending over, and kneeling down in front of the mirror. They were wonderful tits any way she looked at them.

The anesthesia was starting to wear off and they hurt now, but no pain in the world would stop her from posing. She paraded around the room, and her new breasts moved with her. They weighed her down a little, but those magnificent tits were hers now. They were the dream breasts she had watched in the bathroom mirror as George made fierce love to her, bunching up her skirt around her waist. She was mesmerized by them, could not wipe a lewd smile off her face all afternoon, could not wait to show them to George.

She strolled into her closet in the bedroom and started putting on her clothes. Nothing but the skirts fitted. Expenses were mounting. She was going to have to buy a whole new wardrobe—blouses, dresses, jackets. Her new bust was clearly fast becoming the most valuable thing the Cliftons owned, outside of their house, which was not paid for yet. Well, at least the tits were fully theirs. And if the implants were to be the biggest investment the Cliftons had ever made, so be it. You could have worse problems in life than investments.

Mary Ellen, however, could not stop herself from thinking about all that money and feeling guilty. And the new George certainly was not making it any easier for her.

The morning after D-day, instead of Peter-Panning to another feasibility slugfest at HQ, George Peter-Panned to VanCura's Hardware. He bought two rectangular safari-glass mirrors and picked up various nails and tools he needed for his newest investment-enhancing project. The mirrors were long, narrow, and taupe-tinted, with swirls of golden spots. George had Mary Ellen meet him at the train station, where he fitted them into the car. He pedaled his bike furiously behind the car and its fragile load. He could not wait to see how they would look in place.

Mary Ellen pressed the mirrors to the wall for him so that he could step back and regard them from the bedroom door. They looked so perfect in the corner near their bed that George decided to repaint the room before hanging them. So he drove to the paint store and got some rollers and brushes and thinner and a gallon of light-blue paint; he was trying to hit the shade of Mary Ellen's short dress.

In Mary Ellen's mind the investment was clearly getting out of hand.

For the next two evenings George worked on the bedroom. He moved out all the furniture, covered the floor, painted the walls light blue, leaving the ceiling white, then removed the papers from the floor, and dragged the bed and the night table back in. He would go to work right after supper and stay at it until well after midnight. With a schedule like that there was no telling when his bowels would move anymore.

That Saturday, George hung the mirrors around the bed. The mirrors were what the Cliftons' life had been missing—they transformed the room from a space of suburban moderate-mortgage, small-picture fantasies into a boudoir of money-back ecstasy. George put away the tools, washed his hands, and called Mary Ellen.

—So what do you think? he asked, standing in the door behind her, rubbing her ass.

—It looks swell to me, she said after a moment of hesitation.

He lifted up her housedress and started slipping her panties off.

—You wanna test 'em out?

She leaned back and pressed her weight against his body. He began maneuvering her toward the bed. She stepped out of her panties and let him lead her there.

—I think I'm going to put in a Jacuzzi next, he whispered.

—You what? she said, halting abruptly and looking at him sternly. Ever since he had bought his damn army jacket George had been working on matching the federal deficit.

—Or a sunken tub at least.

—In here?

—No, in the bathroom, silly. I'm sick of that bathroom.

—But wouldn't that be real expensive?

—Money's no object, he said.

Holy shit, she thought, except that she was starting to feel too good to say anything. She was kneeling on the bed and watching those magnificent tits through swirls of gold. She would not allow George to take her dress off, however. She had resolved not to show their investment to George for three weeks; she wanted to make sure that she would be presenting the most valuable thing they owned in the best possible light. She wanted to stun him with their new buy, though George was probably going to tear her clothes right off her body any day now.

That would be good too.

For the week after D-day it was easy to put George off. She still had her sutures and her special bra to invoke. And George was busy turning their bedroom into a boudoir of money-back ecstasy. After the mirrors went up, Mary Ellen's coyness became more and more difficult to sustain, but she managed to fight off George's grabbing. The breasts were not yet her own. They still felt like a weight on her chest. They were soft and very tender and yet so hard when she touched them.

For two more weeks the Cliftons made love wearing clothes in front of mirrors, first in the bathroom, then in the boudoir, mostly the same way they had the day George had bought his army jacket. Mary Ellen would keep on a blouse or a sweater or a dress. She would not let George fondle her breasts. They had never played any such games before, so it was good. And any day now George was going to rip Mary Ellen's blouse off. She could not wait. It would amount to a gentle rape. It was bound to be magical.

The bottom line was that Mary Ellen's tits were the best investment the Cliftons had ever made. But now that Mary Ellen had the breasts that were her, their sex, good as it was, never again attained the hot charge of the time Mary Ellen had stuffed her bra with the woolen socks. It was never as new, as fake, as daring, as ingenious, as stimulating. For the purposes of the inner person, wool had it over silicone all the way.

THE BODY SNATCHERS

The Cliftons had bought their modest bungalow on a quiet street a mile away from the commuter station sixteen years before. They cut their grass, trimmed their evergreens, kept their garage door closed, never played loud music. They bought cookies from the Girl Scouts. When a carload of drunken teenagers plowed into a parked car on the corner of their block, the Cliftons signed the petition to have a stop sign put in. They took their garbage to the curb, neatly tied in black plastic bags, so that they would not have to pay extra for the garbage men to walk around their house. They were attuned to the concerns of the collective suburban unconscious: the Bears, the Cubs, the taxes, how much rain they'd got the night before, whether it was hot or cold enough. They had the *Tribune* delivered to their door, kept no pets, owned two automobiles (one of them an old clunker that stood parked in the garage most of the time). They made their social appearances at the block parties but always left early; it seemed George was on the wagon.

The Cliftons were dream neighbors, but they pretty much kept to themselves. Nice people but a little aloof. And, of course, they had no kids to build bridges to the families around them. Maybe they could not have any children. But, in any case, they gave you the idea that they did not need any. In fact, it looked to their neighbors as if the Cliftons did not need any damn body else at all.

Then the body snatchers struck on the quiet street a mile away from the commuter station.

One fine spring day all the clocks in the neighborhood went haywire. The steadiest pendulum of the suburb, George Clifton, did not return from the commuter station on his bicycle. He showed up very late, marching down the street in a used army jacket. It wasn't Halloween. From that afternoon on you never knew with George Clifton anymore. He might ride his bike (the ancient piece of junk weighed more than a Harley Davidson) or he might stroll home carrying a telltale Styrofoam cup; he might show up while soaps were on or not come home till after the news; he wasn't above banging away with his tools till past midnight or mumbling to himself while pushing the lawn mower; he didn't shave on weekends anymore. Throughout, whatever the imperative, he wore that khaki monstrosity.

Someone had definitely bagged his skinny ass.

One week after the bizarre infusion of khaki canvas into the neighborhood, the body snatchers hit again and got his wife. And this turned out to be the real massacre.

That afternoon the mad Clifton woman stepped out of her house in a tight, body-hugging sweater and sauntered in the direction of the train station. The neighbors dropped their dinner forks and threw themselves at the windows to catch a sight of her: the crazy broad's shoulders were thrown way back, her posture was impeccable, so impeccable that you could hear the wind howl, Here she comes, here comes Miss America, as she waltzed down the street behind this unbelievable bumper. The small Clifton bitch had always been flat-chested, but now she carried a couple of stunning knockers.

The first thing that jumped into the neighbors' minds was that the slut was wearing some sort of an absurd costume, that her old man's taste in clothes was rubbing off on her. But everything else about her looked ordinary enough. So maybe she was mocking somebody. Or else the bitch had flipped her lid and had strapped some kind of an orthopedic device to her body. The Cliftons had always been a little different.

Half an hour later the crazy broad strolled through the street again, walking hand in hand with her old man, who was decked out in his goofy army jacket. And he didn't even seem to be paying any attention to her bumper. They just ambled down the street like a couple of teenage lovebirds, airing the humongous pair of tits as though they were the family pooch, while behind them curtains rippled and blinds winked up and down the block.

For the next few days the telephone lines of the entire neighborhood were jammed. Hell, yes, it was true! The Clifton woman really had had honest-to-goodness implants! At her age! And they were huge! Yes, ma'am, there sure was a shortage of silicone around the country now! "Jugs" wasn't the word! And she was going around wearing body-hugging low-cut sweaters! She got her bra made by Omar, the tentmaker. Yes, sir! She was showing them babies off like she didn't get no warranty for the work! And supposedly she had told somebody that her husband just could not get enough of 'em. She did say it! Would anybody kid about stuff like that? He definitely loves it! You can see it in the strange look in his eyes! Because that's not all. Better grab ahold of something. Better sit down too. He just finished remodeling their bedroom!

Swear! Nobody's gonna make up stuff like this, this had to happen!
Because somebody has seen it, and you know what? He put
mirrors around their bed! It's true! It's the truth! Friggin' mirrors
on the ceilings and everywhere else! You're goddam right they're
freaks! Body snatchers got them all right! That whole street will
never be the same!

In the eye of the storm of gossip, the Cliftons got a kick out of
the neighbors' reaction to Mary Ellen's new body. A few people
stopped greeting George. More people would not say hello to Mary
Ellen. One elderly lady spat in front of her. Then there were folks
who seized any pretext to strike up a conversation with the new
Mary Ellen. They had never shown any interest in her before, but
she would talk with them politely, nod, and terminate the
conversation before they could pop the second billion-dollar
question that was now dogging the Cliftons.

Mary Ellen's bridge club had been forewarned about D-day; the
ladies had known about Mary Ellen's breast fantasy for years. To
Mary Ellen's old girlfriends from high school the augmentation
meant an overdue act of women's liberation. Silicone was the stuff
of domestic revolution; the girl was finally flipping her cheap
husband the bird by spending a fortune on herself. Good for Mary
Ellen.

But when Mary Ellen walked into their first bridge party after
D-day in a snug wool pullover, the sheer magnitude of her new
breasts provoked resentment in the other ladies. They could all
understand a little breast fetish in somebody as flat-chested as the
old Mary Ellen, but their bridge partner had evidently lost all sense
of proportion on her D-day; going from a couple of raisins on an
ironing board to cantaloupes was tacky. Her outsized tits now
made her look tawdry; she used to have a dancer's body and look
chic—now all that was left for her to do was to bleach her hair and
go run a Puerto Rican Laundromat in Uptown.

Mary Ellen felt the shock. She sensed that her girlfriends did not
approve of her new body. She did not care. There was no going
back to her chic raisins, so it was up to the bridge club to make an
adjustment to her new figure. The reception she got there,

however, made Mary Ellen worry about how her parents would react when they saw her at Christmas.

She told George about this, and he admitted that he had been a little concerned about it himself. So he thought that they should skip Florida altogether. Maybe they could go to Club Med now that Mary Ellen had a Club Med body.

—No way, said Mary Ellen.

She was not going to stand by while Mr. Big Spender blew more money on their investment. Enough was enough. She would have to face her parents sooner or later anyway. So they were going to Jacksonville for Christmas again; she just had to prepare her folks for her augmented chest first.

Mary Ellen thought that the more time she gave her mother to get used to the idea the better. So the morning after George had finished remodeling their bedroom, as he buried his face in the morning coffee he now could not do without, Mary Ellen announced that she was calling Florida and telling her mother about her cosmetic adjustment.

—Good luck, said George.

Mary Ellen started drinking cognac right after she ate a small tunafish sandwich at noon. She postponed the call until after the next glass all afternoon.

At quarter after five Mary Ellen took a deep breath and reached for the phone. She had just downed her fifth snifter. She had to call now—George would be back from work in ten minutes. Her head was still clear: she had spent the day in such a state of nervous agitation that she had burned up all the alcohol as soon as it had got into her system.

As usual, her mother answered. Mary Ellen had made up her mind to come right out with it.

—Mom, listen, I've got something important to tell you.

—You're finally pregnant!

—No, Mother, no. Not at all.

—Oh.

—Well, all right. Here it goes: I just had implants.

There was a silence on the other end of the line.

—You know, breast implants.

The silence was deep, stretched on. Mary Ellen hung on as long as she could stand it. Finally she couldn't take it anymore.

—Mom?

—I'm here, said her mother and fell silent again.

—Well, what do you think?

—I'm working on it, said her mother. How big?

—Uh, pretty big, Mom.

There was another endless pause while Mary Ellen's mother went on working on it.

—Well, she finally said, I don't see anything wrong with it myself. I know what it is to be flat-chested.

In one whish all the nervous tension flushed out of Mary Ellen's body. She collapsed on the sofa.

—What about Daddy, Mom?

—Your father better not breathe one word about it! her mother snapped back.

A waitress in their favorite Italian restaurant had just had implants too, and Mary Ellen's mother was tired of watching the old fool eat his salad with his spoon and his soup with his fork and dribble sauces all over the tablecloth. So if he even as much as mentioned implants in front of her, her mother would really let him have it.

George was late coming home that afternoon because he had walked from the train again. (The night people, the regulars on the eleven thirteen party train, were getting used to seeing an old, heavy bicycle chained to the long-deserted rack. It was there every other night.) When he entered the house Mary Ellen was still on the phone with Florida. She lay on the sofa in the living room and tears were dripping from her eyes, making large wet stains on the beige satin. Her voice was under control.

George threw up his hands as if to say, What's the matter now? And she gave him a Madonna smile right through the maudlin cognac tears.

THE ONE TWELVE

In the three weeks since he had dismissed Mussolini and his yellow sponge George had managed to put on over fifteen pounds; his inner person was growing faster than a fetus. This was clearly unhealthy, so he was getting his minimalization right.

Mary Ellen had had to let out several pairs of George's polyester pants: he had started to sprout a little belly. She did not mind that he was putting on weight. She rather liked it. She had been telling him for years that with his slim body and pale complexion he didn't look healthy. At his age a red-blooded American was supposed to pack a little fat. She also appreciated that George's body was changing at a time when her own had undergone such a drastic transformation. In a way George's new belly would balance Mary Ellen's new tits.

George did not care that he was gaining weight; his army jacket would easily cover another hundred pounds. He now arrived and departed from his empire in the General Patton's buy. He kept his black overcoat in the imperial wardrobe and used it only for the trips to headquarters. The overcoat was getting a little tight, but the weather was warm now and he did not have to button it up any longer.

These days George lunched on pastrami or corned beef or haddock sandwiches in a stand-up bar around the corner from his deucedom, ambled to the big-picture joint for pussy rock Reubens, wolfed down pizza at sit-down feasts with the rogue district man. At home George was eating large dinners. And he put away two or more beers with his lunches, sipped cocktails out of Styrofoam on the four thirty-three, pushed the bar cart around the house at night.

His bowel movement was now a shot in the dark. Some mornings he would still Peter-Pan it to headquarters. At other times he had to drag a full gut there. On the other hand, George's life was free of stress now. He sat next to Fat Fred in the meetings, his pulse ticking softly: Fat Fred was the best godfather you could ask for in a performance review or a feasibility study. So all George needed to accomplish anymore was to make the right conference room. Then he could sign the attendance sheet, relax, smile or stare vacantly out the window, openly study the barometric pressure on his watch, wait for the coffee cart (George now shuffled into the hallway for his caffeine fix same as all the other dynamos), and amuse himself by listening through the white noise of what was said to the merciless, unstated punches, whacks, and kicks the inner persons of his fellow corpo lifers were trading.

One workday morning before coffee, through with eternity, his desk clean for the day, George sat in the imperial office with an empty gut wondering where to stick the drab file cabinet with his collected works, which he had not unlocked in weeks, while leafing through his *Newsweek*. His eyes hit on a short report. There had been a train wreck in Ethiopia where they had that horrible famine everywhere. Five hundred people had died, but the story rated only a couple of paragraphs in his magazine. The motorman had taken some curving bridge too fast. It sounded like a bad scene. There had been a thousand passengers aboard the train: half of them had died; most of the rest had been injured—gory, wartime numbers. Reading on, George realized that the goddam train had had only three cars. Holy fuck.

He tried to picture the four thirty-three pulling out of the commuter station with three hundred and fifty corporate dynamos sardined into each car. Hell on the Styrofoam cups. He imagined the crumpled suits, the sweaty smiles, the briefcases held above the heads. You sure could not fit too many Freds into such a cattle car. Or too many of George's fearless leaders either. You would do better with the big-picture crowd—they tended to be skinny shrimps. Three hundred and fifty of George's clones would be all right too. His mind coiled back and attempted to load three hundred Freds onto the last car of the four thirty-three. He laughed out loud. Even if you were to press them in with a forklift, it would still take a plutonium-powered locomotive to pull the train out of the station. He chuckled again; the rails would curl up. Then he checked himself—this was sick. Jesus, how many kids had bought it on that curving bridge? All this deucing and empire-leading and having nothing real to do was clearly getting to him. He would take the afternoon off. He owed it to his sanity. He had never been on the one twelve in his career. And it was time to make Mary Ellen a happy woman anyway.

The night before, the Cliftons had put a lot of miles on the old bar cart as it traveled between the sofa and the Lazy Boy. They were feeling no pain at all by the time the news came on. Mary Ellen had disappeared and returned in her short light-blue dress. She had lifted her skirt slowly to show George that she wasn't wearing anything under it. You couldn't help but like quiet evenings at home when they progressed like this.

George had hung all these mirrors all over the damn bedroom, but Mary Ellen dragged him into the bathroom again. He took her from behind in front of the mirror, and she teased him by touching their investment. When he wanted to rip the dress off her tits, however, she started clawing and biting back in earnest. Hell, even this was slowly becoming a habit. Suddenly George decided that he had had enough of it—he was going to see and feel and kiss those magnificent tits this very afternoon if there were to be blood still pouring out of them. Hell, yes. He'd blow the deucedom off at lunchtime and get his hands on the real things.

At the station there was no mistaking Chicago for Addis Ababa: only a young family and a couple of escapee corpo lifers with briefcases boarded the one twelve with George. No one brought any Styrofoam from the kiosk bar, though George had two tall cans of cold beer in a brown bag. He claimed the last seat of the two-car train. It faced away from the direction of the ride, and he watched the shiny rails the train laid as it glided through an industrial wasteland. This was like looking into the past.

The city that pushed its sooty silhouette out of the ocher horizon seemed undiminished by George S. Q. Clifton's departure. He had withheld his hundred and fifty pounds of input from it, and there were no visible holes in the compact mass. He sipped his beer. The beer was cold; the train picking up speed; the colossus behind shrinking; the moment philosophical: you could quarantine a million deuces out of the massive downtown and you wouldn't be able to tell a goddam thing from the back seat of the one twelve. The iron rails caught a few rays of the strong sun and pricked his eyes. It was too warm for his army jacket now. He could wear it unzipped, wide open, sleeves rolled up, and it still would be too goddam warm for it. He would have to leave it home tomorrow and go back into the tough, colossal city bare-assed. It didn't matter. He could not make a dent in the fucking town any goddam way.

Oh, well.

But maybe he could surprise Mary Ellen in her bubble bath. He wished the train would hurry up and get there; he was going to scrutinize his big investment venture, bubble bath or no bubble bath. You could be as philosophical about it as you wanted, but if you were pulling out of the shrinking downtown on the one twelve, sipping a cold beer, babying another one on your lap in a brown bag, if you were in love with your wife and had invested your money wisely, and if you had a bicycle waiting for you at the municipal rack like a span of albatross wings, life was grand.

THE AFTER PICTURE

When George stepped into the house he heard the noise of water rushing into the bathtub. Mary Ellen was still preparing her bubble bath: he was too early. He slid out of the army jacket, undid his tie, and took off his shirt. The pants were tight again around his brand-new belly, so he removed them too. And his socks. He raked his fingernails through his armpits and smelled them. His sweat stank of alcohol, but it wasn't a disagreeable smell. He went on sniffing his fingertips as he stole toward the bathroom in his shorts.

Inside, Mary Ellen was humming to herself—probably admiring her new tits again. She had not heard him come in over the thundering water, and George was thrilled to be sneaking around the house on bare feet, as though he were a robber or something. Feeling the skin on his throat tighten with excitement, he slowly lowered himself to the floor, but all he could glimpse through the gap between the door and the floor were the bottoms of Mary Ellen's bare feet. They looked small and dainty. The nails were painted ruby red. He swallowed hard. The tough, flat colossus behind him may have been undiminished by his departure, the utility company might never miss his input, but he was going to make one hell of a difference in the operation of one suburban boudoir of ecstasy. Because Mary Ellen usually wore slippers or flip-flops around the house, whereas now she was barefoot. So she had to be naked as well. She had nothing over her magnificent tits.

George quickly pulled his shorts off and barged into the bathroom.

Mary Ellen shrieked—the door flying open like that had almost stopped her heart for good. Then she saw who it was and broke into wild laughter. Here was her dear hubby, stark naked, kicking the door in. Even better than stark naked, he had an erection. He had just blasted through the door like a SWAT team, and when he saw her he froze.

Mary Ellen had just finished washing her hair, so she had it wrapped up in a purple towel. It looked as though she were wearing a fez. She also had on a pair of shiny white panties and a low-cut body-hugging sweater. She had been wearing nothing but tight sweaters for weeks now. This one was synthetic and burgundy.

What was the deal here? Was Mary Ellen now taking her bubble baths in those goddam sweaters too? Suddenly it hit George that maybe something had gone wrong at the hospital and her new breasts were disfigured and that was why she was afraid to show them to him now. Maybe the Cliftons had not made such a killing on their family investment after all. He pulled her laughing face toward him so she would not stare so hard below his waist; he was going to get to the bottom of this right now.

—You walked out of the house like this this morning? she asked, giggling.

She could smell the beer on his breath. This was exciting.

George did not say a word: he was still being the robber. He reached for the burgundy cardigan and ripped it open with one jerk of his arm. The buttons hit the mirror above the vanity as they flew off. Now he pulled on her bra. Something snapped and the bra lifted up.

—Ouch, said Mary Ellen.

But it was a throaty gasp, and she was not fighting back at all. She was smiling, standing there with the biggest, most luscious, gorgeous, fabulous pair of tits sticking right into George's face. He saw no scars from any incisions—it looked as though Mary Ellen's inner person had just sprouted these forty-five-hundred-dollar breasts. And they were perfection itself: the nipples proportionate and hard and erect and darkly amber, crowning the most magnificent white half-moons of breasts that George had ever seen anywhere, Mary Ellen's collection of pornography included. If his name were Rockefeller and he had lived a hundred and fifty years, George S. Q. Clifton could not have made a shrewder investment than these babies.

He bent down and started rubbing his face against the killing tits. They felt a little harder than they looked, but they seemed ripe and ready to shoot geysers of sweet milk. He pressed his cheeks and his eyes and his lips into them, running his fingertips around the borders of their amber nipples and tugging on them gently, whispering, They are gorgeous, Mary Ellen, they are fantastic, these tits are incredible, while she was moaning, Yes, yes, yyees, oh, yyyyeeees. He reached for her groin and pried his hand into her smooth underwear and buried his fingers in her moist, hot flesh.

George had not shaved that morning, so sharp little whiskers were covering his chin and his cheeks, and when he started rubbing his face on her new tits he sent shivers down Mary Ellen's spine. When he went on to tug on her nipples, she thought that she would come right there. She was wrong; it did not happen until a few delicious moments later, after George had grabbed her melting crotch and his fingers had spread her open and everything had gone black and she knew she was screaming though she did not hear herself and he had spun her around and entered her doggy style again in front of the mirror, watching her un-fucking-believable breasts and squeezing them with his rough hands and molding and lifting and stroking her silicone inner person, which was now her skin and her nerves and her body.

The best afternoon of their marriage ensued, and though wool still had it over silicone, it was pretty goddam nice. It had cost George forty-five for the army jacket, but the body snatchers turned in good work: you no longer knew with George Clifton— he might show up right after lunch, before the bubble bath, stark naked, with an erection, and tear clothes off your body. And even his physique now felt different. Mary Ellen was used to feeling his pelvic bones slam into her. Now a small belly rose against her ass when he stood behind her and cushioned the thrust of his hips. The thrusts were still hard but not bone-hard anymore. They felt soft-hard now, as though it wasn't her husband's body at all. As though it was a stranger's body behind her, making love to her.

George had a similar sensation of embracing a new body. It cost three thousand bucks a breast (by the time you cost-loaded all the mirrors and clothes and everything else), but what the hell, you only lived once, and this was worth it—this wasn't the Mary Ellen he had known. This busty siren was a different woman. Yet she responded like Mary Ellen.

The two new bodies in the Cliftons' bungalow were unfamiliar and exciting, but at the same time they did not need to overcome any inhibitions. They knew exactly how to give the most pleasure to each other. This family investment definitely rated a killing.

Their rawest passion spent, George splashed some water on Mary Ellen's magnificent breasts and posed her by the potted palm. The afternoon sun was shining into the living room now through the lacy curtains. It projected a frilly shadow on Mary Ellen's fine, fine breasts and on her face and her flat stomach. With his Polaroid, George snapped a close-up of her upper torso first. Then he stepped back and took a picture of her upper body with the palm. Three more steps back and he got her entire body into the last shot. He did not have to tell her to watch the cheese or birdie a single time.

The colors gradually seeped into the black square on a white rectangle, and a perfect "after" picture emerged. This time Mary Ellen was beaming into the camera, her shoulders pressed back, her stomach flat, her skin lacy with the play of sunlight and shadows. And those tits were a phenomenon. She could not take her eyes off the small photograph.

—I wonder if you can blow up a Polaroid, she said.

QWL II

As the company propaganda pamphlets said, QWL was an ongoing people-oriented process. And the rogue deuce and the rogue district man were starting to make a little headway in QWL: they now had a special, private conference room where nobody could track them down with urgent messages or phone calls. No coffee cart ever stopped there, but there were flowers on the table. And there they retreated to kick around various innovative QWL ideas.

Glass for glass, the rogue deuce still could not keep up with the rogue district man, though he was starting to provide noticeable support in letting you see through a pitcher of Michelob.

George's deucedom ran on autopilot, the way it had for months. Fat Fred's people held the fort well too, even though his bloated district had just swallowed another department. (Fred Foss liked getting his two-cent input into redrawing the organizational charts. He was a big emperor at heart, but, then, he could afford to be. He had the bodies in place for departmental takeovers, and they did all the dirty work for him.) So the two corporate dynamos were able to devote themselves to meeting the challenges of QWL head on in their special conference room.

Fred Foss now regarded the cigar-store Indian as a real buddy. He had even, to his amazement, learned a lot from him. He got his first lesson from George on the wave-shaped bench on State Street when he discovered the dizzying depths behind George's shallow smile; he had been dead wrong to underestimate the cigar-store Indian. This meant that it was a bad idea to underestimate just about anybody. Everybody had a little something on the ball, so Fred decided to try to curb his unfortunate tendency to blow people off without hearing them out first.

Then there was George's goofy notion of inner person. It sounded mighty kooky, but it turned out to be a good comprehension tool. With inner person in mind, Fred was able to read people a lot better. In meetings now he could concentrate on dealing with the collective inner corporate dynamo. He had always operated on the gut level, but his new understanding saved him a great deal of time. Fred also liked the image of his fat, cumbersome, disgusting-whale of a body, destined for a funny funeral, as a mere dummy of a robust, muscular, chipper, suave ventriloquist. This made it easier to wash and dress and parade the dummy through meetings.

Finally, Fat Fred had a good time with George. At first watching George sip his beer had made Fred feel as though he were corrupting a minor. In a matter of weeks, however, George matured to where he was putting the steins away with the best skinny shrimps of his size. He now gnawed his way through a pizza with the shortest of gut and the longest of tapeworm. He hit on creative combos for park-bench lunches, such as a Whopper and a hip flask of white port. And all the while George talked talked. He reported openly how he had decided to age gracefully: he was giving up his vitamins, was through with sit-ups, had moved his bowels at 3:00 A.M. one night, was gulping so much coffee now he would shake in his imperial chair as he listened to the Cubs games on the imperial transistor radio all afternoon.

The most memorable QWL quorum Fred and George held took place on a sunny afternoon of the early summer when the Cubs were out of town. They hit their special conference room right after lunch. George had on a plastic-looking tie. They were both in short sleeves. Fat Fred had been taking a pounding from the summer rays outside. His shirt was completely drenched with sweat, so he grunted with pleasure when they walked into their watering hole; the room was cool and dark and restful. Morose Marty, the utility-style bartender, waved a pitcher at them from the bar, then leaned it on the Michelob tap without procrastination. They were regulars here now.

They sat down at their table, where an eternal daisy went on blossoming away among the transient ketchup and mustard bottles. George pulled out a Polaroid picture from his shirt pocket and threw it on the table. Fred did not bother to pick it up. His eyes were not yet accustomed to the darkness of their QWL conference room.

—My old lady's getting implants, said George.

—No shit.

—Something she always wanted to do.

—Well, we're gonna have to have you guys over then, said Fred.

They laughed. George poured beer from the pitcher that Marty had slammed on their table. Fred was very curious about the Polaroid. He lifted it up and tilted it toward the weak light that got in through the opaque window by the door.

The snapshot showed the profile of the upper torso of a flat-chested woman. Her shoulders were hunched and she stared at a bunch of outsized leaves of some plant a foot away.

—That her? asked Fred.

—Yup.

—Nice palm tree, grunted Fred.

His was an inimitable way, and they chuckled again—George

especially. Then he fished another Polaroid out of his shirt pocket and laid it softly on the table.

Fat Fred thought it polite to have a gulp of Michelob before he reached for it. He tilted it to the dim light again and studied it for a long while.

—Holy fuck, he finally gasped.

—Yup, said George.

They sat in silence.

—I mean, she don't have a twin sister or anything, right? That's her too, ain't it?

George nodded with a ton of dignity.

—This is quite a shot, George.

—Yup.

They sat on that for a moment.

—So how much did it set you back, George?

—Four and a half. Grand.

They sat on that too.

—Peanuts, said Fred.

—Not counting the clothes. She didn't fit anything from the waist up.

—Peanuts, considering, said Fred and swallowed a long draft of Michelob.

—So when did she get 'em?

—Three, four weeks ago, about.

—Damn.

—Yup.

Fat Fred waved Morose Marty over and ordered a couple of shots.

—The thing is, said Fred, I don't even have a palm tree that's as good-looking as yours. But like I said, we're having you guys over.

George threw his shot in.

—Yup, he repeated apropos nothing. His inner person was a big boy now, and it was pumped up with all the exuberance of the moment. He loved Mary Ellen, and he was glad to have Fat Fred for a buddy. Real glad.

Then Fat Fred pursed his fat lips and blew some beery air through them.

—Where the hell did you say you got that army jacket, George?

A MIDSUMMER NIGHT'S SERENADE

The cookout was to be a nothing-much backyard belt-buster, but George wanted Mary Ellen to put on her white cotton blouse and her burgundy hot pants. The blouse was very revealing. It showed off George's savvy as an investor.

George wore a pair of Italian loafers Mary Ellen had just bought for him. They were light beige and wire-mesh airy. His white socks showed.

When the Cliftons waltzed out of their house their neighbors dropped water hoses, squeezed beer cans, stopped talking, smoking, laughing. The easy summer breeze howled Here she comes, here comes Miss America as George led Mary Ellen to the car, his white socks gleaming through his imported shoes. He unlocked the passenger door, Mary Ellen slid in, he slammed it shut after her. The tits barely fit. Not a poodle barked till the car pulled away.

The Cliftons found the Foss's house easily. Fat Fred drew a lucid map. The rogue district man welcomed them on the front porch of an old Victorian mansion. The house was huge, but Fred Foss managed to make it seem small. He was wearing a kimono-like deal over his massive body. His feet were bare.

Mary Ellen gave George a dirty look.

Fred's wife, Gwen, was setting the table on a big patio behind the house. It overlooked an oceanic backyard. A thin trail of smoke rose from a big-bellied barbecue. Gwen was still in her twenties. She looked pleasant and pretty ordinary, though next to Fred she seemed young and beautiful. Her solid hips were dwarfed by Fred's. Her large nose shrank beside Fred's cascading chins. She wore a pink housedress and a pair of low sandals, so George got stung with another dirty look.

George took Mary Ellen's dirty looks like a man. He saw that the Fosses did not notice their clothes at all. Fred eyeballed Mary Ellen's bust and lost all composure, but he had the grill to keep him busy. Gwen took in the implants and proceeded to drop silverware and walk into chairs. She was trying to do three things at once: set the table, carry on a conversation, eyeball the silicone bags.

The Fosses had five kids—a big family. The oldest three, all girls, were Fred's from the first marriage. Their mother had died in an auto accident. Gwen and Fred crossed their chromosomes in two darling boys. All the kids were well brought up, and they were not allowed to sit with the grown-ups on the patio. (The oldest was watching television in her room, burning incense, smoking pot; her younger sisters were keeping the telephone wire white-hot; the boys were already in bed, bashing each other with teddy bears.)

The adults sat on the patio. They talked utility company and they sipped Bloody Marys. Over the oceanic backyard the summer had four dimensions. Swarms of fireflies left traces in the sticky air like bright-green subatomic particles. The coffee evening was thick with them, bringing out several graceful nighthawks and scores of jerky bats. They swooped through the fading daylight under high crowns of tall Dutch elms like black holes, swallowing the miniature green flares.

Fred served his showcase spinach salad. There were eggs and crabmeat and slices of tangerines, marinated in some aromatic liquor. It tasted awesome, but Fat Fred never did finish describing the recipe to Mary Ellen—Gwen cut him off. She spoke with an operatic diction and a breathless animation and reported that Fred was an unbelievable cook he was almost as good in the kitchen as he was on the dance floor now Fred didn't really look it in fact he probably looked a little too healthy to be a wonderful dancer but he actually put Fred Astaire and Baryshnikov to shame he danced

with flair style grace and he did not sweat doing it like other people
his size Gwen always did go for big guys one felt so protected so
secure so babylike in Fred's arms but she'd known Fred for almost
a year before there was any chemistry you see she used to be
corporate herself though now she left the utility company all to
Fred Fred asked her to dance at one of those meet-the-executives
seances in a hotel downtown and that was it right there he wrapped
those darling big arms around her and she let go completely and
they went gliding through the air a foot above the floor as though
they were on skates as though Fred had banished all friction from
the world all she felt were waves of rhythm pulsating through the
mellow saxophones and those big hands lifting her away from the
hotel downtown the city of Chicago the world the universe time
and space too her body melting away she came to understand that
what modern physics teaches us is true the universe is nothing but
pulses and vibration even a piece of dog turd is nothing but a
bunch of beeps but anyway the big band was blasting away and
electric utility couples were spinning around them and necking
and whispering and Gwen felt she was merging with the weak and
the strong forces and becoming just a series of beeps and by the
time the music stopped and Fred had spun her around one last
time in silence she was madly in love she had comprehended the
universe with her brain before this of course she did have a
master's in computer science after all she'd had her fill of physics
courses but Fred made her feel all those nutty concepts through
her body there is nothing like it in the store of human experience
and on that dance floor when the music died and the musicians
were shaking saliva out of their instruments she just wanted to
clutch Fred forever which she'd been doing ever since and not
regretting a nanosecond of it—

    It was clear that tonight was serenade night at the Fosses. The
Cliftons were picking at the last remains of the awesome salad that
was starting to turn sour in their mouths. Suddenly Fat Fred
burped.

    The Cliftons roared with laughter.

    Gwen squealed with joy. Now wasn't Fred wonderful now show

her a man who had the guts to be this spontaneous there wasn't a whole lot of balls left in the henpecked American menfolk but what was left Fred had cornered he was as good a lover as he was a dancer which made sense because both were a matter of rhythm plus he was a wonderful father and a matchless provider and a great speaker and an even better writer he could slap together such a mean memo that it put Proust to shame not to speak of Joyce or Tolstoy and she knew what she was talking about even though this may have sounded like an overstatement she knew her literature she had dozed off over every great book and masterpiece novel there is in her school days so she knew Fred was a powerful stylist and she hadn't even started to approach his truly great qualities the man was romantic and wildly macho at the same time and like everybody with an advanced degree Gwen had read all the great social thinkers Marx Freud Plato Nietzsche Adler Dr. Spock but none of these big guns had a better handle on the human animal than Fred Fred had developed this amazing notion of a dichotomy between the inner person and the body and there wasn't a theory that came close to its potential of explaining the human beast once and for all and locking up all the universities and smashing all the punch clocks of philosophy departments and think tanks subconscious eternal soul operant behavior capital *Übermensch* they were all nice shots but no cigar if you wanted the ultimate key then you had to look at the inner person as a ventriloquist of a dummy which was the biological body *qua* itself and the thing was Fred's theory provided you with as much insight into your mailman as into your Immanuel Kant and come on Fred you shouldn't feel ashamed because this was the stuff of genius pure and simple and this was only a statement of fact and these ribs were celestial too—

The ribs *were* tender, their juice spicy, their outside crisp and redolent of hickory—but Gwen kept serenading. They finished the ribs, cleaned off with steaming hand towels, consumed fruit and rum-treated melon slices while Gwen went on singing odes to Fred. Everybody else was drinking. There was nothing else to do but drink.

George tried matching Fat Fred beer for beer, though this was a welterweight bladder going against a cruiserweight tank. He felt himself getting very drunk. He decided that it was a good thing. This was an amazing evening. George had never been to a meeting that had Fat Fred this hamstrung before.

Mary Ellen was deep into her second bottle of wine. She had come here full of self-confidence in her revealing white blouse and had sat erect on her lawn chair, pushing her shoulders back. Then she had begun arching her back, then hunching her shoulders. While Gwen ran her mouth she was staring at Mary Ellen's chest. As was Fred. As was George. So now Mary Ellen was holding her right arm across her breasts as though she were cold, wondering if the elephantine host and his hysterical serenader could see through cotton. She was not at all sure that her right arm was doing her any good: Fab Fred probably possessed X-ray vision too. In any case, it seemed that pound for pound Fred was stronger than a grizzly bear especially for somebody who didn't train he had once practically lifted Gwen's car off the ground she used to have this Volkswagen bug before they were married and they got into this fight once and she ran into the car and she was going to drive off and never see Fred again and she got in and punched the thing in gear and lead-footed the gas and the engine was roaring away and the car wouldn't move she couldn't understand it kept checking to see if the hand brake was off which it was and if the damn thing was in gear which it was too and it had had her completely dumbfounded so she took her foot off the gas and over the purring engine she heard Fred's demonic laughter the sweet guy had grabbed the rear bumper and lifted her back wheels off the ground they had just been spinning in the air while the engine had been thundering and he was now laughing so hard he was about to drop the car it was scary is what that was—

The operatic serenade would have gone on if nature herself had not revolted and made Gwen choke on a piece of pound cake. So Fat Fred whacked his wife very helpfully across the back, and George thought that Fred's strength at least had not been exaggerated in Gwen's odes: the blow was a bone-crushing hit. A yellow chunk of cake came flying out of Gwen's mouth. Her eyes watered; she started coughing; the serenade was over.

It was time to clean off the table.

With a lump of dread in her throat Mary Ellen asked Gwen if she could help. Gwen said that that would be very nice of her, so the women started collecting dishes and taking them into the kitchen through the patio door.

THE FOURTH DIMENSION

—I bet you got a dick bigger than a horse, said George when they had been left alone on the patio.

—I couldn't help but notice, said Gwen to Mary Ellen as they began loading up the dishwasher in the kitchen.

—She does this to me all the time, George, said Fred, struggling with shaking hands to light up a big cigar. I think she may be nuts—I'm serious.

—Notice what? Mary Ellen asked coldly, knowing very well what Gwen meant and feeling like being bitchy with the crazy dame.

—It's just that I've never seen you outranked in a meeting before, said George, waving the cigar smoke out of his face.

—Your outrageous breasts, said Gwen, as though her inner person and her body were one.

—The thing is, I'd have to kill her, said Fat Fred. I've thought about it too.

—Oh? said Mary Ellen, going on being a bitch.

An inner-person silence fell on the patio while Fred puffed on his cigar nervously.

—I'm not a lesbian or anything you understand though I do have a master's degree, said Gwen. I was just thinking that Fred's been such a dreamboat of a husband to me that he definitely deserves breasts like yours—

—Changing the subject, said Fred, ho-ly fuck!

—Well, we don't rent them out, I'm sorry, said Mary Ellen, not smiling at all.

—Yup, said George. And by the way, you can get them too. I noticed your old lady seemed kind of thunderstruck by them.

—I'm so sorry, said Gwen. I don't know what's happening with me anymore I can't seem to be able to help it anymore I think people are beginning to hate me too do you hate me I am very sorry for being so indiscreet and rude I really don't know what made me say that can you ever forgive me I wish I could grab ahold of myself it's as though everything had been speeded up by a couple of beats Fred really is a rotten son of a bitch you see if you want to know the truth but I am going to get those tits anyway if it were to kill me I've been taking any courses that popped into my head professional student is what I am and I don't know what's happening anymore it happens if you hang around higher education for too long I better sit down I can't get over how Fred kept staring at your bust he's a fabulous husband otherwise whereas me I'm a rotten stepmother to his girls I think I better sit down I have a master's in computer science did I mention that and here I am a housewife I think I may be lesbian your tits turn me on—

—That's all I need, a pair of tits, said Fred. I'd love to see them, though.

—Sit down, Gwen, Mary Ellen ordered the lady of the house, who was leaning on the dishwasher. She did not feel bitchy any longer. She just wanted out.

—Personally, I think everybody should see them, said George, but I'll have to talk to her first.

—You know this has been a hell of an evening. Gwen sighed, sitting down on a kitchen stool.

—I'm not trying to swap out the old lady or anything, said Fred, plus my old lady's been having some serious problems lately anyway.

—No shit, said Mary Ellen's inner person, speaking up for the first time that night.

—That's all I was talking about too, said George.

—I feel better now I don't think I'm going to go off again tonight, said Gwen and turned on the dishwasher.

—Maybe we can go skinny-dipping like in high school or something, said Fred.

—I think I'm going to be sick, said George. Then I'll go and talk to her about this.

—Don't puke on the rosebushes, George, said Fred. Use the tomatoes.

But it was too late: George vomited all over the rosebushes. Then he moved to the tomato plants and was sick all over them as well. Then he puked all over his Italian shoes. The fireflies now flew in pairs, and they were cats' eyes spying watching recording it all in their magnetic suburban feline brains.

—You got it all covered now, George, said Fat Fred.

—Well, if you're serious, do you want me to give you the address of my surgeon? asked Mary Ellen in the kitchen, just to say something.

—I'm awful sorry, Fred, I haven't done this since senior prom, said George. Lemme hose it down or something.

—Oh yes yes please I have a fabulous husband who I think deserves tits like yours, said Gwen.

Mary Ellen took the large Ansel Adams calendar off the kitchen wall and scribbled the name of the TV-compatible surgeon on it. She did not remember the address or the phone number of his office, so she made them up.

—Don't worry about it, buddy, I take this as a compliment to my culinary expertise, said Fred, snuffing out his cigar on the patio and throwing it into the spotted rosebush patch.

—Can I put you down as a reference? asked Gwen.

—I'll go and talk to my old lady now, said George.

—By all means, said Mary Ellen, thinking, I gotta get out of here now. This minute.

George opened the patio door and entered a real domestic scene in the big kitchen: the dishwasher was humming away and the wives were talking softly. They seemed to have hit it off real well.

—Can I talk to you a second, Mary Ellen? George asked.

—You can talk right here I gotta run out anyway, said Gwen.

This put the Cliftons in the kitchen and the Fosses on the patio, where the warm, cloudy, starless night now sported an offensive odor.

—I love you so, Fred, said Gwen outside.

—I just threw up all over the rosebushes, and we're thinking about going skinny-dipping. What do you think? asked George inside.

—Jesus Christ, Gwen, said Fred.

—What is this?! She's crazy, George! She's a stark raving lunatic! And I'm not so sure about him either! And now you're starting to go off too? cried Mary Ellen.

—I'm gonna get implants just for you, you no-good son of a bitch, said Gwen.

—I am going home! said Mary Ellen.

—Get ahold of yourself, will you, said Fred. Because we're thinking about going skinny-dipping.

—All right, let's go home, then, said George.

—Let's go! I'm dying to see those implants, said Gwen.

George held the patio door open for Mary Ellen and followed her outside. The Cliftons stood facing the Fosses again. The Fosses were searching the faces of their guests for skinny-dipping clues.

—It's getting late, I think we're about ready to go—we've got quite a drive still, said George.

—A real wonderful party, said Mary Ellen.

—Thanks for everything. I'm real sorry about those rosebushes, said George.

—Really, we've had a great time here, said Mary Ellen.

Fat Fred now turned red as a brick. He lunged forward and grabbed George by the elbow. His grip carried a tremendous force. Mary Ellen jumped back. She was scared.

—You can't go yet! Fred yelled. You haven't seen my kids yet!

The plea was a shriek from Fred's inner person. George did not like it. He had never seen the rogue district man lose his cool this badly.

—Yes you gotta see our kids they're wonderful children just the best, said Gwen.

—But do we want to wake them up? said Mary Ellen, looking at George.

She was, however, ready to go and shoot all the Foss kids if that were guaranteed to spring her out of there.

—All right, but my shoes are a mess, said George.

He tore his elbow out of Fred's grip and headed off the patio. There was a painful silence while they all listened to the splashing of water at the side of the house and looked at the floor. George returned barefoot. He was carrying his Italian shoes and his white socks in a wet pile on his left forearm.

—I'm sorry about the rosebushes, I really am, said George. They look pretty bad.

—Please, George, said Fred. Ready?

Fred started through the patio door and toward a big staircase. The Cliftons filed behind him, trailed by Gwen.

—Don't know about you but I've had a wonderful time myself, said Gwen.

—Absolutely, said George, same here.

—Oh, me too, you bet, said Mary Ellen and thought: I don't believe this is happening.

The two little boys never really woke up. Fred strolled into their room, turned on the lights full blast, pointed at a disoriented chubby face with tousled blond hair and introduced him as Brad, the two-year-old, his prince; a wonderful baby, said Gwen, not a trace of terrible twos; Jesus, Mary Ellen whispered under her breath to George, who ground his teeth in reply and ordered her to admire the Foss's baby with a tiny movement of his chin; he's so cute, said Mary Ellen. Brad's eyes had stopped squinting at them already. He was out again. His brother John, the four-year-old, never budged. Fred had pulled the light-blue blanket off his slender body, and John went on snoring daintily. He had an urchin's face, freckled and clear and pleasant. He did not look like either of his parents. That's my best kid, said Gwen; he's so cute, said Mary Ellen; nice kids, said George; this is my king here, said

Fat Fred, staring at the curled-up little body and avoiding eye contact with everybody else.

The bedroom of the two younger daughters from Fred's first marriage was empty. The nine-year-old and the twelve-year-old were busted faking sleep on the double bed in the guest room. The television was on: Dustin Hoffman was banging the mother of his girlfriend in *The Graduate*. The girls were both skinny and dark-haired and clear-complexioned and curious. Fat Fred blasted them with full lights, took in the situation, and said: Gotcha, girls. He looked up at the Cliftons for the first time now, radiating parental pride, returning to his old utility-company self again. This is Ophie, my princess, he said, and this is Susan, my queen; aren't they darlings? said Gwen; sure are, said Mary Ellen; you're telling me, said George. Meet the pillar of the company, girls, said Fred, meet the devil of QWL, meet my good friend George; hi there, said George, standing there barefooted with a wet pile of footwear in his hands and feeling royally stupid; hello, said Susan. Ophie, the nine-year-old, said nothing. Now can we go back to sleep, Dad? said Susan; yes, ma'am, said Fred and turned off the television, right now's a pretty good time.

The Cliftons and the Fosses filed out of the guest bedroom, walked to the end of the hallway, and barged into a small room. This was Freddie's bedroom. Freddie was fifteen, and she had her blanket all the way up to her chin by the time Fat Fred had flipped the switch. Hi, beautiful, meet the Cliftons, said Fred; Dad! said Freddie; what? said Fred; nothing! said Freddie; isn't she a doll? said Gwen; this is Freddie, my chairperson, said Fred; she sure is, said George, hi there; you can say that again, said Mary Ellen. Freddie was not amused: she had freckles and blue eyes and a high forehead and a nice direct way of returning your look if you looked at her. George stared at the wet shoes in his hands. Mary Ellen was giving Fat Fred dirty looks. Whaddaya, sleeping naked these days? said Fred, snatching Freddie's blanket; Dad, I hate you! screamed Freddie. She wore a long frilly nightgown. Underneath she had small breasts. Gwen, tell him to give me back my blanket, shrieked Freddie, I'm gonna run away from this place; Freddie, I want you to give my good friend George and his wife a good-night kiss and then we're going, said Fred; you're out of your mind, Dad! yelled Freddie, I hate you; please, please leave the poor girl alone, said Mary Ellen; come on, a little kiss, said Fred; come on, Fred, said George, good night, Freddie; yes, good night, said Mary Ellen; good night, sleep tight, said Fred and threw the blanket back to Freddie; sweet dreams, dear, said Gwen. Fat Fred turned out the lights.

—Wonderful kids, said Mary Ellen, but we've really gotta go.

—Aren't they? said Gwen.

—We're gonna have to have you guys over soon, said George.

—Just gimme a holler, said Fred.

—Yup, said George.

—Good night, everyone, said Mary Ellen, stepping to their car, waving. She was afraid that the Fosses might want to buss her cheek or, more likely, cop a feel.

—I don't know about you guys, but it's been a slice for me, said George.

—We're gonna have to do it again soon, said Gwen. And thanks for that address.

—Use me as a reference, please, said Mary Ellen, closing the door and rolling down the window.

—QWL meeting tomorrow? said George, strapping on his seat belt.

—Let me call you in the morning on that. I don't know what I've got hanging, said Fat Fred.

—Bye everybody, said everybody.

The Cliftons' car pulled out of the Fosses' drive.

—Wow, said Mary Ellen.

—Yup, said George.

—Wonderful people, aren't they? said Gwen.

—Damn, said Fred.

CORPORATE CULTURE

During the next few meetings in Morose Marty's conference room QWL was slow. At times the conversation even got to be a job. Both rogue dynamos made sure that they did not avoid the subject of their four-dimensional cookout. They referred to it copiously. Fat Fred even went so far as to submit a humorous bill for dry-cleaning the backyard. It came out to three pitchers of Michelob, since the tomatoes had to be destroyed. But they never talked about Fred's kids or Gwen or Mary Ellen's breasts. They joked, laughed, and talked utilities, but the old reliable pitchers of Michelob did not function the way they used to anymore, though beer tasted better than ever to George.

Beer tasted very good all over Chicago that summer. The season lay on top of the hot city like an airless big top. The air conditioners hummed; the fans whirred; the commuter trains smelled of deodorants in the morning and sour office sweat in the afternoon; the Cubs were a disgrace; the hydrants hemorrhaged translucent curtains of water; the murders went up as blood donations headed down. Atmospheric lids clamped down on the city with depressing regularity, ozone warnings were issued, asthmatics gasped for oxygen. Then violent thunderstorms rolled in, torrential downpours tore through the lids, sewers backed up into Lake Michigan, and beaches were closed for days on end. By the time the bacterial count in the lake had dropped again and the beaches had been reopened, a new atmospheric lid trapped the polluted air. The dog days of August and the hay-fever season lay ahead. The record beer sales would not level off till sometime in October.

In the Clifton suburb lawns and tall trees absorbed some of the heat, and the streets were cooler. But Mary Ellen was spending the summer in the bathtub anyway, reading, sipping cold white wine, admiring her new bust. She could not wait to be on the lake in

Michigan this year. She wanted to give their investment a full tan. She had it all figured out: there was a spot in the back of the cottage, protected by the toolshed and the ravine, that would be ideal for sunbathing in the nude.

George hardly noticed the ugly summer. He was busy at work. He rarely made the four thirty-three these days. The telephones in his deucedom died at four and you could finally get some work done.

In the past George had always operated in the reactionary mode of management that was practiced throughout the utility company: you held her steady as she went, didn't monkey around with any off-the-wall crap (including alleged improvements), and waited till a corporate reportable struck you from the blue. Then you quickly covered your ass, snowed 'em, and pointed your finger down and outside your district. Since he had bought his army jacket, however, George had changed his deuce philosophy. He now belonged to the anticipatory school of management, in which you created your own corporate reportables. He had appraisals to write again, and he was getting started early this year.

Like the opera subsidies, appraisals were a part of the corporate culture. And George was going to give his snotty underlings a dose of culture all right. He was through combing his file cabinet for ideas and phrases; this time around all he was going to need was a pen, paper, and memory.

For the first time in his career George did not dread appraising.

He printed the name of the walrus mustache on a blank form and found himself in front of the imperial wardrobe again, striking the pose of a Bureaucrat Returning from a Meeting in Springtime, his face the hot pink of a baboon's ass, his hands hurting. Given the mood, he thought that Subordinate's Weak Points was a good place to start.

Walter is a slimy snake, he wrote, who will stab you in the back and then rush you to a hospital, only so he can stab you over and over again. In my twenty-four years with the company I have met some real specimens but never a bigger two-face than Walter.

George never stopped: the ideas and words were just rushing out of his pen. He appended another sheet when he ran out of space and went on telling it like it was with Walter. When he had accumulated five pages of the walrus mustache's weak points and his creative juices were roaring like flash floodwaters, he tackled the strong points.

One thing about Walter, he wrote, is that he definitely has no end of balls. He isn't as stupid as he looks either. If the son of a bitch ever really applies himself to the company politics, I expect to wind up working for him one day (perish the thought), as I have long ago overshot the level of my incompetence. I am not saying this lightly. Walter's very strongest point is that he definitely does not mind getting his nose dark brown. However, he still needs to develop his corporate instincts. In his youthful ambition Walter tends to suck on the wrong assholes.

George's pen barely kept up with the swirls of ideas that permutated on and on in his head, making him feel slightly drunk. For each supervisor in George's charge, the naked truth took three days of entranced writing. In two more shifts, he edited the reams of output down to the scale of the form. There followed days of putting a corporate coat on the naked truth and making it presentable to his fearless leader and the appraisees themselves.

Walter's weak point, George wrote in the second draft of the appraisal, is that, on occasion, he tends to come across as something of a hypocrite. On the other hand, Walter displays a willingness to please people. This is one of Walter's strongest characteristics.

As he searched for that certain sound an appraisal had to have in the utility company, George fell back on poring over his collected works again. But even in a perfect corporate coat, the truth was still the truth and there would be problems. Being a corporate leader was a bitch.

The end of July came before George perfected his appraisals, so he locked all the drafts in the sticking bottom drawer of his old file cabinet and went on his summer vacation.

MIDLIFE HONEYMOON

It was the best vacation the Cliftons had ever taken. Mary Ellen talked George into turning the corner between the toolshed and the back wall of the cottage into a nude zone. As a consequence the Cliftons did not bother with a lot of water-skiing or fishing. They went out to eat a lot, but George did not fell any trees until the last day of their stay. He spent the two weeks watching Mary Ellen on their nude beach. She lay on the blanket reading a tempestuous romance, glistening with suntan oil, twisting her body into pornographic poses. She would lift her buttocks, arch her back, spread her thighs, weave her fingers absentmindedly through her pubic hair, smooth the taut oily skin on her breasts. Some of these positions she had copied from glassy, gauzy photographs were uncomfortable as hell. Being a siren was damn hard work, but she knew what these poses were doing to George, and she held them as long and as naturally as she could. At night, under their influence, George turned into a lecherous beast.

There were only two problems with the Cliftons' midlife honeymoon: the bed in their room and George's old cousin behind a thin wooden wall. The bed squeaked, and the apoplectic cousin would bang an ashtray on the wall all night long—even after the Cliftons had taken their passion off the bed and onto the floor.

The old man had had it with George. Never more. He couldn't sleep with that racket every damn night. At their age, for Christ's sake. It seemed unbelievable what a pair of tits, fake ones at that, could do to a guy brought up in Flat City. The cousin remembered George as a nice, sort of a timid nice, kind of guy. But now that his crazy woman had got herself those tasteless implants, George was coming across more like a Hell's Angel—fucking like a rabbit every night, burning his bony buns behind the toolshed, drinking like a fish, leaving the buzz saw and the lawn mower alone, wearing bummy clothes, the works. Only thing George was missing now was a life-size tattoo of a hammer and sickle on his burned skinny ass. Probably just hadn't got around to it in time down there in Chicago.

The old man not only hadn't slept a wink for two weeks, he had had to put up with tons of jokes. Them silicone knockers really fired up their imagination at Don's, at the store, and at the gas station. How did they all five of them fit into that little shack of his, his neighbors demanded to know, cackling. Then some kids saw George and his crazy woman behind the toolshed, and now the people in town were really giving him the business. He was so sick of it all that he considered asking the Cliftons to pack up and go. He could never get himself to broach the subject though; there had been too many nice summers behind them. But George and his wife were not coming back again. That much was for sure.

The Cliftons noticed how rude George's cousin had become this year. As an ashtray percussionist the old coot had talent to burn. But they did not have the energy to worry about him. They were too wrapped up in their sexual heat, though there would be problems down the line.

One afternoon Mary Ellen slipped on her new minimal swimsuit and headed down to the lake for a swim. Passing by the blanket on which lay the sixteen-year-old daughter of their neighbor, she glanced at her breasts and marched on to immerse herself gingerly in the cool water.

Nice tits, she thought, almost as nice as mine.

Then she caught herself and shot out of the water. She rushed around the blanket where the teenager lay drowsily on her back. Standing behind her, drying herself with a towel, Mary Ellen proceeded to stare at the lovely breasts. They were on display under a flimsy white nylon bikini. They were showcase tits too.

They did absolutely nothing for Mary Ellen.

She felt not a tinge of interest or jealousy or desire or whatever the hell it was that used to give her such a charge. Panicking, Mary Ellen ran her mind's fingertips from the flat stomach over the springy mounds of their mass, across the stiff nipples, and down their receding swells. But she got no physical sensation from it at all. The shiver was gone.

Mary Ellen climbed back behind the toolshed, slowly pulled off her wet swimsuit, and dropped onto her solar pad. She was worried. For so many years all intimacy in her marriage had stemmed from sharing with George her fascination with breasts. But this had somehow withered away. An imaginary lover used to press the Cliftons together on the squeaking bed of the cottage. Now they had new bodies to arouse them and they were making love on the floor, but the room was empty: their implied lover was screwing somebody else.

How much did they need her and her fat tits? Could George keep on attracting her forever if he didn't help her conjure up their imaginary girlfriend? Was she going to hold George's interest alone? Had the implied lover vacated only her half of their bed? What could she do about any of this?

Mary Ellen had a thousand questions to which she'd rather not have known the answers, meant to air them all out nevertheless, really wanted to, but never actually got around to it. Things were going so well otherwise.

On the last day of their vacation the buzz saw kept roaring away beyond the ravine. Mary Ellen was busy fine-tuning her full-body tan, and she did not see George all day. He felled and cut up two large trees and made his cousin noticeably less morose. The old man was also no doubt glad to be finally getting rid of them.

Mary Ellen drove the old Ford workhorse home, because George was too sore from all the wood cutting. While she went through all the accumulated mail George fell asleep on the sofa. He just stretched out for a minute and was out like a light. Mary Ellen pulled his shoes and his pants off, threw a blanket over him, put out his clothes for the next day, brought his alarm clock into the living room, and set it for the eight fifteen. She ended up completely alone on their bed. Both George and their implied lover had walked out on her tonight. She stripped and admired her tanned breasts. They looked maddeningly gorgeous. They certainly belonged among the swirls of safari gold.

To hell with the implied lover.

CORPORATE CULTURE II

His first day back to work George was late getting into his modest
empire. He wore cool cotton over his full-body tan. He felt
relaxed. He dropped into his phenomenal chair and gazed through
the open doorway of his office at his underlings racing through
their crossword puzzles. They had just attacked them, were still
going strong, hadn't started passing the Webster around or swearing
yet. Peering at their hunched backs George was reminded again of
how microscopic was the importance of his underlings in his life
these days and what an awesome good their pathetic character
assassination had done him. He unlocked his filing cabinet, pulled
out the appraisals he had spent the first weeks of July composing,
tore them in half, and filed them in the imperial circular file. He
felt at case with the world, and he didn't want to lose the feeling
in pointless discussions. He just didn't have it in him to fight the
system anymore. He was through with anticipatory management.
He was returning into the fold of corporate culture, where the
appraisals said nothing and where there were no problems from
anybody.

On the four thirty-three that day the corpo lifers had pink,
sunburned faces and stiff muscles from the weekend. George
grabbed the last seat of the last car and watched Chicago shrink
behind the train. Shock-absorbing for a Bloody Mary and peering
at the gleaming rails that ran straight back into the past, George
knew that he had been right to be big about the appraisals; careers
in the utilities were too short for truth. He was a corporate dynamo
at peace with the system. He wanted to tell somebody about this.
He decided to call a no-bullshit QWL session soon. There was
nothing else to do for the entire month of August.

THE SAVIOR OF CAPITALISM

While Mary Ellen mourned the loss of the implied lover, Gwen Foss managed single-handedly to prove that liberal capitalism was in deep trouble in America, particularly in the affluent suburbs. There was not enough greed around anymore to keep it going. Socialism was creeping in.

Gwen had thrown away two mornings trying to sell Fred's car at the most expensive shopping center on her side of Chicago. The shops were exclusive, the shoppers sophisticated, the car gleaming. These people stank of money and Gwen was waving the title in their faces and it was costing her a fortune in baby-sitters, and she just could not unload the car. People glanced at the beautiful machine and walked on. They made snide remarks. Sure, they said. I'll trade it for a bridge, they said. For that piece of junk, they said. You gotta be out of your mind, they said and walked on.

—I'll give you a quarter for it but not a penny more, said one elderly gentleman in a seersucker safari suit.

Gwen could have talked to him. She was ready to talk money. She was ready to make reasonable adjustments in price. She had but one object in this transaction and that was to sell, so she was ready to go wherever the market would take her. But before she could explain any of this the old buyer was gone. He moved past her at the furious clip of someone whose only exercise is the walk from his car to his job.

The car certainly wasn't the problem here; Fred's cranberry-red Buick Regal had only eighteen hundred miles on it. Fred still had thirty-four coupons in his payment book. He had always insisted on all the body comforts in his cars, so there was air conditioning, cruise control, extra-wide steel-belted tires, four-speaker sound design with a tape deck, power everything.

The car was a knockout. The problem was the price: Gwen was asking one dollar for the Buick.

Gwen had her lucid moments. Most of them occurred around three or four in the morning when it was quiet everywhere and the lights of cars rounding the curve in the Fosses' street blew up the shadows of the flowerpots on the windowsill to the size of wardrobes and soundlessly slammed them against the plaster walls of the bedroom. She lay in bed on her back. She watched the fast-moving lights pump up the shadows and ram them against the wall. She listened to the raggedy silence, a silence that was built from peripheral sounds: the hum of the engine of the car outside, the tires licking the dewy blacktop, the wheezy breathing of the huge body beside her, the rustling of the Dutch elms in the steady wind. She was afraid to go back to sleep. She was afraid of her dreams. Her thoughts came and went as they pleased. She knew she was in trouble. She decided to do something drastic. So she did, and she ran head on into the greed-deficiency of her fellow citizens.

On the third morning of Gwen's career in used-car sales the July sun was blazing down so hard on the parking lot that she decided to adjust her price to the creeping socialist tendencies in her neighbors before she passed out from a sunstroke. It had to be a hundred and twenty degrees on the cement sidewalk. The sound of the flashers was slowly moving from the Buick to the inside of her head. If these people refused to make bundles of money off her, Gwen would give them a break and let them make less. America was clearly in trouble, but she could not worry about the country much today. She had her work cut out for her: she was selling a car, not saving the fucking nation.

She started asking for two hundred in cash.

Right off she got her man. He looked healthy, though not as healthy as Fred. His fat was all a matter of a sagging center of gravity—it was all in his belly. He wore blue coveralls with oil stains, had a graying mane of long blond hair and half-moons of dirt under his fingernails. He was an alien too; spoke with an accent so thick that to understand him you had to replay everything he said in your mind.

—Lemme look on dz tile, he said.

He ripped the title out of Gwen's hands, studied it closely, handed it back to her, walked around the car, opened the driver's door, slid inside (for all his bulk he moved with a feline ease), drummed on the steering wheel with his fingers, pulled out his wallet, ran his fingers through the bills, and made his counteroffer.

—I got tory-seven bugs. Maybe two bugs in chansh, he said.

Solemnly Gwen handed him the title. Here was a savior of liberal capitalism. It took an immigrant, but this man's greed was in perfect working order. Solemnly he handed her all the money from his wallet, then conscientiously searched his pockets for every last penny he could find.

—You marry, lady? he asked.

—None of your goddam business, said Gwen, thinking that the savior of capitalism was getting fresh with her.

—Yours husban is kill you, he said.

Amazingly enough, he wasn't far wrong. Gwen hadn't expected a saint like Fred to take the sale of one goddam pile of metal so badly.

The girls must have ratted on Gwen after she had got home in a cab that day. She had barely taken a shower and kicked her feet up when Fred was in the door.

—What happened to my car, Gwen?

—Your car?

—Yes! My Buick! I told you not to drive it! Did you have an accident?

—I gave it away.

—You what?!

—Well I sold it if you want to get technical with me I sold it for thirty-seven greasy dollars and I was lucky to get that little for it capitalism is in trouble I tell you nobody's greedy anymore I've learned more about this community by trying to give away that damn car than—

—I am dead serious, Gwen! Where the hell is my car?!

—Well you know we live a pretty selfish existence we give no money to charity we don't go to church we hog it all it was time to do some good deeds I figured it's better to make one concrete person happy than to spread your good works thin you should try it too it felt fantastic it felt like taking the vows of poverty the Fosses are through with low materialist ambitions—

Gwen was not sure if Fred would squash her against the wall like a bedbug or not, so she kept on talking. She was sitting in a chair and Fred was standing above her eyeballing her. Suddenly he took off. He ran the five steps to the television set and kicked it off the stand.

—There you go! Vows of poverty! he roared.

The television screen broke into a thousand shards. Fred lifted the glass coffee table and shattered it over the TV stand with one blow, screaming Vows of poverty, that's right, vows of fucking poverty, just what I say, vows of poverty, yes, ma'am, vows of goddam fucking poverty.

—Doesn't it feel good, Fred? Gwen asked calmly.

This shut Fred up; he did not want to admit how good it felt. He said nothing, lifted a lowboy and heaved it through the window on the driveway. Glass flew everywhere. The kids were sobbing loudly. More Fred's girls than her boys. She felt bad for them all, though the little bitches were getting what they deserved for double-crossing her. They did not know what they had been bargaining for when they had called their daddy behind her back.

Something happened when the lowboy crashed through the window. It was as though a pressure gradient between the outside and the inside had cracked, and all the tension in the room dissipated. Fred was about to throw a speaker through another window, but he stopped. He put it down gently. He ordered all the kids upstairs. He waited till they had gone. Then he walked over to Gwen, who was acting hurt.

—Okay, go get your toothbrush, we're going, he said.

She said nothing, got up, and headed for the bedroom.

—Vows of fucking poverty, he said softly, apologetically.

—Well I had to do something, damn it! she shot back fiercely and slammed the door behind her.

She was back almost instantaneously, carrying a small leather traveling bag.

Fred realized that she must have been all packed, and his heart went out to her, but she marched right past him and brushed off his halfhearted attempt to embrace her.

—We're going, let's go, then, she said.

QWL III

An ozone warning was in effect and city beaches were closed the morning George found a message taped to the door of his office as he strolled into his empire. It was from Fred Foss, said please call, RE: QWL.

Morose Marty was holding the fort, keeping it as dark and soothing as ever, watching over the eternal flower on their table. He waved a pitcher at the rogue QWL quorum: Fat Fred grunted with pleasure; Marty put it to the tap. A smile passed over his sullen face, appalling Fred.

—Did you see that? he asked.

—I thought I saw something too, said George.

—God, I hope he doesn't hit us with a "long time no see" or some goddam thing.

Marty sauntered over and slammed the pitcher and two steins on the table.

—You guys pour your own, right?

—Damn right, said Fred.

—All set, then, said Marty and sauntered back behind the bar.

It was a great utility-company performance. They felt at home. George poured the beer. When he looked up, one glance at Fred told him that they were going inner person on inner person this afternoon like in the old days. He was ready.

Let's go, he thought. It will be good for everybody.

—God, said Fred, sighing, lovingly watching as Marty poured himself a short one behind the bar, why do there got to be broads? Why can't there just be guys in the world?

—Cause you can't live without 'em, explained George.
—Fuck, said Fred.
—Yup, said George.
George sipped his beer while Fred downed his stein, George refilled it. Fred wiped the droplets of sweat off his forehead with a napkin. George took another sip of Michelob.
—Yup, said Fred.
—So how you been, said George.
—Had Gwen committed it's been three weeks now.
—Oh, God, said George.
—Yup, said Fred.
—Damn, said George.
—Yup, said Fred.
They sat on that for a long time.
—How are the kids taking it, said George.
—We go for visits. You can't begin to imagine, said Fred.
They both downed their steins. Fred poured them full of beer again and motioned for a refill.
—To tell you the truth, Fred, said George, she did talk kind of strange that one time. Who knows, maybe it'll be for the better.
—I'm hoping like hell.
They sat on that.
—Gonna need your help too, said Fred.
—Anytime, said George. Just gimme a holler.
—Gotta burn my Buick, said Fred.
—Yup, said George.
Fred had to torch his Buick was all. George trusted Fred completely, was going to be glad to be of help, had no need for any gory details. He sensed that Fred had tracked the goddam alien down to his basement apartment, stinking of fungi, where cartoon characters giggled as in a nightmare. The guy opened his door but kept it chained. He was wearing only a pair of soccer trunks. Fred explained what the deal was with Gwen, apologized, offered to return the thirty-seven dollars, cover any and all additional expenses, throw in a few more bills for the aggravation.
—I kip dz car, is mine, said the son of a bitch.

—I really miss my Buick, you know, said Fred.

—I am terrible sorry, said the alien.

—Okay, said Fred, I'll just have to take it from here then.

There was no point in getting mad. There was going to have to be a bonfire on a parking lot somewhere while Fred went on mailing his payment coupons.

They drank their beer in long and short drafts, saying nothing.

—Goddam, George finally said.

—Yup, said Fred.

But complications in torching the Buick set in right away: Gwen got released from the hospital; the bad-actor DP capitalist moved from the fungi-stained basement and Fred had to put in a lot of legwork tracking him down again; George's implied lover put his job on the line. Before any of that occurred, however, the door of the gin mill flew open, the street roared, and a slender young woman in a short dress charged in. She halted by the door and waited for her eyes to adjust to the underlit room. With her short blond hair and a fashionably bony butt, she was pretty easy on the eyes, but Fat Fred got totally disgusted by what he saw.

—Fuck, he said.

The young lady stopped squinting around, chuckled, and made for their table.

—Here you are, Fred! she cried. Ms. Lewis has been waiting for you in your office for an hour now. I thought you might wanna know.

—Uh-oh, said George.

—Shit, Sharon, said Fred. Why do there got to be broads? Why can't there just be guys in the world?

—That'd be fine by me, said Sharon.

But Fat Fred could not live without Ms. Lewis—Ms. Lewis was division. She was Fred's fearless leader, and she never bothered him unless there was a very good reason to, so corporate report-ables had to be raining down like cats and dogs.

THE IMPLIED LOVER

The implied lover had been many women. Sometimes she passed by the Cliftons on the street. At other times they caught a glimpse of her in the shopping mall. In the summer the implied lover lay around on a blanket below the cottage of George's cousin a lot. The faces of the implied lover changed, her age fluctuated, but what she always had were full breasts. Then Tanya Mendez stormed into the imperial office early one afternoon, and it turned out that the implied lover had an ironing board with a couple of raisins for a chest.

It did not matter. George set his eyes on her and he fell in love. In love, tits did not matter. Love went deeper than that.

At the time George already had a tanned ass; his midlife honeymoon had peaked the week before. He was lying back in his phenomenal chair, his feet resting on the imperial desk, on the verge of dozing off. Suddenly a young woman barged in and assaulted him with a stream of words. She spoke with a slight Spanish accent, looked very lovely and very familiar.

George hurriedly kicked his feet off the desk, thinking, My, my, we are hot about something.

He knew he had seen this thin, fine-boned, long-legged woman before. She had feverish black eyes, long purple-black hair, a pale heart-shaped beautiful face. She wore tall red heels, tight blue jeans, and a loose blouse with red polka dots, and all George wanted to do was stroke her soft, hairy arms. They were covered with long, smooth, dark silk.

You're the emperor, he had to tell himself. Everybody's watching.

The accent finally clicked and George recognized his weekend part-timer in the fiery broad: she was on his payroll.

Her name was Tanya Mendez and she had been working for his department for years, but her shift ran from noon till midnight every Saturday and Sunday. So the last time George had seen her

was eight months before, at the office Christmas party. The last
Christmas was centuries ago: George had still been maximizing
then, worrying about his Swiss-clock biorhythm, paying no mind
to flat-chested dolls like Tanya.

Tanya's full-lipped mouth kept going a mile a minute. It
sounded as though the company had asked her to mop the floor
around the urinals and chew the mop clean, or lick the cobwebs
and lint balls out of the corners of the imperial lounge or
something. Then it started dawning on George what her beef was:
Walter had given Tanya her job-performance appraisal the day
before (George's first-levels had to put in one weekend a month in
the computer room), and she was not about to take the intimations
of insignificance the corporate culture mandated lying down. She
was outraged; her job performance had been rated only as very
good, and she still couldn't believe that. This was a joke, this was
almost funny, this definitely sucked.

George glanced into the first-level office: the walrus mustache
was poring over a stack of printouts, but his ears were turning
crimson. Tanya had stormed past him, thrown a copy of her
appraisal on the imperial desk, and was now making sure Walter
heard every word of her shrill tirade.

Her approach was to tell it like it was in George's empire on
weekends in general and with Walter running the ship in particular. There was enough dirt there to discredit a whole payroll of
saints:

1. Walter was a half hour late coming to work the day he gave
Tanya her appraisal.

2. This was Walter being himself.

3. Walter didn't know his job, couldn't make decisions, give
orders, cold-boot a system, mount a disk.

4. Walter slept on the job a lot, usually on the sofa in George's
office. Often on weekends he failed to make it into the computer
room for a single inspection.

5. Walter had come in with the Sunday *Tribune*, the Sunday
Sun-Times, *Hustler* and *Penthouse* under his arm on Tanya's
appraisal day.

6. This was Walter being himself.

7. Walter mocked the dress code. He usually wore sneakers on weekends, never a tie, had shown up in wrinkled shorts once. His legs were hairy, fat, white, and disgusting. The ladies had to look at them all weekend long, which was not even sanitary—there should be a memo sent around to these supervisors: no trousers, no tie, no business.

8. Walter was a walking health hazard. He never washed his filthy hair, always sniffled, never had any Kleenex, was always spreading germs.

—This is all news to me, George said.

—I thought so, said Tanya.

She had never burst into anybody's office like this before, never had been this upset in her life, loved her job, was proud of it, got along with everybody, trained everybody on her shift, regularly kept the sky from falling, put in the same effort as every other year, when it always said on her appraisals that she walked on water. So the problem here was Walter.

9. Walter was on the beeper more than he was off the beeper on weekends. He disappeared out of the office for four, five hours.

10. All the supervisors did this, but Walter wouldn't even have the doggone beeper on.

11. If you needed Walter, you had to go look for him at Steve's Fine Food & Cocktails (where the help barfed on beer cans) or Papa Accardo's or Stash's or the Filipino joint (which billed itself as a Chinese restaurant and where Walter regularly lost his shirt in poker).

12. Walter was good at only one thing: bringing his portable TV to work and watching everything. Walter was the only person who didn't care if he was watching golf, a mad preacher, the Three Stooges, or two giraffes screwing on channel eleven.

—As long as he doesn't watch a mad preacher poking a giraffe, said George.

—Don't laugh, said Tanya, because that would be right up Walter's alley.

13. Walter had patted Tanya's ass once and had got the hell slapped out of him.

14. Walter drank on duty while on beeper. He often staggered back in smelling like a brewery. One time he wound up stuck in the hallway on his way home, hitting the UP button with his fist and waiting for the down elevator, getting pissed, yelling, What the hell is the matter with this building, who's running these goddam elevators—anybody? This had really happened, and who got to put Walter on the right elevator? Who else but his very good, not excellent, employee?

15. This was only Walter being Walter.

—All news to me, said George.

16. Walter also called Tanya the rose of Spanish Harlem on a regular basis, though she had been born and bred in Texas.

17. This was Walter being himself all right, but the EEO/AA hotline would be very interested in pursuing this.

—Do me a favor, Tanya, close that door, will you? said George and pointed at the imperial gate.

Swaying her trim, angelic butt, Tanya aimed her red suede shoe at the door stopper and kicked it all the way under George's desk. As the door closed the last thing George saw through the opening was the walrus mustache shooting out of the office. Now his face was the color of chalk. He would be lucky if he made it out to embrace the handicapped crapper before he was sick. It looked as though even Walter had a tiny humanoid somewhere in his guts.

POETRY

Tanya had shut the door, and George motioned to her to sit down on his green love seat. Her beef was absurdly petty; nobody read the goddam management appraisals, so nobody, certainly, ever bothered with the craft appraisals. Those things were nothing more than file fodder. Yet here was Tanya wasting so much inner person

on them. Could her hold be a little tentative on what the priorities
were on this planet? Still, what a passionate inner person it was!
What a drive. What sweetness. What beauty. And what a burst of
black silk her Venus mound had to be. How could his buddy Fat
Fred ever say that he didn't need any broads?

Jesus.

George had never been one for fainting over roses or steaming
up the windows every time a full moon swung out from behind a
cloud. Looking at his part-time weekender, however, George was
ready to run to a card shop and start memorizing the merchandise
in the Love & Friendship section. The only poetry George ever
read was scratched into the stunted beige wall of the handicapped
crapper:

> *happiness is a tight pussy*
> *and i don't mean a drunken cat*

While George was dealing with eternity, swinging his feet in the
air and staring directly at it, the inscription looked like poetry to
him. But the minute he stepped out of the john, George started
having his doubts.

Yes, it did say something that was true.

Yes, it did play with words.

Yes, the second line did catch you with your pants down.

Yes, it was about love, like all poetry should be.

And nowadays it was probably okay to use language like that in
poetry. (At any given moment, chances were that there was a
published poet somewhere on the planet Earth sitting in a bathtub
chain-smoking, wiping away tears, committing to paper words like
"cunt," "asshole," and "cockcheese.")

But it did not scan. There was no music, and George could not
warm up to this modern shit. It was all right for a wall of a
handicapped crapper, but it would not make it on a page of a book,
and that was about the size of it.

Why, then, did the damn verse peal through his head as he held
on to the gorgeous, hairy, demonic Tanya for two hours behind the
closed imperial gate? He did not get to say much. He sat there. He

smiled. He watched Tanya's sexy motor mouth open and close and her pink tongue wet her ruby lips and heard not a word that was coming out. He undressed her slowly in his mind. . . .

But all good things come to an end in the utilities, and Tanya had to run to get her boy from the baby-sitter. She said So long, gave George a long (meaningful?) look, fished out the door stopper, and, swaying her angelic ass, kicked it back under the door. She never once glanced in Walter's direction. Then she was gone.

In the imperial office the poetry feeling lingered on: George kept swiveling around on his phenomenal chair and staring at the love seat where Tanya's trim ass (and her sweet hairy pussy too, the way she sat leaning forward) had left a slight depression in the rough green fabric. Such a maddening-charming accent. Such goddam Latin passion. Yet she was as American as George was.

Oh, Mary Ellen, he thought. Help.

The afternoon wore on; George meditated over the small dent in the imperial love seat. In the first-level office outside Walter was working hard on making himself conspicuous: he kept crossing George's field of vision, clearing his throat, hanging around the door. He wanted to discuss Tanya with him, hoped to make his case. George ignored him, then strolled out of the office and headed for the elevators. He needed to be alone. He wanted to think about Tanya.

He walked swiftly down sun-beaten sidewalks till he crossed Michigan Avenue and entered Grant Park. In the distance the green-blue lake palpitated and rocked and blew a cool breeze inland. George ambled down the lawns, marched across the Lake Shore Drive, and lay down on the gentle slope overlooking a sailboat harbor. He chose a sheet of soft grass in the thin shade of a crab-apple tree, and he stretched out on his back. The earth under him was warm. He loosened his tie, spread his arms, and closed his eyes. Pink light shone through his eyelids. There was a faraway whir of a helicopter, the faint smell of hay. The water splashed against the hull of a boat. The tepid breath of the lake passed through his hair. And he was earning money here: the utility company was paying him for this. His was the job. He let out every muscle in his body. The hard light of the summer was getting through the crimson membranes of his eyelids. He could see his own blood, the blood of a corpo lifer in love. Being in love made him feel important: suddenly the warm round planet under him seemed no bigger than his skull. He could not imagine that the earth could survive his death. He could not imagine that the utility company could survive George S. Q. Clifton. If he did not exist, nothing would. He was the world. He was the pink light radiating through his eyelids. He was the lake making suckling noises against the boats. The end of him was going to be the end of everything: no more crab-apple shade, helicopters, appraisals, love, cool breezes, or QWL.

When George awoke the sun stood low over the downtown behind him. He looked at his watch. It was six o'clock. He had put in two hours of overtime. Mary Ellen was waiting for him with dinner.

The rush hour and the happy hour were over; the cleaning crew was sweeping the deserted commuter station. The air sat still and hot and ozone-tinged. George got on the half-empty six forty-six. He didn't care to look at the haggard workaholics aboard, so he sat on the last seat of the train (another routine was creeping into his life) and watched the downtown high-rises glint in the slanted sun. The inhuman mass of concrete now struck him as being as full of romance as a hotel bed. Poetry echoed through his head. Happiness is a tight pussy/zero boobs/company time/life is grand.

He was proud of himself as he pedaled leisurely through the suburb, where dogs were being walked again: he had been able to doze off in a park full of muggers. And he got paid for it.

He explained to Mary Ellen that he had got engrossed in his work. She didn't mind. She was serving a crab salad and a cheese plate, so she didn't have to reheat anything. And she had been tasting the good dry white wine all afternoon. She wasn't wearing any underwear.

George ate his dinner in silence, sipping wine. He seemed lost in thought, and the moment was dear to Mary Ellen. It was a part of his transformation; George used to leave his job behind before he had bought his army jacket. Now he was taking it home with him more and more often. And George, the passionate company man, was a man plugged into his world, immersed in life—the very opposite of the old monkish maximizer. It was healthy for George to be absentminded at the dinner table.

Mary Ellen cherished the moment.

But when the Cliftons made love (in the bathroom again), George still did not seem to be all there. And he did not touch Mary Ellen's breasts a single time. She had to do it herself. But, then, that was nice too sometimes.

STICK SHIFT & VITAMINS

Poetry made you do funny things: the next morning George got to work on the seven fifteen. He had not been on it for weeks. He entered his modest empire, ignored Walter, who was staring at him every time he looked up, pulled out the clerical records, wrote down Tanya's address, told his underlings to take messages, Peter-Panned it to headquarters on a full gut, and signed out a company coupe at the garage.

George pulled no weight at the motor pool, didn't know a single dynamo in the office, so they stuck him with an old beater with a stick shift. The garage lay in the bowels of the building, and George had to drive the coupe up a steep ramp. Grinding the gears, popping the clutch, he jumped the coupe up the incline in jerky lurches. He smelled the clutch burning by the time he had made it out of the building. The engine went on dying in the thick morning traffic. The fearless leaders around him (with only two pedals to worry about) were honking their cheap opinions. The cabbies yelled their ten-cent driving tips. A pack of snotty teenagers in a convertible gave him a standing ovation. This tended to deplete the poetry charge of the morning considerably.

Ten red lights into his outing George finally prevailed over the tricky clutch of the beater and got the poetry feeling back. He steered the car with his left hand, kept his right hand on the stick, wove smoothly through the morning traffic, keeping to the major arteries, avoiding the expressways, feeling like a young man again, fresh out of the navy, driving his first car, the throbbing manual black Mustang. He was a deuce in love, and, like the poet said, happiness was a tight pussy.

George was heading west, to a two- and three-story neighborhood where people new to the city were squeezing time out of old houses and streets were full of potholes. There were neon signs missing letters that stayed on day and night. Sidewalks were caving in. They had been raised several feet in an achievement of Victorian engineering to prevent the streets from flooding, but this had been done generations before, and the worn concrete was giving out. If you were not careful, you could park your car in a crack in the sidewalk and never drive it again.

George found Tanya's apartment. She lived above a FRUTAS Y LEGUMBRES store. The sign was hand-painted, but the pyramids of peaches, oranges, apples, cantaloupes, pears, and mangoes had been constructed with precision and beauty. A locked door with a triangular window showed a dark staircase rising up. You could not see the top of the stairs. There were two rusty mailboxes, sprayed with orange graffiti. The name on one of them said Mr. Sage Mendez.

—Shit, said George.

The company files had listed Tanya as single. This figured. Love and poetry got to be a bitch after forty. The feelings themselves were hard enough to come by at his age, but then you got lucky and there were husbands, wives, kids, careers, and every other goddam thing getting in the way. He almost drove off again. Then he decided he at least wanted to see Tanya, if nothing else. So he bought a pound of peaches and a bunch of grapes, parked the coupe across the street, and sat there watching the door and getting his vitamins. But Tanya never showed.

That was Tuesday.

On Wednesday George bought pears and spent an hour baking

in the coupe. He tried to think about what to tell Tanya if she popped up. Happiness is a tight pussy? That was a hell of an opening line from a boss. Mostly he just wanted to see her.

Thursday George got tangerines and bananas. Tanya sure was keeping him in vitamins, but the door with the triangular window never budged.

Friday morning George had to Peter-Pan to a propaganda meeting about a rate increase the utility company was requesting. Yawning, he sat through the graphs and colorful charts (the public owed the company unconscionable sums of money, and the hurting utility philanthropist wanted a laughably minuscule part of it back), waited for the coffee cart, and thought about Tanya's hairy body. He was happy that Fat Fred didn't show up for his dose of company propaganda and he didn't have to shoot the breeze with him. As soon as the meeting dispersed George checked out another coupe.

Right away, even before he had pulled up to the fruit stand, George saw Tanya sprinting down the sidewalk. She was chasing a tiny dark-haired kid. She grabbed him and started throwing him up into the air. They were both laughing and loud and happy. They looked beautiful.

George followed them in low second gear to a dusty park. There were scrawny, sick-looking trees. The slides and swings bore graffiti. A beat-up chicken leaned at an acute angle to the sandbox; green-painted sun-beaten El tracks vaulted beyond. No wonder Tanya and her son had the park to themselves.

Parked half a block away, George stared at his dark angelic weekender. Tanya wore blue-jean hot pants and a loose gray T-shirt. She sprawled on a sun-dappled bench, her elbows hooked behind the back slats. Her lovely thighs were thrown wide apart. Her boy went racing around the playground, setting all the swings, frogs, horses, chickens, and ladybugs into motion. Then an El train rumbled into view. The kid froze in the twitching field of toys and watched the four silver cars pass through the crowns of sickly trees. He stared at the train as hard as George was staring at those velvety thighs. Because George's mind was made up: he was going to have the smooth long delicious thighs. He didn't care what it took, what it would cost him. His body was pumping with poetry. He started the coupe and drove off before Tanya put her knees together.

He didn't get much work done that Friday beyond deciding once and for all that the poem on the wall of the handicapped crapper definitely qualified as poetry. While modernist and dirty, it was also deep. Screw the music.

He left the office in time to make the four thirty-three, then decided to get a drink. He did not feel like facing Mary Ellen. He thought a couple of Scotches would make him a better husband. He chose a bar near the commuter station where he had never been before, then got his Styrofoam usual as the kiosk bar was closing. He barely made the six forty-six, but he was feeling no pain.

This time Mary Ellen was not happy with George. She warmed up the fiery chili for him, poured his cold Michelob, and tiptoed around him with a heavy heart. Something was wrong here; something had gone wrong already. It hadn't taken long at all. She headed into the bathroom and slipped on a pair of panties; their midlife honeymoon was over.

On Sunday morning George confirmed Mary Ellen's suspicions. Mary Ellen wanted to go out for a brunch, but George had work to do. He had to drive downtown. He needed to make a special inspection of his empire. There had been a lot of problems between his weekenders and his first-levels lately. He had to case the situation before it got out of hand. He was going to be back in three to four hours.

George drove off and left the stunned Mary Ellen to draw the only conclusion that suggested itself: George was having an affair. (The emperor still could not be mistaken for a rabid company man, had never gone to the office on Sunday before, had never let any work problems reach his imperial perch.)

George had twenty-four years of catching up to do. He was clearly getting started on the job. Mary Ellen had been waiting for this to happen ever since the implied lover had deserted their bedroom. So now she did not have to wait any longer. But she was not ready for it, had no idea what to do. She made for the bar cart, then called Florida and stayed on the phone for an hour gabbing with her mother and wondering all the while: Who the hell is she? Do I know the bitch? Probably not. Chances were she came with the imperial territory. So George was likely to be with her right now, even as her mother was running down Aunt Dorothy's raspberry jam.

Mary Ellen abruptly closed the open-ended conversation with her mother, and she quickly dialed George's office. She had news for the slut, whoever she was: this was going to be a war. Emperor Clifton of the little belly and an inner person was definitely worth fighting for. Fighting like hell. Biting and scratching and pulling hair.

A woman's voice answered the call. She sounded young and sexy.

You bitch, thought Mary Ellen, you goddam slut.

—Is Mr. Clifton there, please? she asked.

—Yes, he is. May I tell him who's calling?

—This is July.

—Thank you, July. Hold on.

You goddam man-stealing cheap syphilitic whore!

—This is George.

You two-faced son of a bitch! What are you looking for? The clap? Bigger tits? Herpes?

—Hello? Who is this?

Come home. Will you? Hurry up! I love you. I want to bite your cock off.

There was a click on the other end of the line. Mary Ellen went on holding the phone to her ear till the dial tone cut on. So it is somebody on the job, she thought. Okay, then, it's war. She slammed the phone down, pulled the cork from a sloppily plugged bottle with her teeth, and went to take a hot bath.

THE BUST

Walter had weekend duty again. George figured that if he could bust him, he could make Tanya Mendez a very happy woman. He stabbed his plastic card into the stainless steel box that was the lock on the main gate of his empire, hoping to walk in on a typical Sunday in his department.

He got his wish.

He found the office of the first-levels deserted and checked the lounge. As foretold by Tanya, a small portable TV was hollering away on the little telephone stand, though nobody was watching the Bears lose another preseason game. As foretold, the long table at the center of the room was covered with newspapers. As foretold, there was the *Tribune*, the *Sun-Times*, and *Hustler*.

George walked up the ramp into the computer room and into history. Tanya and her young coworker Ann were astounded to see the big boss. They had been making tape backups on one of the minis. While mounting, dismounting, labeling, and logging tapes they were discussing George. Tanya was just telling Ann what a nice guy their big boss was and how she had fixed Walter good when she looked up and there was the man himself strolling into the computer room—on a Sunday!—smiling away. The empire would never be the same.

—Hi, ladies, he said. Where is my friend Walter?

Tanya wore a tight beige designer sweatsuit and maroon sneakers and maroon lipstick, and she was ready to kiss the big boss. There had in fact been words between her and Walter this very morning. So she stared George down, smiling as if his hands were already sticky with Walter's blood.

George could not get enough of Tanya's smiles and looks. He waited a full hour before he allowed Ann to beep the walrus mustache. It did not do any good: evidently Walter didn't have his beeper on.

Two more hours would elapse before Walter finally showed up. In the meantime George received a mysterious phone call. Ann said that some July wanted to talk to him, but when he lifted the phone, someone held the line and would not say anything. This was pretty odd, because nobody knew that he would be here, but George did not think about it much. He had been digging up information about Tanya's marital status, and Tanya's answers were pure poetry: she was married, separated, and scraping up divorce money. Her husband, Sage, couldn't hold a job, was a jerk, hadn't been seen in two months now. He used to get drunk and beat her because he was jealous. He was venting his insecurities was what was really going on. Now he was venting himself on the "bar lady." The bar lady had a fat ass, but Sage took off with her anyway. She was going to be hell on Sage, she would talk to anybody. Sage was sure to kill her. Tanya was relieved. If Sage or his bitch gave her any trouble, Tanya was going to have them both deported. They were Mexican Mexicans, had zero green cards between them.

George would have paid cash money to hear more of this sweet music. But then the light came on in the lounge, and the imperial bloodletting got under way.

George gave Walter ten minutes to come in and inspect the computer room, but the walrus mustache blew that too. All the ten minutes bought him was a chance to get comfortable on the sofa in the lounge. He had kicked off his sandals, stuck his bare feet on top of the phone stand, undone his old gray canvas jeans, and unbuttoned his wrinkled green rugby shirt. He was yawning and scratching his white fat paunch when George walked in.

Tanya and Ann snuck behind the first band of disk drives and watched the two men through the glass wall of the lounge.

In five quick steps George loomed over Walter.

—Let me have your ID, he said in his deuce voice. You're suspended.

The walrus face was stunned. Walter slowly swung to his feet and started groping for his sandals. He wasn't saying anything. He lifted his left leg to strap his sandal on, lost his balance, made three stutter-steps to regain it, and stopped himself by ramming into the table. This performance pissed him off.

—What for? he said defiantly.

—You really want me to go down the list with you?

—I didn't do anything different from what everybody else does, said Walter and continued to strap on his sandal while leaning on the table.

He succeeded before long.

—I don't care what anybody else does, Walter, said George, but I've been here for four hours now. You're through doing this.

Walter reached into his breast pocket, threw his ID card on the newspapers covering the desk, and with one jerk of his arm unplugged the portable TV. The picture collapsed into a blip and the screen went blank.

—Goodbye, George, you're a goddam pain, said Walter.

—You didn't say that, Walter, said George and watched Walter stagger out through the main imperial gate.

NTR

While Tanya and Ann sprinted from the disk drives back to their work station, George marched up the ramp. He crossed the long, harshly lit space and walked into the sweetest smile a fearless leader ever got returning with corporate blood on his hands. Ann headed to her locker to get ready to hit the streets, and Tanya went on giving George doe eyes. Her smile said power was sexy.

George flashed his best cigar-store stuff at Tanya. He was a deuce in love, and he was old, and there were wives and husbands and kids all over the place, and none of it would stop them now.

—That Walter's so stupid! said Tanya. He heard me tell you—

The tone of her voice let George know they were swooping down to where inner persons interacted.

—He's a jerk, he said. There's only one thing I honestly couldn't blame him for.

—What? Patting my ass?

—Yup.

—Well, I don't blame him for that either, but I don't usually like to get my meat where I get my bread, said Tanya and burst out laughing.

George roared. She was incredible: all that superficial innocence, calling Sage's paramour a bar lady and all that and underneath it such scathing wit.

—Rules are made to be broken, said he.

—Come to think of it, maybe there would be a way, said she.

—Shoot, said he.

—I've got this passport. I've had it for four years and I don't have a single lousy stamp in it, said she.

—How fast can you pack your bags? said he (though he didn't have a passport himself).

—Only country I don't care to see is Mexico, said she (meticulously defining every clause in their love contract).

—Mexico is out, said he.

Power was sexy, and this was love after forty, and there would be no misunderstandings. The implied lover was welcome to have George on any terms she wanted. He stepped up to Tanya and stroked her dark, soft forearms. He said that she would be hearing from him real soon. She laughed and said that she was looking forward to having her passport stamped.

George conducted a brief shift change with the astonished evening-shift supervisor, who arrived in hair rollers. She almost keeled over when she saw George. She had never run into the big boss on a weekend before, never hung around while history was being made. George was amused by her reaction. He reported that Walter had been suspended and that the rest of the shift change was a big fat NTR—nothing to report.

MEMORY & CASH

In utilities, however, life is not only QWL and the sexy power to
suspend subordinates. Life is bookoo ass-busting, decisions, deals,
unquotable understandings, cups of turtle soup, rivers of coffee,
and marvels such as the 300-megabyte memory disk.

Computer memory is stored on smooth light-brown metallic
platters, mounted on an axial piston. They are the size of hubcaps,
remember everything if they are bit-error-free, spin around in disk
drives at the speed of 3500 revolutions a minute, and cost seven
hundred dollars per.

This had not made any difference to George S. Q. Clifton until
he fell in love. Then he suddenly saw the bottom line: disk packs
were money. He had several machines that needed twelve disk
drives to keep their reams of technical gibberish. With three-week
retention of backups, this meant that a single computer had to
have thirty-six memory disks. So George kicked up his feet on the
Kremlin desk and he called Fred Foss.

Fat Fred's big empire had extensive memory needs, and Fred
appreciated turtle soup, good wine, fine cigars, and damask
tablecloths. Consequently Fred was buying all his disk packs from
one salesman. The guy was a real bullshitter. His wares were a
little on the expensive side, but he was funny and he had good taste
in conference places: they were wrapped in damask. He was
making a bundle off Fred's purchases, knew it, was fair, didn't
mind spreading a little of it around. This was the American way;
you had to be brain-dead to order your disk packs any other way.

Fred gladly put George in touch with the guy. His name was
Steve DeVries, and he was just the man a deuce in love needed:
short, pudgy, bald on top, quick-witted, and big-picture all the
way. The sleeves on his tweed jacket had real holes. The buttons
were fishbone. The maître d' of the French restaurant where he
met George greeted him by name. They bantered familiarly as he
led them to a choice corner table at the back of the room, away

from the bar and the kitchen door. The damask tablecloth blazed with whiteness. A crystal vase held an obscene purple cattleya.

George had been passing by the joint for years. It lay on his train-station route. He had never even thought to walk in. The place was always full of big shots and VIPs, investment types, high-powered lawyers, three-martini CEOs and orchid secretaries, infirm tycoons and their young wives who ordered everything for their husbands from armies of waiters.

A few months back, over a bare table with a plastic daisy splattered with beer and ketchup, Fat Fred had confided in George. He said that he would give up his district for a deuce's job in purchasing in a minute. Dealing with salesmen on behalf of the company was where it was at in the utilities. The sales reps dragged you to seven-course lunches, smothered you in tickets for ball games and plays, lured you aboard planes for weekend seminars in California, had even been known to hold a gun to your head and stuff your pockets with cash. Purchasing devastated you with job satisfaction.

Sipping turtle soup, George saw Fred's point. The soup tasted fine, a little sour maybe, but it definitely had the chamomile tea beat. George could have been coming here and stuffing his guts with paté for the past five years. But there were so many other boats George had missed that this particular one did not really bother him.

Life in management gave not only devastating job satisfaction, it provided constant challenges as well: you had to pry these nasty-looking escargots out of their housing. At the same time you had to think about what you were saying: in purchasing you couldn't just blurt out what was on your mind. You didn't spell anything out. You talked around things in case there was a grand jury down the line. So you complimented Steve on what a fine place for doing his homework he had found and assured him that you had no gripes with the power lunch, but you were ready to go it bigger.

How big?

Well, George needed an infinity of bits just about, needed it yesterday, but he had· been hit with some heavy hospital bills lately, so he didn't have the exact number of memory disks he needed. He hadn't been able to think about anything but his bills.

Steve was damn sorry to hear about George's money problems. He had an idea, though. If George could accommodate some soft errors on his packs, then a margin would open up. You could always ship some cheaper disks and bill them as top-of-the-line merchandise. No one would ever know the difference.

George agreed, because how would they? People didn't understand memory-disk specs.

Right. And the important thing was that you would create a billing margin this way. Billing margins were what killed money headaches. Because what happened to the margin depended only on how much creativity you had.

That would work, but George didn't want anybody to cook the books or anything kinky like that.

Of course not, and the margin could be paid out in cash.

Good. Because cash was cash.

Was cash. Now George had mentioned that he needed an infinity of bits. But, Steve argued, some infinities were bigger than others. That's what the theory of infinities taught.

George had not made it to school that day, but this was very interesting. Except how could an infinity be smaller? It was infinite, wasn't it?

Well, an infinity of integers was obviously bigger than an infinity comprised only of odd numbers, right?

But George was not talking a bigger infinity. He was talking a *smaller* infinity; he could match any integer Steve threw at him with an odd number and never run out of them. So he still wasn't getting it. ·

A very good point. Steve was impressed. But this was philosophy, not math anymore, and philosophically speaking, they had run into a brick wall as far as infinities were concerned. So how the hell many disk packs were they talking?

George needed forty 300-megabyte disks up front and more later.

Which was a goddam infinity of bits by any measure, and they had a deal. And Steve was going to structure the purchase in a way that was fair to everybody.

Steve then picked up the tab. The purchasing lunch had been a spectacular success: George had never picked apart dizzying ideas like this before. Infinities were right up there with going inner person on inner person. However, he had a feeling that he should have gone over the specs of the memory disks that Steve was going to ship him. But their philosophical conversation had never dipped that low, so now Steve was sure to send him some real shitty disks. Not that this would mean the end of the world: the company would pay premium for them; George would get his kickback from Steve, charge the money to the users, and then junk the disks when they got to be a problem. No one would ever know.

George and Steve parted outside the damask-and-snails joint. Steve killed George with his big-picture handshake: firm, dry, great eye contact, perfect timing. He said he would be talking to George the next morning. He had to run the numbers through his PC, but roughly speaking, they were talking a margin of three and a half grand in cash.

George headed for the nearest travel agency thinking: a chicken-shit three and a half grand—fuck, I've easily saved the company that much in cab books alone over the years.

All George needed now was a passport. Life was grand.

THE GRAND LIFE III

Chicago was one of the most racist cities in the country. The ethnics hated the blacks. The blacks hated the Mexicans. The Mexicans were glad to be here, though they hated the Puerto Ricans. The Puerto Ricans hated the ethnics. The progressive element on the Gold Coast and in the lake wards thought money and style important and race or ethnic origins irrelevant. And there also were a few suburbs somewhere where money counted more than what you looked like. But these were big-picture places. The heart of Chicago lay west of Ashland Avenue, and it was working class and bigoted. So George Clifton and Tanya Mendez made a great stride forward in Chicago ethnic relations on the firm, clean bed of a fancy hotel abroad.

The city was a major financial center of the world. They flew first-class, because money was no object this weekend. Aboard the plane George discovered that happiness was static electricity. He began lightly to stroke Tanya's shins, smoothing out the tender cover of tiny black hairs, and he wound up generating so much static that her light skirt clung to her long delicious thighs.

The plane landed at an airport that looked like every other airport. The customs officer, however, refused to stamp Tanya's passport. They did not do that here, she said. George got hot. He started arguing, holding up the line, but Tanya grabbed him by the elbow and pulled him away.

—Oh, forget it, George, she said.

—You don't have stamp one in this passport, said George and went on waving the booklet at the customs bitch.

—Details!

—Why did we come all the way here, then?

She pulled his face to her and gave him a long, wet kiss.

The hotel towered on the rim of a sweet-water indigo sea. The sheets were lemon-scented, the bed king-size, the sex furious: George had slowly undressed Tanya and kissed her quivering thighs, her hard stomach, her musty Venus mound, her eager life. In sixteen years of married life George had never before been unfaithful to Mary Ellen (though he did have two women in her). Tanya had not had a man touch her in months. It had been years since Sage was this passionate, grateful, obliging. (In the Mendez bedroom the oral sex had always gone the other way.) So inner person did not enter into it, but the grandeur of love had it covered.

After they had recovered from their orgasms George called room service. He ordered two lobster dinners and a bottle of Chivas. The hotel room cost a hundred and twenty American, but the service stank: George and Tanya were back on the bed studying each other's bodies, slowly, gently, tenderly fucking before anyone knocked on the door. George waited till the knocking was upgraded to pounding.

—Leave the tray near the door, he shouted.

But the voice behind the door insisted that he had to have a signature. He was sorry, but he didn't make the rules.

—Oh, yes, the rules, said George, pulling his pants on.

The rules, the signatures, the responsibilities, the utilities, the corporations. You could get this same room in all the major cities in the world. It always came with a sauna, a pool, squash courts, restaurants, bars, and a corporate astrologer's booth in the basement. The color scheme of rusty browns, magentas, and dark blues set off the sparkling sheets, emitting the hum of countless feasibility studies and performance reviews. The sturdy, edgy, modern furniture was penetrated with the funny questions of the chin-scratching big-picture crowd that pitted woodworm against depreciation schedules.

Tanya had been curious about the astrologer's booth, so George sent her down for her corporate horoscope, poured himself a glass of whiskey, and called home.

Punching out the number, he suddenly remembered that Mary Ellen had wanted to spend a weekend in this same corporate-feasible hotel room. She had been talking about it on and off for years. And she did not mean to travel abroad for this; she merely wanted to drive downtown, check in, and drop two birds: a good musical and a Bears game. The phone was ringing in his house, and George felt miserable already. But he told himself that this was something he had to do: he had to make Tanya come, and he had to make her happy, and he had to piss money away with her if it were to destroy him.

George never succeeded in drawing Mary Ellen out of her bath. She knew that it had to be George, letting the phone throb on and on. She didn't care to listen to his lies again. They hurt. George was a terrible liar. Mary Ellen didn't want to sound bitter, wasn't ready yet, still had to purge her feelings, still had more investing to do. First she had to turn her heart into silicone so she would be perfect for George again. For another four months. Then she could get a silicone spleen for four more months. Until, piece by piece, she became all silicone, and the Cliftons lived happily forever after. Meanwhile she turned on the hot-water faucet and let the roar of rushing water answer the stubborn ringing. George and his fucking phone were about to make her go out of her mind.

George was a pretty good theoretician but a lousy practitioner of lies. The story that he had made up about his weekend abroad had seemed plausible. They were adding a critical billing system to his empire. (True: George no longer asked his hard questions in meetings, and the planners were hitting him with headaches right and left.) This one was a real money pipeline for the company (true) and it had George's fearless leader sweating bullets (true). Boston, Massachusetts, had a model operation of this ulcerative machine (true), so the company was sending George to eyeball it (false). George didn't feel like going (false), especially as the damn trip was going to gobble up the Cliftons' weekend (true). He had tried to wiggle out of the assignment (false), but in the end the boss hadn't left him any choice (false). George was a company fool (true), so his was to do or die (true).

As she listened to this preposterous bullshit Mary Ellen had tried to look at the potted palm. George was making her sick.

George had noticed that Mary Ellen's face was draining of color, and he was losing his confidence fast. He had prepared his lies carefully, and here they were grinding to a halt. He took a long draft of beer to regroup, but then Mary Ellen got up, went to his closet, and started packing George's things. She chose his ties, folded his shirts, rolled up his socks, and saved his ass. Didn't say a word. The last thing she did was to stick a bottle of generic aspirin and two rolls of antacid tablets into the corner of his light suitcase.

—What are you doing? George had asked.

He never had headaches or stomach troubles or any other leadership health problems.

—What's that supposed to be for?

Mary Ellen had had no comment. She just looked up and stared back. And George had not had the balls to pull the pills out in front of her. They were still there among his socks now.

Tanya took the first two aspirins the next morning. She was impressed with George's packing. George swallowed three aspirins. Articles of clothing, empty glasses, plates, bottles, shoes, and trays lay scattered around the room. It had been a wild night. Tanya was hung over; George's brain felt compressed into his skull. He declined Tanya's invitation to take a shower with her.

While his hairy angel sang in the shower in melancholy Spanish, George reread her corporate horoscope: Beware of Geminis, grazers, passive-aggressives, and macrobiotics. Opportunities are opening both for your id and your ego, but you have to be careful not to spread yourself too thin. Take care to anesthetize your superego. Limit your carbohydrate intake, keep your holdings liquid, engage yourself in the world more than is habitual for you. *Talk to strangers.*

A fortune cookie for the big-picture crowd, thought George and smelled his fingers. He didn't understand half the babble. Neither did Tanya. There may not have been anything there to understand. It didn't matter. Happiness was having Tanya's fragrance on his knuckles. He nailed his three aspirins with a slug of Chivas. Gotta take his medicine like a man, show this headache who was the bigger son of a bitch. Then he stopped himself.

Jesus, look at me, he thought, I sure don't have to worry anymore about blowing out a hundred and fifty candles. At this rate he was going to make a good-looking stiff. Good. Chivas Regal was the best medicine this goddam vale of tears had.

He got up and followed his hairy angel into the bathroom, where clouds of steam hung in the air. Tanya was singing in a clear, high-pitched voice. Her Spanish song sounded enigmatic, haunting, religious. She did not stop singing when he came in: she was giving him a performance, went on with it while he slid the shower door open and stepped under the steaming jet of water. He recoiled, the water was scalding, she started giggling, he lifted her by her thighs, spread them, and pinned her to the magenta tiles. This was the best pill, the best whiskey, the best religion in the world: both their headaches melted away.

The rest of George's weekend abroad was more aspirin, whiskey, and religion, and the loud sound of time ticking away—they had only so few hours together to begin with. George raged at the slow service in the dining room; the waiter took a chunk out of their affair just serving the soup.

George and Tanya never set foot outside the hotel. They ended up doing their shopping in the gift shops of the crowded airport, where Tanya found a thin wristwatch with a golden face and a snakeskin strap. It cost half a disk of memory, so George bought two of them—one for Tanya and one for Mary Ellen. Their flight was about to take off when Tanya went crazy, buying a satin tuxedo suit for her boy, then a train set, a fighter plane, and little boots. Finally they had to sprint to the gate.

No one asked them for their papers, so Tanya's passport remained clean. Tanya thought it funny.

—You gotta take me to Russia the next time, George, she said.

—Yes, ma'am, said George.

Toronto fell away from the plane. They burrowed into the gauze of acidic clouds, then surfaced into the hard russet light of a summer sunset. The weekend abroad was over.

While Tanya watched droplets of water sizzle on the edges of the porthole window, George pulled a wad of bills out of his pocket and glanced over it. It still had a thick spine. He ordered a bottle of champagne, less than half a platter of smooth, light-brown memory. There had to be over a grand still left. He didn't want to let go of Tanya. He wanted to go home and lie to Mary Ellen even less. He had one more idea left.

All weekend long neither George nor Tanya had brought up the subject of their relationship after Toronto. Remembering Tanya's crack about Russia and her lawyerly bent, George now figured they were staying lovers for abroad. So to see her again he would have to grind gears of coupes and stalk her through dusty parks shaken by El trains. Now and then he could descend on his modest empire for a weekend inspection and help Tanya with the tape backups to be around her (blowing his imperial image). A few months down the road he could maybe buy a few more shitty disks from the suave salesman, take Tanya to the Bahamas, and get another hit of religion in a shower.

He could not wait that long, but he did not know if he could keep Tanya away from her kid for another night to establish a binding precedent in Chicago. He had had no experience with mothers.

George composed his best cigar-store Indian smile, reached for Tanya's hands, and held them. Tanya looked tired, sleepy, content. George told her that he needed a little hand from her. They hadn't done a good job abroad. He still had a grand to piss away. And he had thought of a nice way to do it.

Then he laid out his plan. Tanya looked at the wad of bills and revived. She certainly was not going to be a drag on liberal capitalism. She would have to check with her baby-sitter first, but one more night away should not be the end of the world.

The sun had set before the plane landed. Chicago was a million lights. George stroked Tanya's electric shins in the backseat of a cab. They were headed for the same room in Chicago as the one they had just left in Toronto. They got the same color scheme, the same bed, the same shower, the same window high over a different sweet-water sea.

The astrologer's booth in the basement was closed, so George had to call Mary Ellen from the lobby. She had not been answering the phone when George really wanted to talk to her, and now he was hoping that she would not answer again.

She lifted the phone on the first ring.

—I've been calling you all weekend, said George.

—I know, said Mary Ellen.

—Where were you?

—Oh, I was here. I read three books.

Mary Ellen sounded almost cheerful, which was a relief to George. He plunged into his lies.

—Something came up, and I won't be home till tomorrow night. These people here are incredible—

He really was an awful liar.

—George, she said, I love you. I'll always love you.

She did not wait for George to pull himself together and think of something to say. She hung up and left him with the last thing he wanted to hear ringing in his ears.

George took the elevator upstairs, where Tanya lay naked on the corporate-feasible cost-effective bed ordering steaks and champagne from room service. She wasn't the same lover in Chicago as she had been abroad. Now she was doing her big boss a big favor by blowing his memory grand, and she went about her job assignment with a grim determination.

George stepped up to the window. The lake amounted only to an absence of lights. There was a pair of amber ribbons of sodium lamps directly below and a black mass of water and night beyond. In the distance, planted in the dark volume, a tiny red light of a beacon blinked like a turn signal, running off a dying battery.

George lay softly down behind Tanya and started stroking her back, her ass, her thighs, her small breasts with dark nipples, her back, her thighs. He caressed the back of her neck with feathery touches of his dry lips, his tongue, his warm breath. He had to forget Mary Ellen.

The electric Tanya just lay there. For all she cared, the big boss could have turned into a bull, a cloud of butterflies, a herd of swine, Julio Iglesias—they were no longer abroad. Even though her body was getting excited from all the gentle rubbing and squeezing and exploring, she felt as though she were performing marital duties. In the end, reluctantly, she went with her body; George was the big boss and she was his weekender in this city.

George entered Tanya, and she just lay there. All her Latin sensuality was gone now. No more religion here. Gently he turned her over and moved on top of her with fierce urgency. Tanya kept her eyes closed as she lay there like a Victorian bride, gritting her teeth, thinking of England.

Mary Ellen had never once thought of England in the sixteen years of the Cliftons' marriage, so this went on for a long time. George tried to concentrate on the soft, moist pussy of his hairy

angel, on her beautiful face, her tender skin, her smell. His mind
kept slipping away, worrying about the phone ringing, the room
service knocking on the door. He couldn't help it. In his mind he
was timing the sizzling steaks Tanya had ordered. He wanted to ask
whether she had ordered them rare or well done. He caught
himself hoping for a well-done steak. Was he stark raving mad,
having angelic Tanya and cutting up raw onions in his mind,
pouring steak sauce, waiting for the service elevator? So he lifted
himself up on his hands and looked down at where their bodies
joined and separated and came together again and separated and
clashed. This was better, but then someone was coming down the
hall, and he was sure that it was the waiter with their dinner. His
spirits fell; the faint footsteps passed their door and marched on,
and he was hurling his hips against Tanya's soft and tender life,
and happiness was Tanya's tight pussy, and there was no end to
this in sight. Nothing was going on in his erect flesh; Tanya lay
there submitting to it, keeping her beautiful black eyes closed.
George closed his eyes too. He imagined Mary Ellen's gorgeous
tits and running his hands over them and her stiff nipples and her
flesh spreading hotly; he had Mary Ellen's eager body under him,
and he rammed into her with the full force of his hips and froze
and let out a muffled scream.

Which was answered by three crisp knocks on the door.

ILLUSTRIOUS CADAVER

Shortly after lunch the following day George arrived in his modest
empire carrying a suitcase. He glanced at his messages, filed them
in the imperial circular file, changed Tanya's vacation days on the
attendance sheet to EP (excused, paid—death in the family),
locked his suitcase in the imperial wardrobe, told his first-levels to

take messages again, and was gone for the day. He hired a cab and spent the rest of the day in flower shops. He bought roses of three colors, carnations, irises, petunias, gladiolas, lilies, daisies, orchids, tulips, asters, and chrysanthemums.

He got on the second car of the four thirty-three, where no one knew him, and sat buried in flowers like an illustrious cadaver. Exotic fragrances wafted through the car. It was the allergy season; the pollen and mildew counts had been going through the roof all weekend long, and here was a deuce in love, hugging two hundred bucks' worth of flowers. The corporate dynamos and fearless leaders around him started sneezing and eyeballing him over their papers and Styrofoam cups. George was too tired to care.

He revived as he neared home, looking like a gigantic bouquet with two dragging legs. The neighbors were throwing themselves at their windows again. Old Clifton was clearly in the doghouse at home, and he must have done something terrible—he was lugging a whole flower shop in his arms. He could barely see where he was stepping over it. His white socks showed through his gigolo shoes.

George paid no attention to his surroundings; he was going down the list of his lies in his mind. In theory they sounded pretty convincing, but he already knew that he was going to trip himself up on something. He always did. But Mary Ellen knew everything anyway.

George never had to get entangled in his sordid lies. Mary Ellen was touched when she saw her illustrious cadaver. He looked so sallow, drawn, and anorectic in his flower bed. She pushed her way through the thorns and petals and she kissed him. Then she darted through the house rounding up vases. She combed the pantry and the basement and still ended up sticking daisies, tulips, and carnations into kitchen utensils. Then it took her half an hour to distribute the bouquets around the house.

Mary Ellen had her own two-way mirror through which she had been observing George, and the whole mess had been clear to her for weeks now. Her mirror did not show her the particulars, such as who the bitch was and where Boston lay on George's map, but she got the essential picture in sharp focus. So she had spent a miserable weekend purging herself of bitterness. To keep George, Mary Ellen was prepared to smother him in kindness, but now it no longer seemed necessary. Because as soon as Mary Ellen had planted all her flowers in water, George pulled out the watch.

Mary Ellen froze; with one look she appraised the gorgeous thin work of art on a snakeskin strap at three to five hundred dollars.

—You don't like it? asked George fearfully.

—Oh, George, cried Mary Ellen.

She threw herself around his neck. She held him tight so he couldn't see that she was blinking away tears.

—George, she whispered, I don't care where you've been or what happened. I'm sticking my head in the sand, because it's all my fault anyway—

—Oh, no! Don't say that. Not at all, said George.

He no longer had any idea about what he wanted. Mary Ellen's breasts looked so good, so huge, so firm after Tanya's angelic chest. Tanya had her refined features—the silky jungle on her underbelly, and she ordered her steaks well done, which was a stroke of genius—but Mary Ellen made George feel guilty. He hated what she had said: he never wanted her to stick her head in the sand again. He was going to make everything up to her. He was buying a few more disks his empire didn't need, and he was taking Mary Ellen to the Bahamas. He still had a week of vacation left, and if happiness wasn't making up with your wife, he didn't know what was. So George announced that he was treating Mary Ellen to a dinner in a fancy French joint.

Mary Ellen refused to go. She felt no less guilty than George: it was all her fault. Because all the mirrors in the world could not make up for the implied lover.

George insisted that they go.

Mary Ellen insisted on driving at least.

In the car George did not touch her shaven shins. He was busting his brain looking for some way to tell her about how, listening to the footsteps in the hallway, he had made love to her last night in a downtown hotel. He thought he had paid her the ultimate compliment, but there was no way to break it to her.

The Cliftons smiled at each other while flickering candles cried beige wax all over damask tablecloth; they pried a battery of snails from their housing; they blew what was left of the billing margin. Mary Ellen had the most beautiful tits on the premises. Her bust stopped conversations cold. But she had eyes only for George. And George was going to make love to her under the rustling coconut palms (so he could close his eyes and imagine that he had Tanya in his arms? What a mess).

In the car on the way home, leaning his back on the passenger door, George kept talking about going to the Bahamas. Mary Ellen stopped at a red light. George made a long pause. She set the car in motion again. George wasn't saying anything, so Mary Ellen looked at him and saw that he was out. He had to be exhausted. Mary Ellen felt almost protective of the philandering son of a bitch. At the next light she bent down and sniffed his body, but the only smell his body gave off was the stench of bone-weary fatigue. She couldn't smell the slut on him at all. She turned the radio down; George needed his rest. The streets sliding by slept their Monday-night sleep; the soft streetlights and the thick suburban shadows flowed and ebbed. Mary Ellen listened to George breathe deeply and regularly, and she felt at peace.

FUNNY MONEY

Before he cashed in on his imperial memory needs George had never taken a cent of company money. Throughout his deucedom he had strictly rationed pencils and Scotch tape, never used cab books, Peter-Panning to headquarters through blizzards, never gone on frivolous junkets, never lapped turtle soup, never eaten snails. He had held his grim line on costs and had paid for it with his reputation; it made George a little different as deuces went. So he figured he had a pile of company funny money coming to him.

The morning his shipment of forty 300-megabyte disks came in, George called Steve DeVries and left a message. Minutes later the salesman was on the horn.

—Don't tell me you've got some problems with my disks already, George, he started out jovially.

George read the strong undertone of anxiety in DeVries' voice to mean that his disks were total crap and chuckled. (The quality of the disks made no difference to him; he had the responsibility codes of the project manager of each machine in his empire. And he could charge any crap that came down the pike to them. They didn't know any better. If they did, they wouldn't care. Company money was funny money.)

—Don't worry, Steve, George told his fellow theoretician of infinities, the only reason I'm calling is because I need forty more, as it turns out.

—And you didn't know that last week? the salesman shot back.

—What's the matter, Steve? The paperwork's too much trouble to make a pile of bucks?

—Let me get back to you on that, okay?

—Fine, said George.

His feelings were hurt. He had expected the guy to be beside himself with greed, and here was DeVries talking to him as though he were a little kid. And why? For steering so much business his way? Was socialism creeping in again?

But it was not just DeVries, everyone was getting on George's case lately. He couldn't get a QWL quorum out of Fat Fred for the life of him. George called him two days after his weekend abroad.

—So when are we torching that Buick? he asked.

—Maybe never, said Fat Fred, sounding as down as he had sounded on that State Street bench.

—Well, how about some QWL brainstorming, then? George proposed.

Fred declined. Things were too crazy in his empire: his boss was on the rag; he was soaking up another department; Gwen was finally coming home; the kids were in a state. Fred was rushing around not knowing which fire to put out first. He sure did not want to start any new ones right now. In fact, he had been slowly getting himself ready to forget the whole thing and move on.

—Ooookay, boss, said George.

He asked Fred to call him the moment he felt up to QWL again. Fred promised that of course he would. They hung up. While he was into communicating, George dialed Tanya's number.

His hairy angel didn't sound overly thrilled to hear from George either. She was glad that he had changed her vacation days to excused paid time—that was very nice of him and she thanked him. Then she had to go because her baby had just woken up from his nap. She would try to get back to him when things were a little less crazy.

George waited the rest of the week for things to get less crazy all over the city. He also waited for his memory connection to come to his capitalist senses, but DeVries never called. George spent his time in the imperial seat reading, immersing himself in abstracts of planetary griefs, because he did not trust his underlings to take messages on his behalf. They too were cold and professional with him. Walter had his suspension to brood about. He wouldn't talk to George, felt persecuted, spent his time in the tape library in the back. He listened when George had something to tell him, turned around, went and did as he was told, and never said anything.

The whole world treated George as though he were an auditor. The only exception was Mary Ellen. She was a woman in love, and she treated George like royalty. She pampered him. He could do no wrong. She got up and made his breakfasts; she walked him to the train in the morning and drove to the station to get him off the four thirty-three; she had a hot bath ready for him when they got home. And she was the only person who had any reason to be sore at him.

At work, George's first-levels had not been denying George any calls. His empire had grown tremendously after he had stopped asking his hard questions: the computer-room floor had filled up with hardware, tape racks, disk cases, and data cabinets; the phones were ringing off the hook. The main five-number office line seemed lit up all day long. There were crowds of dynamos, users, support people blinking on hold all the time; the crossword puzzles would soon be a thing of the past in George's empire. Yet hardly any of these calls reached George. Now and then the clerk answering the phone would page him, the emperor would leap at the phone, and there would be a fellow hardworking deuce hitting him with another feasibility meeting or a retirement party or a golf-outing raffle.

For six days George watched the phone blink and listened to the static of the intercom. Then he snapped. He called Steve goddam De fucking Vries and left an urgent message: he needed to hear from him immediately as in presto as in yesterday.

He sat in his imperial seat and stared at the phone. The calls were coming in as usual, the callers were put on hold, and the clerks paged the same lucky sons of bitches who were always in demand. No one needed George for anything. The goddam salesman just refused to return his calls.

George dialed DeVries's number again. The secretary who only thirty minutes before had hummed soothing assurances now told him curtly that Mr. DeVries was not available. No, she did not know where he was. No, she could not track him down to deliver a message. No, tomorrow Mr. DeVries was going to be out of town. She did not know for how long, no. She was very sorry, but that was all she could do.

George conquered the urge to tell her and her useless boss to go and fuck themselves if they couldn't take a joke.

—Well, all right, he told the bitch, have Mr. DeVries get in touch with me the minute he can. I've got some very good news for him.

He went out and got a pussy Reuben rock, three beers, and one for the road in the big-picture greenhouse. Then he wandered around the hot city for an hour. The air still lay over downtown like a big top, but the shadows were going from herbal tea to thin, watery coffee already. The girls were still out in their thin summer dresses, though, giving you a pain in the neck.

When he felt better (calmer, cleaner, ready to move on), George returned to the office. He got back just in time to get a call that finally meant something. The voice sounded like another basic corpo dynamo; the name said nothing to him. The guy was friendly and not at all suspicious. But he was from the company security. He had got some report about some funny stuff that was going on regarding some computer disks or media or whatever these ghosts were, ha-ha, and he had to look into it. Like he had nothing better to do. These irregularities always turned out to be just a lot of smoke anyway, but a calling was a calling, so he would be by to talk to George sometime next week.

They knew.

They were about to blow him out of the water. George's deucedom was over. He would get fired. He had saved the company thousands and thousands of dollars, pens, pencils, cab tickets, warehouses of paper and oceans of turtle soup, and they were going to nail him for a lousy weekend abroad. Now everything would come out, and Mary Ellen would get all the gory, sordid details, the name, the face, the hairy legs, the dates, the place, the hotel. . . . George was washed up everywhere. Jesus, he could even wind up in jail. He had a clean record, but the judge could have a hangover, or his teeth might hurt, or the FBI might be after him. It would just be George's goddam luck. As soon as a guy starts coming into his own and soaring here and there, they shoot the ass and the balls off him.

George locked his office and headed for the bar near the commuter station where he did not recognize a single face. He ordered a double Scotch. He was going to think things over and find some way to strike back at Murphy. He drank his Scotch, then ordered some bourbon as his feeling of utter impotence grew and his panic increased. There was only one thing he could think of: End of Job. Stick his head in the oven, turn on the gas, stamp a big EOJ over everything and make Mary Ellen the richest widow in their suburb with the biggest tits in the collar counties. He couldn't come up with anything else. Bearing it like a man seemed out of the question. Hundred and fiftieth birthday, hell. He had a week.

Despite the long string of drinks, George managed to figure out the mechanism of his undoing. The fucking sharpie memory salesman had got scared of George. He had felt tainted by their first deal, George was putting too much pressure on him, so the suave asshole had lost his cool and decided to cover his ass first: the idiot choirboy DeVries must have thought that George had got greedy, had lost his fear and his sense of proportion, was going to start ordering forty disks a week, so he had evidently run and squealed to company security. The son of a bitch had a tailor, stuffed his mug with snails, but he thought small. He couldn't deal with people who thought big. They scared the snail shit out of him.

George, however, was through thinking big himself. Big Fred was going to be the only thinker left anymore.

Yes, big Fred.

Why hadn't he thought of him right away? He was the one person George didn't mind facing, the one guy he could tell. Fat Fred was a genius, and maybe a genius could think of something. The pink slip and the arrest warrant had not been issued yet. What if there was life after EOJ after all, even in the utility company that got so worked up over its funny money?

QWL IV

QWL had been on hold all summer, too goddam long, but now Fred was holding the door of their special conference room wide open for George again. It was good to be back. George bowed slightly, stepped inside the bar, and froze. The jukebox was gone. There were no more dusty cacti by the opaque window.

—Be right with you gentlemen, a bright voice sang out from the bar.

—Fucking shit, said George.

They had an energetic young man on their hands: Morose

Marty had disappeared too. George exchanged a disgusted look
with Fred. He was not sure if they wanted to sit down. This was
not their watering hole anymore. Then he glanced at their table
and relented. The new management had not yet got around to
junking their plastic daisy, so he made for his old chair.

The bartender came rushing around the far end of the bar. He
had a neat mustache, wore suspenders, had slapped a checkered
rag over his shoulder, carried a fountain pen, was ready to take
their orders. Fred asked for a pitcher of Michelob and two steins.
George wanted a double Scotch also. Fred passed on the hard
stuff.

—Salad with your Scotch? the waiter asked.

George shook his head sadly. They looked on in disgust as the
bartender hurried back behind the bar. The homey utility-
company tempo paced one fewer work location on the face of the
globe.

—Fucking Murphy, said Fred.

—Yup, said George.

It figured; George hadn't had a break in weeks; it was starting to
be almost funny now.

Fred was talking a blue streak. Things were looking up for Fred.
George was happy for him. It was good to know too that something
could still go right.

Fred reported that Gwen had finally come back home a week
before. She had made great progress, was really doing well, didn't
think Fred was a genius at all anymore, called him a slob, a bum,
even a son of a bitch. So all that damn therapy had done some
good anyway. It gave Fred the goddam thrill of his life, Gwen
calling him a son of a bitch. So the Fosses were seeing some
daylight anyway. Good things came in bunches, so Fred had run
into his goddam capitalist alien too. Spotted his Buick in traffic
while going to the liquor store Saturday. Tailed him for the better
part of an hour. The jerk was just cruising around, showing off
Fred's good taste in cars. Made the bad mistake of eventually going
home. So now Fred knew once again where to organize a bonfire
soon. His DP took his opportunities when he saw them, but he
had the soul of a mole: he had moved into another basement. An

ideal place for what Fred had in mind. There was a bank of an expressway on one side and a factory down the block, and nobody hung around there much. There might even be a way to watch the goddam Buick go up in smoke from the shoulder of the expressway.

Fred went on and on, and every time someone opened the door, the slanted light of a September afternoon lit up the shiny blossom of their daisy. George sipped his Scotch, gulped his beer, was starting to warm up to the idea of torching the damn Buick. What the hell, he had nothing else to look forward to in his grand life but blowing his brains out. After a while George felt that their inner persons were good and ready and that they could hit some real QWL.

—Fred, he said, you ever been in love?

They sat on that.

—Fuck you, George, said Fred.

—I've been thinking about sending a bullet through my ears lately, said George.

—What the fuck is that supposed to mean? said Fred.

In the deep silence of inner person, George threw in the rest of his Scotch. Then he dripped the last drops of Michelob into their steins. Then he ordered another pitcher. Then he poked the plastic daisy with his finger and swung its shiny blossom away from him. Then he told Fred everything. He mentioned the silky hair on Tanya's forearm and that you could have a small infinity and how he had called Mary Ellen and she said that she would always love him. He even told Fred about the room service timing the well-done steaks perfectly.

While George spoke, whetting his parched throat with beer, battering the daisy about the vase, Fat Fred just sat in the chair. He watched the plastic daisy and he looked gloomier and gloomier.

—So I dunno, George concluded.

—Oh, boy, said Fred.

They sat on that for a long, long time.

—You asshole, said Fred.

—Yup, said George.

—Goddam, said Fred.

—You fucking turd, said Fred.

—Oh, boy, said Fred, covering all the angles.

—Yup, said George.

They sat in silence. George pulled out the plastic daisy, shined it up on his sleeve, and smelled it.

—Sometimes I'm a chicken about it, said George. It can get messy when your hands shake.

—Cut the bullshit, said Fred.

—I mean it, said George.

—I know you think you mean it, said Fred.

They sat on that.

Suddenly Fred was strobing. He threw the rest of his beer in, refilled their steins while motioning to the frantic bartender for another pitcher, wiped his sweaty forehead on his shirt sleeve, saying, We're gonna fix that goddam DeVries stop playing with that fucking daisy put it back you're gonna have to loan me a tie I have a light-blue shirt for this so get me something red with stripes I can't believe you got suckered into this you son of a bitch I hope she was worth it at least I don't see the hair thing at all myself and zero boobs too talk about kinky shit when you got Mary Ellen at home Jesus I still don't give you anymore than a fifty/fifty chance of keeping your job we'll just have to see will you put that goddam daisy back god damn it?

George obediently threaded the wire stem of the daisy back into the narrow ceramic vase. Those funny speech patterns sure ran in the Foss family. He had never seen Fat Fred this worked up over anything.

THE DUMMY

For the next six days George made the seven fifteen and got home on the four thirty-three. He checked his calendar as soon as he entered his office; he now looked forward to performance reviews and feasibility studies. They gave him something to do at a time when workdays crawled at the speed of continental plates. The harried security guy was leaving George hanging, and George struggled with weird feelings. He felt as though his inner person were shrinking, withdrawing, deserting the body. He had never had enough time to see it fully developed and now it was slipping away again.

When George had no meetings to go to he crashed conference rooms. He sat down and smiled. He took discreet readings of the barometric pressure. No one asked any questions. He still cut a dashing cigar-store Indian.

In the imperial office he spent a lot of time on the phone with Fred. When he talked to Fat Fred, George was the dummy and nothing but the dummy. Fred was the ventriloquist.

Fred thought that George definitely should not go and turn himself in before the audit. Every day the security people put off their investigation was a gain.

—Yes, Fred, said George.

Fred thought that George would have to come clean as soon as the security hound finally stuck his head in the door. He had to look relieved as he incriminated himself.

—Okay, said George.

Fred thought George would have to make DeVries look like a real shady, unscrupulous son of a bitch (which he was).

—That's true, said George.

Meanwhile George had to come across as a misguided victim.

—I'll do my best, said George.

Fred also thought that, before anything else, George had to tell Mary Ellen what had happened and iron it out with her. He absolutely had to have her support.

Fred was a big goddam thinker, and some of his brainstorms didn't work out badly. Fred wanted George to be hitting the bottle pretty hard; this proved to be no problem whatsoever. But in making George enlist Mary Ellen's support for his memory deal, Fred's mind had collided with a hell of a concept.

George took care to time his confession carefully. The seven

fifteen was rumbling through the town when he told Mary Ellen
she had better sit down because he had something pretty rough to
tell her. Then he gave her the gist of the news.

Mary Ellen's face went limp with cold fury, and George
regretted not sending a bullet through the roof of his mouth
instead. She started pacing across the kitchen, then blew up. She
had known what was going on, but she had had no idea that the
slut was a spic. She just couldn't believe that George was so stupid
that he bet his career and their entire future on this dirt. He made
her stomach turn. She wanted him out of her face. She was giving
divorce a long look. She was seeing her gynecologist. She wasn't
waiting till the herpes broke out. George was a sleazy thief, and it
was going to serve him right to get fired for this.

Mary Ellen finally ran off and locked herself in the bathroom.
The bathroom was her empire. George could have kicked himself.
He was stepping out of the house when the bathroom door flew
open and Mary Ellen demanded to know if the bitch had big tits.
She sounded hysterical.

—No, I'd say Tanya's pretty flat-chested, said George.

In reply Mary Ellen had another go at busting the bathroom
door.

After that morning Mary Ellen would not say a word to George.
She could not forgive him for cheapening the implied lover like
that. She was miserable and lived in a daze. She continued to shop
and to keep the house clean and to make George's dinners. But she
stayed in her empire after he got home, slept on the sofa, and did
not bother to get up anymore to make George coffee in the
morning.

George bought his wake-up coffee at the bar kiosk downtown. At
night he couldn't sleep, so he lugged booze to bed with him and
clinked right back at Mary Ellen through the bedroom wall.

The demise of George's inner person occurred four bottles of
Cutty Sark and nine six-packs of Michelob later. It made everything easier. At the time George was reposing in the imperial
chair, staring at the imperial picture on the half wall beside the
door. He had been doing this a lot. Three white cows were

chewing cud in a foggy pasture below a huge orange sun that hung in the bare branches of massive oaks. The sun had hypnotic powers over George. He could stare at it for hours on end. After a while the orange disk always brought back that odd feeling he had had while working overtime under a crabapple tree in Grant Park: the warm earth was shrinking under him. If he did not exist, nothing would. The security dynamos, the wife, the company were an illusion. He went on staring hard at the picture: the sun, the oaks, the cows, the fog, all illusory. But how soothing it would be to roll around the dewy grass and damp oak leaves in that heavy, foggy, gray light of a cold orange sun.

The clerk paged George on the intercom, and he snapped back. The utilities at least were no illusion. He picked up the phone and there was Fat Fred, sounding happy. He had some great news. He had been busting his ass working on something big. He hadn't even mentioned it to George yet because it was a long shot. He still wasn't prepared to go into details, but he had pulled all the strings he could think of, had called in all the favors he had coming, and it looked as though he might have a big surprise for George. His chances had definitely gone up: he was maybe as good as seventy-five/twenty-five. So Fred thought the thing for George to do now was to get back into playing the emperor.

George did not get dizzy over Fred's news. He found it hard to care about anything. He was the dummy, and he did as he was told. Fred wanted him to play the emperor, so he pulled out his ancient master appraisal, burned off twenty copies of it, and grabbed a pair of scissors.

When four o'clock rolled around George called his evening first-level into the imperial office and administered to her her prefab glimpse of insignificance. It was corporate culture, so she did not take it too badly and signed. Not that it mattered either way.

On the shaded streets of George's suburb the dogs were sniffing around bushes while their owners puffed on cigarettes, watching them. The air was warm, the sun pretty low already. George leaned into the pedals of his old workhorse, thinking about the foggy landscape, the cows, and the cold sun. More than anything else (more than a threesome with Tanya and Mary Ellen, more than a million bucks), he wanted to lie down on the wet oak leaves and brown grass under that large heatless orange sun and have the steaming white cows lumber toward him through the mist and stand over him and bend down and lick his face with their warm, drippy, hand-sized rough pink tongues.

He was losing his mind so what.

When George stepped through the doorway of his house, Mary Ellen headed for her bathroom. A cold plate lay on the dinner table. A golden can of Michelob stood beside it. George ripped its top off and downed it in one breath. Fred would have been proud of him.

He didn't see Mary Ellen again that evening. Her empire was off limits, so he went and pissed on the evergreen behind the house before going to bed. Nothing mattered anymore, and he slept beautifully that night. When he awoke the sun was streaming into the bedroom. The house was silent. The clock showed quarter to eight; he had forgotten to set his alarm. It had not been necessary lately, and he had got out of the habit. Now he would be lucky to make it to work by nine. Oh, well. He felt great. The sheen of unreality had been stripped from the world. No need to wallow in the dewy goddam grass anymore with the white cows.

The air was clean and fresh. George hopped on his bicycle. He had to watch out for the schoolchildren. Energetic flocks of them animated street corners; yellow buses picked them up, stopping all traffic but George.

George was flying on his old workhorse. He wasn't chasing any trains. He didn't care what time he got to the station; Chicago was going to be there whenever he got there. He wanted the sensation of speed: the cool air pressing against his face; the trees whishing by; the sweat; the lungs gasping for air.

The leaves of sycamores were turning yellow around him, and George felt his luck was turning with them.

CORPORATE CULTURE III

At the office George had a message to call his fearless leader. He got on the phone. His boss's voice dripped with significant meaning. He sounded as ceremonial as a district man in the utility company ever got.

—Well, George, said the district man, you've heard the one about the kink in the wood?

—What kink? asked George.

He felt betrayed already by the buoyant mood of the morning; Murphy was still walking all over him.

—Didn't you see the eight o'clock announcement?

—I just got here.

—Oh, said George's leader. Well, Georgie boy, we're not on the same team anymore. They shuffled the deck again.

—Damn, said George, though he didn't care either way.

—That's what I said. Well, the best of luck to you, George. It's been great working with ya. So long, buddy.

—Same here, said George. So who's gonna hold my hand now? Do you know?

—Sure do, said George's former boss, who did not like surprises. You heard of a fellow by the name of Fred Foss?

—Damn! gasped George.

—I know what you mean, George. Be careful around that guy. He's different, but don't quote me on that. Well, it's been a pleasure.

—Sure was, said George.

George had no sooner hung up than he was paged on the intercom. Fat Fred was on the horn.

—I can't talk yet, said George. I just heard the eight o'clock announcement.

—You fucking son of a bitch. You cost me three mainframes.

—I can't believe you pulled this off, Fred.

—Management appraisals are due on my desk in three hours, Mr. Clifton, said Fred.

—My old boss said you were a son of a bitch, Mr. Foss, said George.

—By the way, Mr. Clifton, Gwen managed to call me an anus this morning, only she phrased it differently. Things are rebounding, said Fred proudly.

When George got off the phone he scrambled to find a copy of the eight o'clock announcement. It was five pages long. A new organizational chart was attached. It seemed that everyone in the utility company had taken one step over. George's empire was now a part of something called ISS. That was the big picture. Many fearless leaders had lost their intrepid followers. Scores of followers had been torn away from the succor of their leaders.

The human reality behind the chart was worse. Life was misery: in offices all over the utility company, people were gorging themselves on aspirin. Coffee-cart arrivals turned into mob scenes. The phones were lit up all morning as corporate dynamos desperately sought independent confirmations: Was it true that their new boss was a nitpicking paper-pusher? Had he ever been known to stick up for his people? What was he like on a long ride in an empty elevator?

On the big-picture floor of headquarters the leaders of leaders and the guided missiles were confused. Where was this new frontier of their empire located? What was their absentee rate again? Roughly what did these people do? Hope they didn't run payroll. Payroll they could have. Payroll was the biggest headache of them all. Did these folks kick in their fair share? Had they bought a lot of savings bonds last year?

All this chaos and corporate suffering had been loosed on the utility company because Fat Fred wanted to hold the hand of a deuce in love. George had never felt so important in his life.

He unlocked the drab file cabinet and pulled out the collage appraisals he had pasted together for his troops. Walter's lay on top, so George paged the walrus mustache. Walter showed up in the imperial doorway looking nervous. George pointed to one of the hard chairs and solemnly read the mind-bending phrases off the form. When he looked up, Walter wore a tiny, sweaty little smile on his face. He had never dreamed that his boss would rate him average after he had got busted and had spoken hastily to him. The precise wording did not bother him. He dove at the form and signed it. In the comments section he scribbled: This appraisal, I feel, is in the ball park in terms of the kind of a year I had. I intend to improve drastically. Then he waltzed back onto the computer-room floor. Walter was a busy first-level these days.

Watching him, George felt like a true leader. The secret of leadership rested in being big about the petty shit and petty about the big shit, in knowing when to close your eyes and when to slap on a suspension. And also, as he now so sadly knew, in keeping your hands off the hairy shins of your part-timers. In the sundown of his imperial career George was becoming a pretty decent deuce.

In swift succession George passed out the rest of the imperial appraisals. None of his other employees liked their chunks of corporate-certified nonsense as much as Walter did his. They fretted, but kept their complaining within bounds. They sensed when it was time to sign and stopped fussing.

Murphy was definitely slipping today.

After lunch George walked the signed appraisals to Fred's new office in headquarters. Only a few short months ago his work for the year would have peaked with this drop-off. From now till Christmas he would have run on autopilot; there was something to be said about the chamomile phase of his imperial career.

Accepting the appraisals, Fred was very official with George. Even after they had ducked into his office, where nobody could see them, Fred never dropped the mask of a stern, fearless leader. He glanced over the forms, thanked George, said he would be by early next week for an inspection of his department, then busied himself with some paper on his desk. George kept standing by the door. After a while Fat Fred looked up.

—Anything else?

—No, I guess not, said George and walked out.

That night Fred called George at home to say that he was real pleased with how everything was going. And especially with that little drama in his office. That was good practice for both of them. They were about to bite the bullet, and this way they would give better performances when the chips were down. They would have to cool the QWL for a good while now.

—Yup, said George and went to sleep and slept like a baby.

On Saturday morning George slept late. By the time he got up, Mary Ellen was back in her empire, floating in a bubble bath, sipping white wine, reading. George tried the bathroom door. It wasn't locked. He was dying to tell Mary Ellen what Fat Fred had pulled off. He eased himself inside, closed the door, and stood there, looking down at his wife. She looked pretty as a summer night. Their investment remained unbelievable.

—I haven't washed your back in a long time, he said. Need it washed?

Mary Ellen gave George a long look. He locked his eyes in hers, then looked away. She slid down toward the faucets a little and turned her back to him. George lathered up a tornado on Mary Ellen's soft skin. He ran his fingers up and down her spine. He massaged her shoulders. He felt very grateful that she was forgiving him.

On Monday morning the dick finally showed up to bust the emperor George Clifton. He looked haggard, was completely bald except for a tuft of gray hair at the top of his forehead, didn't know where to put his hands. He rang the imperial bell by the departmental gate for one timid beep, then tiptoed into George's office like a cold. He must have absorbed some hard hits from corporate suspects that turned out to be beyond suspicion. He flashed his ID card and started apologizing.

—I'm sure it's just another misunderstanding, he said.

George swallowed dryly, hung his head, and ran his fingers through his hair the way he had practiced it in front of a mirror. Then he looked up as though he were about to dive off the roof of a high-rise and couldn't stand to see the sidewalk below.

—I think I can save you a lot of time, he said.

His inner person was back and it was speaking now, passionately believing in Fred's lines.

THE BUST II

The harried dick did not want to believe George at first. He kept looking for some cost-equalizer till he finally realized that there was just no way around busting George. By then George was pretty sure that the man liked him, but in the end the guy was a dick and he had to do his dick job. So he called his boss, and George's chicken-shit memory deal instantly took on a different order of corporate magnitude.

The security deuce, a stocky young man with closely cropped hair, arrived in five minutes, pumping adrenaline. His department had never busted a cozy con like this before; this was white-collar crime at its most sophisticated; you could ride this case way up into the big picture. So he ushered George out of his office, called George's district man, said he needed him over urgently, didn't explain why, then went through the reams of memos in George's filing cabinet while taking mental notes on the suspect's plush office. The room resembled no deuce hangout that he had seen before. This den was opulent AVP stuff, with the thronelike chair, the half-acre desk, the wardrobe, the credenza, the love seat, the pictures . . .

Fat Fred arrived, looking grim: the inner person was frozen out of his district completely. The security deuce took him to the lounge and began reciting his understanding of what was being alleged here. But George cut him off and said that there was no point in wasting everyone's valuable time: he had taken three and a half grand of company money. He had not had a good night of sleep since, so in a dumb, strange way he was relieved now that the whole thing was out in the open.

—Okay, George, you're suspended indefinitely, said Fat Fred sternly. Let me have your ID pass.

—The company will get in touch with you, added the security deuce.

George fumbled in his pockets, surveying the glory and the grandeur that had been his imperial office. The place was damn hard to kiss goodbye, handicapped crapper and all. His inner person had busted free here. He pulled out his ID card, handed it to Fred, strolled out of his modest empire without saying a word, and headed for the one twelve. So this was how great empires bit the dust.

The platform of the commuter station was deserted, the one twelve empty. George sat by the window on the shaded side of the train and watched the tracks crisscross. There were faded billboards, unpainted bridges, truck docks, dusty bushes, piles of materials, and rusted debris of cars. Now, for the first time in his career, the angular pile of high-rises shrinking behind the train missed him: the sensational news about his bust was breaking around headquarters. The sullen dynamos (who had been busy pulling the photographs of their kids from under the glass tops on their desks, boxing up their collected works, calling transportation, hand-carrying their plants to their new work locations, pinning their old cartoons on new bulletin boards) were dropping everything and buzzing with excitement and forgetting their corporate blues.

George himself had one last thing looming on his corporate agenda: he had to get a nice suit for the kangaroo court.

D-DAY II

George wound up with eight days in which to get his new duds. He had nothing else going, so he researched the project exhaustively. He visited all the major retailers of men's clothing. He went and talked to a tailor. He ended up buying a navy fine-wool summer-weight double-breasted two-piece suit. Its thin stripes were spaced so as to convey an impression of power, its cut was conservative. George also picked up a pair of white shirts and a somewhat risky paisley red-and-gold tie.

The alterations were finished the evening before George's D-day. His research had paid off. He modeled his new suit for Mary Ellen, and she could not believe how handsome George looked. She had never seen him this dashing before. Looking at him, Mary Ellen thought that even if Murphy were to get his way in everything and George were to get fired tomorrow, she would go out and get a job just to keep this slim gigolo around the house. She embraced him and gave him a hell of a good-luck kiss.

George timed his arrival on the twenty-first floor of headquarters with great care. He did not want to get stuck waiting for the kangaroos to assemble, grinding out idiotic small talk, making people nervous. He stepped into the conference room at the stroke of ten. When he entered, all the invited fearless leaders were already seated on three sides of a large fine-grained table. (No one had been late for this meeting. The corporate dynamos never got to deal with out-and-out criminals; they always faced survivors who lived by hedging their bets. There was something primal and elementary and thrilling in confronting a bona fide confidence man.) A single chair occupied the short far side of the rectangular desk. Facing it sat the AVP in his big-picture suit with a platinum Crusade of Mercy pin and Fat Fred, who was chairing the meeting and making history. Fred had on a light-blue long-sleeved shirt and George's red-and-blue-striped tie. The supporting cast of kangaroos featured George's old district (home team three), his old division man (home team four), Fred's new fearless leader (an open mind, straddling the divisional fence on this one), the harried security guy who had busted George (dick one), his zealous boss (dick two), and the district man for security (dick three).

George headed for the chair of the accused. He felt bare-assed. For the first time in his career he would not be able to ride out a meeting on the strength of his cigar-store Indian smile. His heart was beating in his temples.

—That's everybody, isn't it? Fred asked rhetorically, getting up and closing the door.

All the eyes in the room dug into George and studied his pinkish face, his stiff sitting posture, his carefully combed chestnut hair, his new suit, the gold-and-red silk tie. The tie was a judgment call: if it wasn't too loud, then it certainly teetered on the verge. The suit was just plain too much; it looked better than everybody else's with the exception of that of the AVP, who spent five times the money on his clothes that George did.

While the corporate kangaroos X-rayed him, peering through his suit at his guts, trying to place him once and for all in the chain of corporate being, George kept his eyes on Fat Fred. His buddy seemed huge in the long-sleeved shirt. George's old, plastic-looking tie lay on his belly, tracing its convex outline and emphasizing it. It looked as though his fellow QWL expert had gained weight again. And the long-sleeved shirt and the tie gave his buddy an unfamiliar dimension of pomp.

—I thank all you good people for coming to this unpleasant, you might even say tragic, meeting, he said as he dropped onto the chair, which squeaked faintly. We don't need much of an overture here, because everybody, I believe, already has the outline of the story.

George did not remember ever having heard Fat Fred talk this ceremoniously. Fat Fred was always gruffer than Morose Marty, so George sensed that there had been adverse developments he had not been told about. Maybe Fred had not managed to cast the right kangaroos for this.

—George, said Fred, I'd like to ask you a couple of questions just to clarify everything in my mind. Let me start out with the hardest one of them all: Can you tell us why? What were you thinking?

—I . . . I . . . I wasn't thinking, mumbled George. I was in love.

A cramp of astonishment seized the room. George had hit the kangaroos with a punch that nobody, but nobody, had anticipated. The dicks thought that this was criminal deviousness at its most white-collar provocative. The home team thought it was pathetic.

—Huh, home team four let out.

—I guess I was in love with my weekender, Tanya Mendez. Fred let everybody sit on that.

—Wait, he said after a while, I don't understand. Let's start at the top here. How does the money tie into it?

Question by patient question, while no one was shifting in his chair or breathing, Fat Fred pulled a mass of unconnected shockers out of George. He kept clarifying each unbelievable answer that George mumbled, and an inchoate understanding of this overwrought company soap opera began to emerge in the kangaroo brains around the table. Fred got George to describe how he had stalked Tanya in the company coupe, how she had sung a Spanish song in the shower of the Toronto hotel, how she had swallowed the aspirins Mary Ellen had packed for George. This knocked everybody's socks off.

—Thank you, George, Fred finally said. Would you mind waiting in the lounge down the hall in case we need to clarify something?

George traversed the distance from his chair to the door in pristine corpo kangaroo silence. In the lounge he eased himself onto a sofa and stared out the purple-black glass of a wall window down at the toy El train twenty floors below.

In the conference room the AVP broke the spine of the general awe.

—Am I dreaming this? he asked.

—Yeah, really, said Fat Fred.

—Anybody ever seen this dolly? the AVP asked.

Ultimately he would be the one making the decision, so he wanted to pursue all information relevant to the case.

—I probably must have seen her at a Christmas party or something, said home team three. Don't really recall her, though, so she must not have been that hot.

—They should have a picture of her on file in personnel, suggested home team four helpfully. (He was curious himself.)

—That's a very good idea, said the AVP.

Fred got up reluctantly. Damn, he thought, I should have anticipated this. He did not want to leave the meeting for a single minute, but there was nobody here to whom he could delegate this.

—Lemme make a call, he said. Be right back.

From the lounge at the end of the hall George saw his buddy Fred step out of the conference room. He didn't look in George's direction and vanished into an office.

In the conference room the lines of opinion were solidifying.

—Has anybody here seen this guy's office? asked dick two. (He and the fearless leader of all dicks were here to make an example out of this lover boy. Ideally, they wanted to put him up on a chair, stand him by his old, heavy file cabinet, open the top drawer, drop his balls in, and slam it shut. Minimum, they wanted to see him fired and thrown into Cook County jail.)

—Why do you ask? said the AVP.

—Talk about opulent, lavish, and ostentatious, said dick two. In fact I doubt that there is a chair to match his the company over.

—Well, to be fair about it, said home team three, George inherited that office furnished. The manager before him was quite a wheeler-dealer I understand.

—This is correct, said home team four.

George's old boss and his old division man were lining up on the opposite side of the issue. They had an ulterior motive for that of course. The incident had taken place during their reign; they were here to cover up their lack of controls. So they had to be circumspect in defending George.

—But you're right, it's quite an office, acknowledged home team three.

—Oh, well, I thought it was the guy's style—clearly the person is a sharp dresser too, dick two went on pitching dirt.

The home team had no comment about the suit. George's suit had spoken for itself, so there was no way to parry this indisputable hit.

—That's neither here nor there, said Fred's new division man.

He had clean hands in this matter, and he had come into the meeting with an open mind. But these vulgar security types were beginning to grate on him.

—Well said, allowed the AVP.

—All we're doing here is wondering about what else we don't know about this person, said dick three.

—Right—that's all we're questioning, said dick two.

—Well, in fact George used to wear an army jacket when it was colder, said home team three, grinning stupidly.

He meant his remark to lighten up the gloom, but he ended up costing George more points.

—An army jacket?! gasped the AVP.

—Well, yes, a regular infantry-type jacket, home team three admitted softly.

—Is this before he had been promoted into management? said the AVP sternly.

—No, that's as recently as last May, said dick two. We've interviewed people.

—After thirteen-some years in management.

—One of those old khaki military things you see on young people with backpacks? asked the AVP incredulously.

—One of them, dick two nailed his point.

George's old fearless leader wished that he had kept his flytrap closed, though the security vultures might have brought up the jacket anyway. They had done their homework and they were not bashful about hitting below the belt.

Now the door opened and Fred returned with a stack of papers. As he passed out the copies of a page from Tanya's employment records he sensed that George was sinking into even deeper trouble with the kangaroos. Everyone in the room strained his imagination trying to make a woman's face out of the black smudge in the corner of the form. After a while you could see that the face was smiling, but you could not guess the woman's age at all. However, her birthday was plainly stated elsewhere on the sheet: apparently Tanya Mendez was now twenty-four years old.

—For this woman? She looks quite Hispanic, said dick three.

—Says here born in Texas, countered home team three.

—Amarillo, said dick two.

—Yes, Amarillo, Texas. Home team three stood his higher-ranked ground.

—She looks pretty Spanish to me, said the AVP, tilting the paper. This meant: case closed; Tanya was a spic once and for all.

Goddam, I better do something real quick, thought Fred.

He might have missed the bus here already. He had lost all that time with the fucking picture, and now George's case was hemorrhaging all over the place. He decided to default to the worst-case contingency and portray George's escapade as a really irrational, mad love.

—I made a couple of phone calls while I was waiting for these copies, he said. Seems that our dear Tanya's kind of skinny and flat-chested, I guess, and hairy too.

—Hairy? The AVP lifted his eyebrows.

—I guess she has beautiful black hair, but apparently she doesn't shave her legs, and they're pretty hairy.

—I see, said the AVP.

—He's probably tired of large busts, dick two allowed.

—What do you mean? Why? asked the confused AVP.

—His wife has jugs up to here, explained dick two.

—But she used to be like this desk. She's had implants, I understand, said dick three.

—That's neither here nor there, said Fred's new division man.

—Are you sure of this? the AVP said, turning to dick two.

—We're positive, said dick three.

—This is getting more fantastic by the minute, said the AVP.

—Seems almost pathological too, suggested Fat Fred.

—This sure is better than *Dallas*, concluded the AVP.

—I think the coffee cart should be out there by now, said Fred, looking at his watch.

He needed to buy time.

For once a meeting was not peaking with the arrival of a coffee cart.

THE KANGAROO PANIC
BUTTON

From George's observation point high in the Chicago skyline the lake looked like an azure mountain of water towering above the city. He was watching the sailboats on its slope. He counted twenty-nine of them. Then the coffee cart arrived, and George watched the kangaroos file out of their courtroom and pour their fixes. They were not talking much. The original departmental groups had not broken up. It had to be an edgy, somber meeting of sharp divisions, George guessed. Fat Fred was the last man to step up to the coffee cart and the last to disappear into the conference room. He did not lift his eyes in George's direction.

Go get 'em, St. Bernard, George thought.

The coffee cart rolled on; the kangaroos were huddling back in their lair; another sailboat pulled out of the Monroe harbor and started climbing up the azure slope. George just knew they were going to skin him alive. He would wind up looking like those raw, flayed bodies of Gray's *Anatomy* on the thin wooden walls of Newport where his kink in the wood lay.

Behind the closed door of the conference room the tie-choked chair of the meeting tore into a vintage Fred Foss riff. He was aiming it squarely at the AVP. In the end, after everybody had got in his nickel's worth, the AVP would decide George's future, so Fred did not waste his time glancing at anybody else; he had not blown his image, had not put on long sleeves and a tie to assist in canning his best buddy.

Fred knew that his particular big-picture ambassador probably was the wrong kangaroo for this. Fred was not sure that this AVP had been around the utility company long enough to relate to the collective inner person of the old-boy network. There were a few big-picture leaders who had come up through the ranks, but this AVP had been a guided missile out of a hotshot business school.

Fred, however, was stuck with him, so he stabbed his eyes into the AVP's face and talked about what a slimy snake Mr. DeVries was and how he had made similar propositions to Fred himself. Then he paused and gave a long look at the fidgety dicks.

—I myself, he said, am a people person. Now, this guy's clearly a little confused, a little pathological, a little out of his depth, and way out of line right now. But look at his record. He has served this company for close to a quarter of a century. Twenty-five years. He has been craft for eleven years, a supervisor for eight years, and now a second-level for nearly six years. Twenty-five years, and until now there hasn't been a single blemish on his record.

Tugging at George's polyester fucking tie that was choking him, Fat Fred serenaded his buddy, repeating how in October, George would have given twenty-five years to the company, the last thirteen of them as unbroken perfect attendance, a quarter of a century, his entire working life, because he had never worked anywhere else. He mentioned George's hiring date, twenty-five years ago this coming month, twenty-five years of dedication and professionalism.

Fred was aiming his speech at the panic button of the collective utility-company inner person. He knew the psychology of the old-boy network, and he was playing it like a virtuoso. What he was saying to the inner persons around the table was:

No one quits this company.
No one quits this company and survives.
This guy has had twenty-five years with this company.
He is useless, just no damn good, outside the company now.
You are throwing him to SHARKS, PIRANHAS, and BARRACUDAS.
This poor misguided, defenseless person
who has twenty-five years of service . . .
You are signing the DEATH WARRANT of a fellow company man.
You are killing the poor son of a bitch—yes, you are.
There are minimum-wage-jobs people busting their asses out there.
Twenty-five goddam years, for Christ's sake!

No company man quits this company and lives.
Do not kid yourselves.
Twenty-five years . . .
This is MURDER.
Fred brought his serenade to a rousing crescendo and stopped.
Pulling on the fucking tie, he checked its effect around the room.
The guided missile met Fred's gaze and remained AVP inscruta-
ble. The dicks had smirks on their faces. The home team had been
hit hard, and George's new fearless leader looked as though he
would start fighting back loud sobs any second.
—Nice speech, said dick two, but the guy is a thief, so maybe
that's what he needs.
—Like I said, I'm a people person, Fred retorted.
—We know you are, said dick three, but maybe we need an
example around here.
—White-collar crime, said dick two.
—The company can't afford to be soft on this, said dick three.
—There have been a lot of problems with just this sort of thing
around the country, said dick two.
—Gotta arrest the cancer before it spreads, said dick three.
—What disturbs me about this, said dick two thoughtfully, is
that we would never have uncovered this.
—Good point, said the big-picture man.
It looked bleak. Fred had always known that dicks were low on
inner person, but the AVP apparently could not bring himself to
forgive George Tanya's hairy Spanish legs, the army jacket, the
implants.
—I am a people person too, said Fred's new leader, and this
person looks awfully mixed up to me.
—Seems to me he knew full well what he was up to, said dick
two.
—Never would of caught him, said dick three.
—Good point, said the AVP.
You fucking narrow-minded, sleazy, two-faced big-picture son
of a bitch, thought Fred, I bet you've swilled enough turtle soup to
hold a regatta in.

—Can we, at least, think about this? Fred pleaded out loud. The guy's got twenty-five years with the company.

—Well, I suppose so, allowed the AVP skeptically.

—Good idea, I think, said home team four, sticking his neck out. Twenty-five years ought to count for something.

—And I could use him in that office in the meantime, said Fred. Innocent until proven otherwise, right?

Even before the dicks could yowl, the AVP set Fat Fred straight.

—This person is not innocent, he said, this person is guilty. The question is: What are we going to do about it? I see nothing un-American here. He stays suspended while we think. Let's just wrap up all this thinking by next Monday.

Yeah, thought Fred, we know you did all your thinking, you goddam fucking guided-missile hatchet man.

The fearless leaders collected their pages from Tanya's employment records (so they could show their wives what the Juliet of this out-and-out company love story looked like) and dispersed into their empires. The harried guy who had busted George left without having opened his mouth in the meeting. He was never getting promoted in the security department.

Fred Foss was a sore loser. He was furious. He did not follow the crowd of corporate dynamos out. He sat by the table and struggled with the fucking tie. It took both hands, but he finally managed to loosen its noose and get it off his neck. He was not going to hang himself ever again.

He had one more idea, but that would be the whole wad right there.

VOODOO DUST

George jumped on top of the printer and onto the tape drive and over the processor and down to the disk drive he went, skipping a console. He sprang from the DEC to the IBM, bounced off a disk cabinet to the Honeywell, hitting his stride as he sprinted across a band of Century disk drives. He dove on top of the data cabinet, broad-jumped to the band of chillers, barely clearing the ceiling. The chillers were tall. He slumped over and recovered his rhythm, plunging from one unit to another, stutter-stepping across their tops to push off his right leg. He ran around the entire computer room, leaving busted covers and drive doors and keyboards and terrified clerks in his wake. He was in late middle age, almost an old man now, but he used to take splendid care of himself, he had maximized his life shrewdly, he still kept in shape pedaling his heavy bike, and it showed. It showed till he attempted an impossible leap from the last chiller to the higher top of the best number-cruncher in his empire, the tall 3B20. He flew through the air, silent, wearing a cigar-store Indian smile, hit the edge of its top with his chest, fell down on his back with a nasty thud, and lay there smiling till the paramedics took him away on a stretcher.

Every jump of George's unannounced inspection of his old empire had been carefully planned. Fred had drawn diagrams of the obstacle course for his dummy. He had smuggled George into the building past the guard in the lobby, patted his back in the elevator, told him he hated to put him through this, but it was the only way.

George's confidence in his director never wavered. He pushed the card key into the metal box by the imperial entrance, sprinted past the office of the first-levels, raced up the ramp into the computer room, and started his inspection. The first printer cover cracked under his foot, and he felt awesome. He moved along at the limit of Fat Fred's imagination till he got ambitious and dove to the top of the chillers. The chillers were the little extra George liked to throw in when he saw himself as a company man. Fred's scenario had called for him to jump off the last disk drive, walk into the imperial office, sit down in his imperial chair, and page the hell out of the intercom, acting his most mercilessly efficient self. But George saw a way to spring on top of the chillers, and he never looked back.

The utility company was a progressive corporation, and Fat Fred figured that a nervous breakdown was George's last shot. The company never fired alcoholics, drug addicts, or madmen. An unannounced imperial inspection was almost as good as voodoo dust; it made more of an impression than Tanya's hairy legs.

Early in his career, as a first-level, Fred had supervised the night shift of another computer empire. He had been putting together a case on one of his clerks, trying to get him fired. The man's name was Gino Goodman, he was black as coal and no end of trouble. Slowly, incident by incident, Fat Fred had painted him into a corner. When he had Gino past his final two-week suspension and on an indefinite warning of dismissal, when he was chilling bottles of champagne at home to celebrate, Gino had showed up for work wearing elbow-length gloves. He did his job, typing the console commands with his gloves on, so Fred said nothing. The next night Gino showed up with the gloves and a cap, pulled down to his eyes. Fred ignored him. The third night Gino came in wearing the gloves, the cap, and a green scarf over his face. Only his eyes and his eyebrows showed, and it was impossible to overlook his costume anymore.

—Hey, bandito, Fred shouted when he saw him, you headed to rob a bank in the morning or what?

—Fuck you, man, said Gino. I ain't gettin' no voodoo dust on me.

Fred left him alone. In the morning he sent him to the medical. Gino refused to talk to the sorcerers in medical because they were in on the hex. They had sprayed the computer room with voodoo dust, but Gino was keeping himself protected. He was never going to take off his gloves or his cap or his scarf. They were nobody's business, because they didn't interfere with his job performance.

By the time Gino got back from his voodoo-dust disability, his final suspension and his warnings were stale, and Fred knew that he would never get rid of him. Gino now had a shaved head and his old easy grin. Voodoo dust was no longer an issue.

Fred Foss had always believed in stealing superior ideas, so Gino Goodman became his inspiration. He and George had gone over George's situation in great detail. They had examined it from every possible angle: voodoo dust was the only thing that could save George's ass.

D-DAY III

The kangaroo court returned to session on a day when the sweet Indian summer faltered. The schoolteachers were still on strike, but the beaches were closed for the year, and dark clouds chased each other swiftly across a cold sky. Only three white sails were still climbing up and down the indigo mountain of water opposite the twenty-first floor of headquarters.

The chairperson wore an open-necked shirt with short sleeves and no tie: Fred Foss was through hanging himself. He reported to his fellow kangaroos that, regrettably, George Clifton would not be making an appearance that day. He had been hospitalized three days before. His bizarre behavior had got a little too peculiar on Tuesday, and Fred was not talking about a *hospital* hospital here. George had snapped, and he was now committed. It hadn't been a nice scene at all.

—I don't believe this! dick two exclaimed.

—Believe who will, said dick three to the AVP.

—Doesn't surprise me one bit personally. The guy was clearly at the end of his tether, said Fred's new division man and his fellow people person.

—I've known George for ten years. He hasn't been himself lately, believe me, said home team three.

—I hope he gets better, said home team four.

—Seems to me George has lost what little value he's had as an example by flipping his lid, said Fred.

—This smells so bad I'm going to choke, dick two said, appealing to the AVP.

—How many years does this person have with the company? asked the big-picture ambassador.

—Twenty-four. Twenty-five next month, said Fred.

—All right, said the AVP. I'm a people person.

And he laid down the big-picture law: George Clifton would be busted from a deuce to a first-level. He would stay in the same department as an added element of punishment. He would, of course, make a full restitution of the company's money. Then he gave Fat Fred a long, hard look.

—These hospitalizations really bleed the benefits budget, so I am going to rely on you to let the patient know ASAP, he said.

The voodoo dust had done its job. The kangaroo court adjourned forever half an hour before the coffee cart made it to the twenty-first floor. The fearless leaders scattered to their work locations, where they had mostly already missed their coffee carts' stops.

The security trio departed hissing. Fat Fred made an unnecessary trip to the john to shake his new leader off his back, then ambled into the lounge, dropped down on the sofa, and watched the toy El trains thunder way down below the mountain of indigo water. That son of a bitch George owed him. He had given up three mainframes and his pussycat of a fearless leader, who always went with Fred's suggestions; he had blown his image by swinging from a flammable tie in a meeting; he had done all the fanny-busting while George had had all the fun: being in love, throwing memory money around abroad. But the thing that really got Fred jealous was George's performance on the obstacle course: God, if only he could do something like that. If once in his life Fred could jump up on the printer and go over the tape drives and the chillers. He would have the time of his career. He would topple consoles and crush printer covers and put his feet through the Plexiglas tops of disk drives and leave such mayhem behind that he would make Genghis Khan look like a peacenik. He could really get his jollies off on that obstacle course, yes sir. That goddam George owed him Lake Michelob just for that, just for having the kind of a body that was up to unannounced inspections. And George was forty-seven too.

Shit, Fred thought, I couldn't have done it at eighteen.

THE UTILITIES OF THE INNER PERSON

George did not care that the company had busted him back to an operation supervisor, a first-level. He stepped down one band in management, took a seven-thousand-dollar-a-year pay cut, and never looked back. The demotion was the least of his problems at the time.

Mary Ellen and Fat Fred made sure that, after his glorious obstacle-course performance, George got the best care there was. They put George in the Orchard Mental Health Clinic, which had only recently discharged Gwen. The starry-eyed, Fred Foss groupie had spent the better part of a summer there. Chicago had no better place for these things. A day of George's stay cost the utility company almost as much as a memory disk. The ratio of white smocks to patients was the highest in the city.

George figured that he would put in his time, say what he had to say, do what he had to do at the Orchard Mental Health Clinic, and move on. He did not belong there any more than the next corpo lifer. His checking in was a great acting performance, an artistic achievement. And he had always thought that his twenty-four-plus years in utilities had prepared him for just about anything.

George was wrong. Thousands of man-days spent smiling in meetings, thousands of coffee-cart arrivals, the passion of appraisals given and taken on the chin, the emotional surge of suspensions did not prepare him for a single minute of the time that was ticking in the Orchard Mental Health Clinic.

After his leap to the 3B20, an ambulance had taken the smiling George to an emergency room, where they dressed the gash on his chest, examined his back, took reams of X-rays (rolling him around a cold, shiny metal table like a meatloaf), pronounced him fit in body, and put him in another ambulance. At the Orchard Mental Health a pretty nurse had showed George his room, then had given him the ten-cent tour of the ward. The joint sucked in a lot of sun, sparkled with cleanliness, smelled of disinfectants. The nurse pointed out George's locker, his washroom, the social room, the cafeteria, the gym, the view from his window: treetops, shingle roofs, a church spire, and the pile of downtown high-rises in the distance. She then decided that there was no point in wasting time, and she took him to his first meeting in the ward.

The nurse walked George into a large conference room, and to his horror, he found himself in a performance-review meeting. A big-picture ambassador in a white smock presided over a team of kangaroos, corpo lifers, and miscellaneous dynamos. Their chairs formed a circle; there was no table to hide any part of your body behind; no one took notes, sipped coffee, or smoked. Turning crimson in the face, George had to introduce himself and describe his performance so that the others could review it. He found he wasn't crazy enough for this. His breath got short, his acting skills deserted him. He was stuck in the utility company of the inner person.

George mumbled that he couldn't recall much about what had happened. Apparently he had snapped and started jumping up and down machines on the job.

—Why? What happened? demanded the dynamos.

George tried to give them his most charming cigar-store Indian. He found that the best, most foolproof tool of his career was completely useless here. The corpo loonies and kangaroos wanted to know what his real problem was. They peppered him with deeply personal questions. They didn't like his answers, knew he was lying, insisted that he come clean. It was like being pinned down by a committee of Fat Freds who hated his guts. Red in the face, perspiring, whispering nonsensical answers, George realized that Orchard Mental Health was inner person unbound. But understanding that didn't make it any easier to survive his performance review.

After an endless while the big-picture man in the white smock designated another dynamo to be the punching bag, and the corpo lifers went after him. George's pulse dropped slightly. He was surrounded by the cream of Chicago's mad. (They still read *The Wall Street Journal* here and discussed *Tribune* editorials; they kept up with the stock market. They were returning to their successful careers, though they would be a little too soft for their decisions now.) George did not dare smile. He sat on his chair and tried to make himself invisible, remembering how those wonderful coffee carts always wheeled in a delicious moment of release. He wanted out of here. He wanted out of here now. He wanted to get up and stroll out into the street. He didn't care if he got fired from the utility company for it. He just wanted out. The inner-person kangaroos now left him alone till their interminable meeting peaked and they headed for the cafeteria in one herd. George's cardiovascular muscles were sore, and he made for the station of the head nurse. She was a tall, thin woman behind a tall shelf in a mental health kiosk.

George flashed his most composed cigar-store Indian smile at her.

—Hello, he said.

—Hello there yourself, she replied cheerfully.

This was the best care the utility-company benefits could buy, and George knew immediately that he was in trouble.

—I think I'm not off enough to stay here, he said, so I'd like to discharge myself as soon as you can get the paper work done. Which I presume won't be until tomorrow, right?

George was trying to be reasonable. He was a bureaucrat himself, and he knew about administrative hassles.

—And what is your name? the nurse asked, enunciating her syllables carefully as though she were speaking to a three-year-old.

—George Clifton.

—Mr. George Clifton. Let's see.

She started scanning a computer printout.

—I don't think I'll be on that list, George said, being helpful, I was admitted only a few hours ago.

The nurse stabbed her thin finger into his name on the printout. There followed his address, his social security number, his abbreviated description (HR BR EY BR NSM), and a field of letters and numbers that probably described his obstacle course in painstaking detail.

—Wow, he said, you sure are efficient around here.

George was still trying to ingratiate himself, but he already saw that it wouldn't work. The head nurse went with what her printout told her.

—I'm sorry, Mr. Clifton, but you'll have to see the doctor first.

—But when I checked in I was told I could discharge myself anytime I wanted.

—I'm afraid your doctor has put you on SP.

—Huh?

—"SP" stands for "suicide prevention" in mental-healthspeak, said the head nurse cheerfully.

—Shit, said George.

He felt like throwing a fit. He had entered the treatment under his own volition. They had told him he could check out in twenty-four hours if he so desired, and now this broomstick of a woman was telling him that he was imprisoned here indefinitely. He wanted to have it out with the nurse. He wanted to tell her just where they could shove this whole fucking fruitcake.

But George restrained himself. He flashed his deucemost smile at the nurse and marched back to join his fellow ventriloquist dynamos for fried chicken in the cafeteria. Entering, he was conscious of being the new kid on the block. Everyone watched him, and he held himself erect.

Like General Charles goddam de fucking Gaulle, he thought, strolling through a hail of assassin's bullets.

Then he caught himself: Jesus, the place was having an effect on him already. They were already bending his sanity: ·the fucking George de Gaulle Clifton, the fearless leader of the best nuthouse in Chicago. He would have to be awfully careful here. The one thing he absolutely could not afford to do was to display any emotion.

George was scared. They could keep him on SP forever. There was no four thirty-three out of here.

It took six days of de-Gaulling it through hails of bullets, toning down his smile, perfecting his invisibility, subduing his feelings, before George made it out of the mental ward. They added up to the most miserable week of his life. He hyperventilated his way through more meetings than he would have put in in a month of electric utilities. He sorely missed the coffee cart, thought about poor Gwen Foss a lot. She had come in wearing her rosy specks. They had wrestled them away from her, then stomped her ass-deep into voodoo dust. She must have gone through hell.

Six days after an ambulance had brought George into the ward Mary Ellen drove into the city to pick him up. She had put on the light-blue dress with the short skirt, had her hair done, sprinkled herself with her most expensive perfume several hours before leaving the house so that the natural fragrance of her eager body would have time to fuse with the aroma of the perfume. When she walked into the place George was still signing some papers. He looked up at her, mumbled hello, and bent down to the release forms again. He didn't notice her hair, her dress, or her lovely smell.

The Cliftons walked out of the Orchard Mental Health Clinic hand in hand. George seemed very distant until they had passed through the entrance and turned the corner into the parking lot. Suddenly George grabbed Mary Ellen and locked her into a constrictor embrace. She melted in his arms. Behind Mary Ellen's back George was blinking away tears.

The Cliftons stood embracing in the middle of the parking lot for several minutes. They were both survivors of their D-days. They had not held each other like this in years. George didn't want ever to let go of his precious wife. He longed to wrap her in his arms and squeeze the breath out of her and smell her intoxicating fragrance and forever feel her hard, soft, beautiful body and never release her again.

But a fish truck swerved into the parking lot, screeched to a halt, and blared its horn. The world kept on turning; the civic-leader loonies had to get their chow.

QWL V

The jukebox, the cacti, and now the battered pay phone and the opaque windows were gone. Glittering glass panes in the old frames packed the bar with the thin diluted light of an El street. You now had a view of the peeling light-green paint on the massive girders of the tracks and the grimy façade of an old factory across the street. You could not call the joint a watering hole or a gin mill anymore. It was now definitely a café, though no tourists were likely to beat down the door for the view.

—Let's get outta here, said George.

—We should of known better than to come back here in the first place, said Fred.

—You wanna stay or what?

—Well, we're here. Anywhere else we'll have to walk.

—So you wanna stay, then? asked George.

—What do you wanna do? asked Fred.

Fred had a point, and George headed to a table. The furniture was no longer grab-bag; the plastic mustard bottles had been upgraded to Dijon glass, the plastic daisies no longer bloomed anywhere on the premises. George had been released from the voodoo-dust cleaners only two days before, and Murphy was still walking all over him. But as the company never tired of repeating: QWL was an ongoing, people-oriented process. So George and Fred just had to grip their QWL torch and chase their plastic daisy and Morose Marty and his working-class clientele to some goddam where else, because the city was sure to be hiding another perfect QWL gin mill in its streets. Meanwhile, though, they had to deal with their unemployed actor. He sprinted around the bar to welcome them with phony affection.

Fred asked him, not a little brutally, what had happened to Marty.

—Ah, Marty! said the guy with a sardonic smile, Marty got canned for cussing out a customer.

—Well, did the guy deserve it or what? asked Fred.

The thing about Marty was that he was from the old school.

—Just what we liked about him, said George.

Okay, but Marty was not going to change. Marty just could not handle the new image of the place. Speaking of which, what did the gentlemen think of the new look of the establishment? There were, of course, many more improvements still to come.

—Your prices the same? growled Fred.

This bottom-line approach put the unemployed actor on the defensive. Well, yes, some of the prices were still the same, but a few items had had to be jacked up a little bit to pay for all the remodeling and whatnot.

—So how much did you jack up a pitcher of Michelob?

On a pitcher of Michelob the price adjustment amounted to roughly two dollars.

Roughly? Did they have soft prices now? Was the joint a bazaar now? Could you haggle here?

Well, no, it was exactly two dollars a pitcher, still one of the better prices downtown. And they would soon be putting some fresh-cut flowers on all the tables.

—Hold the flowers, grunted Fat Fred. Make it a pitcher of Michelob.

They sat in silence until the bartender ran back with their beer. He set down two steins and tilted the pitcher toward Fred's glass.

—We pour our own, thank you, said Fred.

He wrestled the pitcher away from the bartender, then joyfully splashed Michelob all over their table. The unemployed actor stole back behind the bar.

—Speaking about money, said George, I'm having a hell of a time scaring up the restitution dough.

—Don't tell me, said Fred.

—Yup, said George.

—How much, for Christ's sake, said Fred. Not all of it, I hope.

—Oh, no, not all of it, said George.

—How much? said Fred.

—Three grand would be perfect, said George.

—You sure you can swing the five hundred, George?

—I figure you'd have it all back in half a year—with the cut in pay and all, said George.

They sat on that.

—All my dough's locked up in retirement accounts and Mary Ellen's tits, George explained.

—Clifton, you got a hell of a nerve for a first-level, said Fred. I mean, what am I? A wet nurse? How much punishment do I gotta take? You puked on my rosebushes. You got me to wear a tie. You cost me three mainframes and a pushover boss. Now you gonna push your luck some more?

George knew from the tone of Fred's voice that his loan had just been approved. Dripping the beer all over the table, he overfilled Fred's stein.

—I *am* torching that Buick for you, don't forget, he said.

—Goddam, George, you better.

—Yup, I will. I would of anyway.

—You lucky son of a bitch, you're hitting me at the right moment, said Fred. I still feel guilty about the whole deal.

He lifted his stein with one hand and swept a puddle of beer onto the floor with the other. The unemployed actor eyeballed them but said nothing.

George knew just what Fred had meant: Gwen was cured, and now she was getting feisty at home.

—I can't tell you how much I thought about her in there and how sorry I was, he said.

—Yup, said Fred.

They sat on that for a while. George splashed the rest of the Michelob in and around their steins, then paid their last inflated bill.

—We've been at it all weekend long—no holds barred, kids crying, the neighbors turning their TVs down, the whole nine yards, said Fred. Sometimes I wonder which was better.

—Lemme say this, said George with a ton of conviction. I'd have no problem deciding which was better.

—I guess, grunted Fat Fred.

—First day in they had me thinking I was General de Gaulle.

Fred burst out laughing. George indulged a sour smile. Fred got up. There were shiny pools of beer all over their table.

—Let's go, *mon général*, said Fred. We don't want your new deuce to be mad at you.

They shook hands outside. The sleeves on George's shirt were wet with Michelob. Fred said that he would have the money for George the next day. He had a meeting to go to at headquarters— the feasibility of some new micros or something.

O meetings, thought George. O feasibilities.

THE GRAND LIFE IIIB

George was through with meetings, through Peter-Panning it to headquarters, through waiting for coffee carts. He no longer had any use for his cigar-store Indian smile. He was now back in the trenches, supervising clerks, getting a dose of the real world. Happiness was keeping the surprises down to a minimum and making it upstairs for coffee twice a day.

The company no longer wanted George's input at meetings. They sought the input of his fearless leader, the new emperor. They would get about as much out of this deuce as they had ever got out of George.

Fred Foss had given a lot of thought to the subject of George's new boss and replacement. He finally decided to appoint Wayne S. Q. Piper the new emperor of the satellite computer operation. Wayne was a fat dynamo with watery eyes, massive jowls, low forehead, and a thick head of graying red hair. His career ambition was to hang in there for two more years and retire. All Wayne cared about was that nobody rock the boat. He was status quo all the way, and he would leave George alone. He would even gladly step back and let George go on running the empire if George felt like it. And if he didn't, then the place would run on autopilot. So Wayne Piper was Fred Foss's man, and the department zapped him with an out-of-the-blue lateral: Wayne's district, Fat Fred, called Wayne into his office and gave him a week to move from a standard-size toilet bowl to the handicapped number in his new building.

Wayne was walking into a really sticky situation, and he didn't like his transfer. He didn't care to have a demoted old deuce reporting to him. Especially since the guy was a certified loony, just released from a loony bin. But his leader had made the decision, and Wayne's was to do or die as usual. He didn't have any problems with his new imperial office, no sir. In his long career Wayne had never seen an imperial office to compare with his new work location. It made him respect his predecessor, George Clifton. The old deuce had to be a dangerous guy if he could pull off having a million-dollar chair like this. He seemed real chummy with Wayne's fat district man too, which would just be Wayne's luck. The two were going to lunches together and everything else. So Wayne's last two years with the company had the makings of a real crowning touch to an illustrious career, a crowning touch that he needed like he needed a hole in the head.

Returning from the QWL quorum to Wayne Piper's empire, George walked under the El. The day was overcast, the lunch hour almost over. Around him secretaries were rushing back to their phones while corporate dynamos sauntered leisurely behind them. The CTA was sending short midday four-car trains around the Loop. George's four thirty-three was only a coffee break away.

George decided that the later he got back to the office the better. He and the new fearless leader snoozing in his old chair were in the process of defining their relationship, writing George's employment contract. So George did not want to spoil Wayne with short lunches right off the bat. He stopped at General Patton's and went through their pile of long-laced boots. He needed a pair to go with his army jacket now that the summer was almost over. He did not find anything he liked and looked at his watch. There were only two and a half hours of challenges left in the day. He decided to mosey back to his crossword puzzle.

The moment George entered the office of the first-levels Wayne called out of the imperial office that he wanted to see him. George could not believe his ears; Wayne was getting ready to bawl him out for the two-hour lunch even though George had clearly told him that he was meeting Fred Foss, their big boss. He headed into his old den with an attitude, but Wayne grinned at him jovially, and George realized that this wasn't about the lunch.

—Take a load off your feet, old buddy, said Wayne, pointing to the green sofa, where the imprint of Tanya's hot pussy still burned somewhere.

George sat down with a sigh.

—Hell of an office you put together here, Wayne went on.

—Thanks, said George on behalf of his predecessor.

—I don't know how you managed this. You pay for this stuff out of your own pocket or something?

Wayne was getting at George's cooking the memory bills of course. George just gave him a hard look.

—Aren't you supposed to be at that micro meeting, Wayne? he asked.

—Oh, no. No, no, no. Fred didn't think I needed to go, said Wayne (thinking, Shit, this is sure to be a barrel of laughs, having a big boss above and a little boss below—not to mention the wife. His last two goddam years were turning into a real boss sandwich).

—This is a big operation, said Wayne. I'm just starting to get a handle on how big. So I'm going to rely on your input a lot, George. Once a deuce, always a deuce, right? I'll be sending you to a lot of these meetings.

—I'm not sure how bad they want to see me there, Wayne, said George.

—I'm talking down the line, said Wayne. I'm retiring in two years, George, and Fred and I have definite plans for you.

George had to suppress a laugh. He put his hand on the green fabric where Tanya had once sat and smoothed it out.

—Well, you got it made here for those two years, Wayne, he said insincerely.

—Now, about this Sunday, George, Wayne said, squirming. Technically speaking, you're a supervisor now. And the way I read

this damn work schedule, you're supposed to cover this weekend.
Now, if that's a problem, I can reschedule you for later in the
month.

—No problem at all, said George, thinking electricity.

Wayne lit up as though he was hosting his retirement party
already.

—I think we're going to make a hell of a team, George, he said.

—I think so too, George lied.

George got up to get on with his crossword puzzle, then stopped
in the doorway of the imperial office and pointed at the drab file
cabinet.

—Will you need to use this, Wayne?

—Oh, no. I travel light. I don't even have enough stuff to fill up
this desk.

—Would you mind if I kept my stuff in there, then? Locked?

—Oh, no, not at all. Go ahead. You deserve to keep something
for this masterpiece of an office, said Wayne.

George now had something to look forward to—Sunday. But
first he had to make it through three more days with his arrogant
young coworkers.

On Monday morning George's former underlings started out
treating their former emperor with gleeful condescension. By late
Tuesday morning, when the big boss suddenly showed up and took
George to lunch, they realized that, even busted, George remained
a deuce. A curious species of a deuce, a working deuce. Because
George had been making sure to do his share of work around the
computer room. He wrestled with software gremlins, same as
everybody else, argued with the hardware support (and their
flowcharts that always showed that the problem really was in the
software), same as everybody else, oversaw his share of printing,
same as everybody else, did the crossword puzzle every morning,
same as everybody else. He caught himself daydreaming a lot
about another obstacle run around the computer room. He was
surprised to find out how much the first-levels were supposed to
know. They had to master the layout of fickle data circuits,
memorize the maps of gremlin city in a few notorious processors,

find their way around labyrinthine manuals, soothe the feelings of users with plausible lies, make their troops do some work. It seemed that the closer you got to the big picture the less you had to know. But George was resolved to put in the time and learn the job. This got across to his coworkers, and by the end of the week George had a mentor: Walter took personal interest in bringing George up to speed. This confirmed that the essence of leadership was to be big about the petty shit and petty about the big shit, and George set out to apply this insight in the trenches of Wayne S. Q. Piper's modest empire.

THE GRAND LIFE IIIC

After George had got through slapping her with his confession, Mary Ellen tried to make him describe the slut in detail, but it was like asking him for a kidney. So the weekend that George spent at the mental ward Mary Ellen drove downtown, parked the car in front of George's building, put on a pair of shades, and waited to get a lowdown on the bitch.

Stalking Tanya Mendez was getting to be a Clifton family tradition. She spotted Tanya the instant she appeared. A pretty, fine-boned young woman in tight jeans popped from behind the corner and floated into the building on a sail of gorgeous long black hair. She was flat at the chest but wore four-inch bright-red heels. Watching the bitch and gritting her teeth and wishing her happy bunions, Mary Ellen realized that she could be big about George's affair only as long as the other woman remained an abstraction. But once she had a name (Tanya Mendez, for Christ's sake!), a face (pretty eyes, smoldering flamenco features, not at all reassuring), a body (zero tits, yes, but also nice long legs and a bony butt—all in all, still a sultry dancer), a style (weekends abroad), the slut drove her crazy.

Sunday morning, as she was making George his coffee, Mary Ellen was really thoughtful. She knew George would be spending the day supervising the damn Mexican who had bewitched him once before. She served George his morning schooner of coffee, sat across the kitchen table from him, and studied his demeanor for any changes: he did not seem to have put any extra effort into choosing the clothes he had thrown on. He wore an open-necked golf shirt and a pair of cotton jeans (the dress code did not apply on weekends in the utility company). He had not washed his hair. He had used his old aftershave lotion. There was a speck of dried blood on his chin. Yet in her heart of hearts Mary Ellen knew that she was looking at a philandering husband.

Look, she wanted to tell him, I'll stop shaving my legs, I'll dress sleazier than she does, I'll get a pair of red shoes and crotchless panties and push-up bras if that's what it takes. Whatever she does, I can do it better.

She said nothing and only let the wraparound loosen around her bare breasts.

Sitting in their kitchen at dawn, in the fragrance of steaming coffee and the flood of slanted sunlight, the Cliftons were smiling at each other with tenderness. Mary Ellen's beautiful tits were practically hanging out of her wraparound. They looked gorgeous. George could not understand what made him chase small, hairy-nippled breasts. His inner person was in tune with Mary Ellen's. He understood her anxiety, and he grinned back sadly to promise her that he would do his best. He still loved Mary Ellen the most. He just hoped that she wouldn't start talking about what they were both thinking. He got up just to make sure she couldn't.

—Well, I better get going, he said.

There were no commuter trains on Sunday, so George had to drive to work. Twirling the coffee in her cup, Mary Ellen listened to the car pull out of the garage, then halt in the driveway. George came back in, said it was chilly out, disappeared into the bedroom, and reemerged wearing his army jacket. It instantly made him look so much younger, contemporary, open-minded, and macho that Mary Ellen wanted to scream.

He walked over to her and gave her a long kiss. He was telling her that his intentions were good anyway. She had not tightened her wraparound yet, so she pressed her gorgeous bosom against the rough khaki canvas. It felt absolutely ravishing.

George drove off. Mary Ellen went on sipping coffee in the kitchen. Strangely, the army jacket had calmed her down. While George could hardly look any more philandering, the jacket reminded her of the old calculating maximizer that George had been before he got it—and anything, anything at all was better than that.

—Oh, man, she moaned, remembering.

It had been only a few months but seemed so faraway, so unreal—it was almost a different life. She could never put up with it again. One word about George's biorhythm falling out of sync, one quote from Mussolini of twenty-eight years before, and Mary Ellen was walking out the door. So it was better to let George get whatever he had to out of his system. Besides which, their inner persons still conducted pretty deep conversations without saying a word. George still had a lot of feeling for her.

George did have a lot of feeling for Mary Ellen.

He had a lot of feeling for Tanya, too.

He slipped his plastic key card into the box by the gate of Wayne S. Q. Piper's empire and walked in on two matronly white clerks camping out in the office of the first-levels. They showed no signs of alarm—evidently this was where the weekenders operated from. George greeted them, saw that they were looking at him with barely contained curiosity, and retreated into the lounge. They had no doubt heard about his obstacle inspection in long, breathless, squealing detail. They were sure to know about Tanya and the memory deal. His former empire was a place of very few secrets, but so fucking what.

George dumped his ten pounds of local and planetary griefs for Sunday on the table (he had bought both the *Tribune* and the *Sun-Times*, because that was what Tanya had said that Walter did on weekends, and George had found out that the walrus mustache had the supervision down to a science), walked up the ramp, and

made an inspectional round of the computer room, keeping to the
floor only with a supreme effort of will. Memory disks lay scattered
around the back of the room: some weekly backups were under
way. No alarms were beeping anywhere, so George hurried back
into the office before the temptation to go up a printer and across
a band of disks became irresistible.

The weekenders fell silent when he opened the door. They must
have been talking about him.

—So what do you people do for coffee around here on Sundays?
he asked. Don't tell me you drink the dishwater out of the machine
in the cafeteria.

—Did you want us to go to Steve's? one of the matrons offered
eagerly.

—If you go, I'm buying for everybody, said George.

—That will work, said the matron.

They went on staring at him. George headed back into the
lounge.

—I like your jacket, said the second one as he departed.

Well, ladies, thought George, go ahead, cream in your pants,
that's what management's here for. Just don't forget to finish your
disk backups.

Waiting for the delivery of his second cup of the morning (he'd
be so wired by the time Tanya showed, he'd be shivering like a
small poodle), George unlocked the imperial office and slowly
sank into the imperial chair. Then he kicked his feet up. He
leaned back. The whole seat swiveled with his body. He grabbed
the back of his head in his palms the way he used to when he was
an emperor here. He sat there for a delicious minute. Goddam,
this was what he called comfort and luxury. Them were the days.
He tried all the drawers. His fearless leader had them all locked, so
George got up and swung the door of the wardrobe open. He
looked at himself in the mirror. His body now filled the army
jacket nicely. He no longer saw anything of the Bureaucrat
Returning from a Meeting in Springtime before him. Yet it had
been only five months since, on this very spot, his life had started
changing. He remembered the baboon-ass of a face he had had.

Later on in that department store too. But now that shade of hot pink seemed as out of reach as his empire. He attempted to recapture that lost feeling of shame. He had done all right as an actor once—had been able to manipulate his own emotions to fool doctors and dynamos—so he took off his jacket and tried to bring back the hot-pink feeling. It was nothing doing. George unbuttoned his shirt, tossed it over the imperial chair, and posed in front of the wardrobe half naked like the corpo psycho that he was. His face remained pale and cool as a peeled apple.

—George Status Quo Clifton, he said. The asshole with a timer, the senile aunt who keeps the cleanest desk.

The words that had once had claws no longer reached him. His character assassin Walter was his mentor these days; George himself was somebody else. He was much more used up and much younger now. He put on his shirt, grabbed his jacket, locked his fearless leader's imperial office, and attacked the crossword puzzles.

By eleven o'clock George had finished his second coffee, abandoned both crossword puzzles, skim-read through the papers. He was starting to get hungry. He marched into the first-levels' office, pulled out a beeper, turned it on, and told his ladies to hold the fort for him. If something that he should know about came up, they were to beep him. And if he hadn't made it back by shift change, then so long till the next time.

George went to Stash's and had eggs and sausage and more coffee. He had not seen Tanya in weeks. He did not want to face her after such a long time in a room of gossip-mongering women dying with curiosity. He was going to greet Tanya on his own terms.

Stash's Grill was open twenty-four hours a day, seven days a week. Very few people came there for the ambience; everyone sat on rotating stools along a noodle-shaped plastic bar, watched the grill sizzle, and discussed how close last night's numbers in the lottery had got or how slow the ponies had run at Sportsman Park. There were used-up, toothless men in torn coats, nursing cups of coffee that had to last till the liquor store opened at noon, fat paddy-wagon cops wolfing hashbrowns, parking-garage attendants in company overalls, and, all the way back, a fearless leader in a two-piece suit and a flammable tie. He was a part of the big happy family, had the most to say about the crawling asses they were doping up for today's races in Cicero even as he was speaking.

George finished his food and went out to case the neighborhood: Sunday was different downtown. The Loop El did not thunder overhead. The sidewalks seemed wide, the traffic thin. The city was a million neckties down, and the high-rises looked forsaken. On Sunday they didn't fit into the biggest of the big pictures.

George wandered into Papa Accardo's and ordered a Michelob to neutralize all the caffeine in his veins. Beer always tasted fine on company time, and George got caught up in watching the Bears game. The colors of the TV high above the bar were off. On the mauve mud the Bears were losing, but George was being paid for his civic trouble. Suddenly he was in no hurry. Tanya and the old empire weren't going anywhere. Ordering beer after beer, George lasted through all the fumbles and interceptions and blocked punts and missed field goals and dropped passes and busted tackles in garish colors. He used to earn his money smiling in meetings, but he found this a superior way of getting a paycheck. Being a first-level had deucing beat by a mile.

By the time George started back to the office the beer had all that morning coffee pretty much washed out of his system; his head felt like a cloud. The sidewalk rolled and ebbed under his shoes. When he put his mind to it he could still walk straight as an arrow. He just couldn't think of Tanya's shins at the same time. He had to stop to think anything at all, though to walk seemed a better idea than to think.

The evening weekenders were doing something out in the computer room when George walked in, so he got on the intercom. There was a long overture of static, because he had to think about how to put this, and thinking gobbled up time.

—Tanya, please report to the boss, he said finally.

His hairy angel took her sweet time, then halted in the doorway, well outside George's reach. Her hair was tied up in a careless ponytail. She had on a pink turtleneck, a pair of tight jeans, and tennis shoes. There would be no electricity—no way to stick a hand up the leg of those tight pants.

Sitting by the supervisor's desk, George raised his hands and extended them to his hot Latin lover. They stuck into the air like a busted half of a drawbridge. Tanya chose to lean on the frame of the door, three paces away, and smile a wistful smile.

—I like you, George, she said pretty goddam softly.

—That's great news for the labor relations in this fucking department, said George with beery nonchalance.

He went on offering his hands, the blood slowly draining from his fingertips.

—I'm real sorry you got busted because of me, said Tanya.

—Don't cry for me, Argentina, sang George.

It was the first thing that had popped into his head, and it made Tanya laugh while she kept staring at his hands.

—It was worth it, believe me, he said.

He did not just mean Toronto. He also meant the discoveries he had made as a result of the busted disk-pack deal: happiness wasn't just a tight pussy and electric thighs, happiness was cracking printer covers and flying down a row of Century disk drives and bouncing from chiller to chiller at forty-seven years of age; happiness was doing your civic duty and getting paid while watching the Bears eat mauve mud.

—George, you're sweet, and for an old guy, you're sexy, she said.

She was letting him down easy. There were pins and needles in his hands.

—Whoa, said George. Come on, give old grandpa a kiss.

—Listen to me, George. I'm not through talking yet.

George had to let his hands slowly down. He laid them across his thighs, feeling the blood rush back.

—If we didn't work together, I wouldn't even care that you're married, said Tanya, but I couldn't deal with having to be around you all the time when maybe I wouldn't want to anymore.

She sounded definite.

—Come here, will you.

—Abroad is different. Abroad I don't have to worry about it dragging on and on. Like I said, I like you.

George wanted to bring up the precedent but knew that it was useless. Everything was useless, because purchasing was out of the question now. He offered his hands to her again.

—Come on, a goodbye kiss for the old deuce, he ordered.

Tanya finally walked up to him and gave him her small hands, and he pulled her onto his lap, and she didn't care if her coworker saw them or not and gave him a sweet, sweet kiss.

—Goddam, Tanya, he whispered, there's gotta be a way.

—Maybe there is.

—So tell me, God damn it!

—If one of us quits here, then we can party like crazy.

—Fuck, Tanya, I'll be an old coot by then, he said, sighing wistfully. They got me for life.

—You never know.

—I know this.

—You might win in the lottery, Tanya said, giggling, and gave him one last kiss and wiggled her way out of his arms.

That's about the size of it too, George thought, watching Tanya's bony ass in the tight jeans waltz out of the office.

When his shift expired with the basic NTR, before getting into the car George strolled to the filling station down the street and picked up five lottery tickets. He had never bought any before in his life, so he had no system, no lucky numbers, no string of birthdays to ask for. He let the computer choose the numbers for him. What the hell—live by the computer, die by the computer, party by the computer.

He knew exactly what to do if the goddam machine nailed the right numbers. He would jump on top of the printer, busting its cover, then fly over the processor and onto the chillers, giving the utility company one hell of a notice.

TIME

George had wasted twenty-five years on maximizing his life expectancy. He had swallowed his vitamins, followed his routines, and beheld eternity every day at nine o'clock. And all he had accomplished was that he had squeezed his time a little, pulled it out by a few decades, made it stretch to his hundred and fiftieth birthday.

Later he had stopped worrying about Mussolini, bought the army jacket, developed his inner-person humanoid, discovered the grand life—managing only to speed up the linear time. Then he had got busted to a first-level, and suddenly he had found himself in the fourth dimension: time now began to rewind furiously while it kept creeping forward.

As in his youth, George no longer had his choice of commuter trains in the morning. He now had to oversee the shift change, so he had to make the seven fifteen. Instead of leading the general management ascent into the cafeteria, he now followed a fearless leader with the troops. As in his youth, George had to do some work on the job again while his emperor snoozed in his imperial chair. As in his youth, he sat in an office teeming with youthful dynamos and waited for his promotion to a deuce just as they did.

Most of his new peers no longer had the bodies that were capable of soaring around the computer room on top of the chillers, but George got no end of glimpses of his youthful self through them. They were eager, ambitious, easily frustrated, and no guided missiles, so they always fought to go to meetings to make a name for themselves. But Walter and his fellow supervisors rarely got invited anywhere, because in meetings they were still walking monkey wrenches. They fought for their departments too damn hard, spoke out of turn, argued for Cost-Beneficial Truths (instead of aiming at a consensus everybody could live with), got juices instead of coffee from the coffee carts, then refused to fall in line when it got to be time to wrap it up for lunch.

Off the job, George's coworkers were getting their first divorces, buying their first houses, starting families. Music no longer meant as much to them as it once had, and, gradually, they were stopping their record buying. It had also begun to dawn on them that if they went on eating whatever they felt like whenever they felt like it, they were headed for major trouble with the mirror.

George too was putting fat on his anorectic body. He too would have loved to be promoted to sweet deucing again, though he had his coworker's petty dreams of meetings and career paths out of his system. And he too had a wife who wanted a baby.

For the past fifteen years the moon had held no power over Mary Ellen's body. Then she had gone through her silicone puberty, sprouted her magnificent breasts, and started ovulating regularly. Time was rewinding, and Mary Ellen was experiencing the long-suppressed, nail-biting hope of getting pregnant. She had always wanted a baby, though never more than now. The implied lover had been a bust; the Clifton household worked best with three members; a baby could give her life the meaning the implied lover had failed to provide.

As in their youth, the Cliftons were making love all over the house on the spur of a moment. Mary Ellen would seduce George for a quickie on the sofa or on the dining room table as the soup ebbed and flowed and splashed out of the plates. Or George yelled out of the shower, asking Mary Ellen to bring him a clean towel, grabbing her when she opened the door and ripping her bathrobe off.

In fourth dimension, while rewinding, time crept forward. On the work schedule, Wayne soon had George down for another Sunday. Paging through the ten pounds of newspapers, George decided to hang in there through the clerical shift change. Tanya showed up in her trademark red shoes, a tight skirt, short sleeves. Her hair was loose and black and sexy. With the matrons eyeballing both of them, Tanya passed through the lounge, nodded to George, and sauntered up the ramp into the computer room.

George went on sucking his pencil over a crossword puzzle. The matrons exchanged glances of disappointment. George waited till they had left, then paged Tanya on the intercom. She showed up right away.

—So, Tanya, you quitting the company yet? he asked.

—It doesn't have to be me, George, she said, laughing. You can quit too.

—Damn, Tanya, I've been thinking about it.

—No luck in the lottery, huh?

—O for twenty, said George.

—Well, boss, I'm sorry, said Tanya, but I need this job. I'm not rich.

—Damn, I wish I was, said George.

George would have kept Tanya from doing her work for hours, but the other clerk paged him. He had a call. It was from Mary Ellen. She had a little surprise for him. She was downstairs by the guard's desk with it. So George smiled at Tanya, grabbed the beeper, and headed for the lobby.

Mary Ellen embraced George and said she had brought him his lunch. Their old workhorse Ford stood by the building, its windows rolled down, its radio blasting. Mary Ellen led George to its palatial backseat, where she started serving him a spectacular meal. There was a bottle of dry white wine in an ice bucket, a sausage-and-tomato salad, crab cakes, soft cheese and crackers, strawberries in whipped cream, strong coffee out of a thermos, a slice of lemon cheesecake.

George was a stud being fattened for an insemination, though he did not know it yet. He slowly tasted the delicacies, grinned at his groomed, coiffed, perfumed wife, and listened to the smooth riffs coming out of the radio. A celestial guitar ricocheted off acres of tall, windowless, sunlit walls, and George was trying to remember the last time he had put on any of his dusties at home. In music, George's time went back to Elvis. He owned every record Elvis had ever put out, but Elvis was now packing them into the Graceland cemetery. Little Richard had found religion, written a book about it, and pushed it on talk shows. Chuck Berry had long silver sideburns. The cotton picker Carl Perkins went on

224 Jan Novak

hitting them where they lived with "Blue Suede Shoes," but he was a grandpa now. Bill Haley of the Comets rested in peace, free of impostors, unimitated, unexploited, forgotten, heard only on the ghoulish history-of-rock radio shows. The satin-voiced guitar had time busted, and it was rewinding George's memories back to where music was music, while Mary Ellen held on to the moment. Her calendar said that now was the best time to make a baby girl. The Sunday streets of downtown were deserted, the traffic sliding by them thin; Mary Ellen had no underwear on. She was back to her tricks, sliding her skirt up for the old peekaboo.

A tuft of lovely curly brown hair peeked at George, and he thought, What the hell. He unzipped his fly, guided Mary Ellen on top of him, and ground his hips against her moist eager life. The radio was blasting away; cars passed by them and faces jerked around in shock. George tried to think what he would say to the kangaroos if he were busted for this.

His mind was drawing a blank.

Meeting the thrust of her stud's hips in the backseat of an ancient car, soaring toward an earth-shaking orgasm, oblivious of the eyes sliding by, Mary Ellen had a wish: she wanted the Mexican slut to pitter-patter out of the building on her whorish red spikes and see what a happy marriage George had. So letting her magnificent breasts slip out of her dress, she moved her hips with a feverish urgency and kept an eye on the front door of George's building.

Just then the beeper went off. The bitch wasn't coming out— she was calling George back in. She was clutching and grabbing and tearing him out of Mary Ellen's body. She wasn't interested in seeing the happy Cliftons and their investment making a baby.

George reached behind him and shut off the goddam beeper. He never stopped thrusting his body into hers, and Mary Ellen had a powerful orgasm. She did not get pregnant, however. Kids just weren't on the corporate horoscope for the happy Cliftons.

FIFTY POUNDS OF FAT

Three weeks into her meetings at the Orchard Mental Health Clinic, Gwen Foss still insisted that big Fred was a pretty good man. This infuriated everybody in her therapy sessions. They were all awful people, dumped on poor Fred horribly, called him names. Yes, they could not even remain civil about it.

The man was a fat pig, the fellow dynamos in the utilities of the inner person said. They had all seen him—he came around regularly—and the man just looked like a pig. Gwen could serenade him all she wanted, they said, but the only magic quality the man had was that he somehow did manage to make it inside the place, because he was a pig. And he was using Gwen. He was the most frequent visitor here, because he wanted to keep on manipulating her. The man was a snake pig, and if Gwen refused to see this, it all harked back to her lack of self-esteem.

In meeting after meeting the dynamos kept hammering away on her self-esteem. After a month and a half Gwen conceded that they had a point: her lack of self-esteem was the root of all her problems. The group then helped her to formulate a strategy for regaining it. Her self-esteem had a price. The price was fifty pounds of fat.

If Fred lost fifty pounds for Gwen, her self-esteem would shoot up. Ditto his life expectancy. If he refused, she would escalate the situation till she got her fifty pounds. First she would stop cooking for him. Then she would withhold her affection. Then she would leave him.

On paper the strategy looked great.

In reality Gwen was escalating her way right out of her marriage.

When Gwen came home from the clinic and asked Fred for fifty pounds of his fat, Fred flatly refused: things were too crazy at home

and at work to go on a diet. A diet was a major undertaking. It
required a lot of concentration and mental energy. He now needed
every ounce of it to save the ass of his love-stricken buddy George.
So Gwen stopped cooking, and Fred took over their kitchen
without a squeak of protest. He found cooking dinners very
relaxing and started making sumptuous feasts: lamb chops, ribs,
pork shanks, a goose. The kids loved it. The price of self-esteem
was going up as Fred went on gaining weight. It soon rose to sixty
pounds of fat.

In the meantime Gwen started losing weight. Every night Fred
invited her to the dinner table, and every night she locked herself
in their bedroom instead. She did not see how she could eat these
dinners when she was refusing to cook them. It was a mess, so she
upped the ante and froze Fred out of bed.

Fred did not seem to notice. He said nothing. He was so sweet
about it that Gwen felt her love for him growing again, putting her
sanity on the line. She had to leave him while she still had the
strength to escalate.

Gwen rented a navy-blue Cadillac and loaded it with toys,
books, clothes, and shoes while the kids were in school. She had
long lists of things to pack, had everything ready, was very rational
about it. The kids were going to their grandfather's house in
Pennsylvania. They were not coming back till she got her fifty
(sixty, seventy) pounds of Fred's fat. She stated this clearly in her
parting letter, which she wrote while she waited for the kids to
come back from their schools. She had one hour after Freddie's
return to herd them all into the car and be gone before Fred got
home.

As soon as Freddie stepped out of her boyfriend's car, Gwen
chased all the smaller kids into the back seat of the Cadillac. They
were all set when Freddie refused to get into the car. She ambled
past the Caddy into the kitchen, opened the refrigerator, got a
carrot, settled herself onto a chair, leaning her chin on her knees,
and calmly proceeded to munch on the carrot.

—Now Freddie, said Gwen, please do me a favor and cut out
the Hamlet stuff I know a thing or two about the classics and if

anybody's torn completely apart by this then it's me but I've just got to get the fifty pounds of your father's fat or—

—Are you crazy, Gwen? asked Freddie.

—Who the hell are you little girl to question my credentials as a psycho didn't I just spend half the summer in a mental ward didn't your own father have me committed he had his good reasons too every doctor who examined me went along with him we're talking about the best place in the city so you are questioning the whole fabric of mental health in this country by shooting your mouth off like this I mean what sort of a question is that am I crazy—

—Okay, you're crazy, said Freddie, but I'm staying here. Somebody's gotta take care of Dad.

—Will you lay off the Hamlet bit do you think it's asking too much of him to lose fifty pounds he's well over three hundred and everybody in the therapy thought it was rock bottom minimum you would not believe some of the suggestions they came up with—

—What did they suggest, killing him?

—Pretty close but look at it this way how would you like to make love to somebody his size Freddie—

—You're sick, you know that?

—Let me tell you we don't have any sex life and—

—I don't wanna know about that!

—Well you should because you're making judgments about us dear and you don't have all the facts yes it's true I've been refusing to sleep with your father till he loses the fifty pounds and I'm crawling the walls—

—You're disgusting, Gwen!

—Well that may be but here's the kicker Hamlet would love this because he hasn't lifted a finger no pun intended to get a piece of my fanny—

—What makes you think he doesn't have a mistress?

—Please stop shouting at me, said Gwen.

She and Freddie would say many more things, about Hamlet and health and fat and sex and disgust, but Freddie never wavered in her decision to stay. She went on chewing carrots and standing her ground. Gwen could not bring herself to leave without her. Then her time ran out.

A BLUEBERRY FARM

Fred was beat. Ass-busting was not very common at district level, but Fred Foss had had several balls in the air all week. He was also dabbling in agricultural real estate on the side. And he had to wrap everything up before tomorrow. Tomorrow was George's twenty-fifth service anniversary, so Fred knew that he wouldn't get a damn thing done. Tomorrow was devoted to QWL.

Walking home from the commuter station Fred barely dragged his feet. His back hurt. He had not eaten anything all day. He had been on a diet for over a week now, though he had not told anybody about it. He was going to drop the fifty pounds. Fat was his favorite part of himself, but Gwen was so hung up on it. He wanted his shrinking to be a surprise. He did not think he could handle encouragement, pep talks, praise, stats, comparisons. The whole goddam thing depressed him; he had not lost more than ten pounds in that entire week-long epoch of starvation. And those were the easiest pounds to get rid of. He had already cut out lunches and breakfasts and the Big Mac attacks, the snacks, the beer and peanuts, the commuter specials, the coffee and dough-nuts in between. He had not gone on a midnight refrigerator raid in eons. At the same time he had doubled his consumption of cigars. He still ate dinners at home, since he cooked them. He did not think he would last through the night without dinner.

Fred's plan for this evening called for a very dry martini while he delegated the broiling of the steaks to his daughters. Then he would savor his steak, lie down on the rug in the den to straighten out his back, and listen to music. He was going to enlist his boys to change the records for him. And tomorrow he was going to suspend his diet. Mixing a diet with QWL was like mixing amphetamines and gin.

Fred was looking forward to the next thirty-six hours.

Crunching a bank of dry maple leaves under his shoes, he rounded the bend on their street and saw a dark Cadillac parked in his driveway. There were people inside. It did not look good. And the closer he got the bleaker it looked. Those were his kids in the unfamiliar car, wearing grim expressions. They had sat in the car for hours, they told him, because Mom said to. Fred took in the hangers with clothes, the shoes, the toys. Then he marched the kids back into the house. The whole house clearly was one big, wide-open left field again, so opening the door, Fred braced himself for vows of poverty, or worse.

He walked right into Gwen's arms and wet, sloppy kisses, salted with tears. Gwen was a basket case again. She had been awful to him, she mumbled, she'd wanted to blackmail him by kidnapping the kids, and had it not been for Hamlet Freddie they would have been long gone she was a scheming bitch and the whole issue amounted to fifty ridiculous pounds of fat and she was going to get implants to make up for being such a shrew for going on a strike as a wife when Fred was so unbelievably good nothing short of a saint—

—Hold it a second, Gwen, said Fred.

He sent all the kids upstairs. They climbed the steps hanging their heads, unsure whether Mom would still be there when they were allowed to come down again. When they had disappeared, Fred grabbed Gwen by the shoulders and shook her, saying he certainly was no saint. If anything, he was a son of a bitch. He was paid to be one. He bullied people all day long. He schemed more than a crooked politician. He had just caused the entire organizational chart of the company to be redrawn, seeding hundreds of ulcers. He was no better with her, was he? He had refused to go on a diet, hadn't he? And he knew that she was right too. So he was very obstinate about it. He would make about as good a saint as he would an acrobat.

—Gwen, I'm a rotten son of a bitch, he concluded, so cut it out.

—You've made me feel a lot better, said Gwen.

—And I love your breasts just the way they are, said Fred.

—You sweet liar, said Gwen.

—Honest, said Fred and called the kids down.

As long as the rented Caddy was there, Fred piled everybody inside and took them out for a spin. Freddie no longer had a problem getting in the car; Fred was making jokes; the kids clowned and giggled; the ride was smooth as old cognac; Fred's back did not hurt anymore; Gwen made Fred stop, and she bought a round of strawberry milkshakes, then talked Fred into having one too. They were a family again. It had been a long summer.

At one of the lights Fred had to stop behind a cautiously driven convertible with two elderly ladies inside.

—Watch this, everybody, Fred ordered.

He inched the Cadillac forward till their front bumper gave the convertible a gentle nudge. Both ladies flew out of their car to inspect the damage, flapping their arms, getting very emotional. So Fred backed up and went around their car, blowing his horn and waving at them. This upset the ladies no end and increased the speed of their flapping. They looked like a pair of old storks clearing for takeoff, and everybody in the Cadillac just about died laughing.

They got on the expressway and drove for an hour, and nobody noticed it had been that long and nobody cared. They could not get enough of this feeling. Then Fred pulled off the expressway and took them down two-lane rural roads, through stands of trees and vineyards and cornfields. He finally stopped in front of a roadside shack with a large hand-written sign: U PICK. The shack amounted to a padlocked pile of weather-beaten boards with a torn tar-paper roof. Behind it, perpendicular to the road, there were rows of tall shaggy bushes. In the narrow lanes between them a thick blanket of wet brown leaves covered a bouncy rug of weeds.

—Where are we, Dad? the kids asked.

—We're in Michigan, said Fred. The lake and the beach are right behind those trees.

—So what is this here? asked Gwen.

—This here is our blueberry farm.

—Yay, yelled the kids, we have a blueberry farm in Michigan. Can we go in our little house?

—Damn, I forgot to get the combination of the lock, said Fred.

—What do you know about blueberries, Fred? asked Gwen.

—Well, they're bigger than caviar and not much cheaper, said Fred.

—If you know so much about them, how the heck are you going to grow them? Gwen demanded to know, but she was smiling.

—Me? I'm not going to grow them! Fred said, laughing. You are!

—Yes, Mom, you are, shouted the kids.

—No, I'm not! cried Gwen.

—Yes, you are! yelled the kids. Dad doesn't know anything about blueberries!

But Fred knew all there was to know about blueberries: blueberries had no cholesterol and they had zero fat.

THE BIRTHDAY PARTY II

George's twenty-fifth birthday party came with the territory of the fourth dimension. Technically speaking, George was only celebrating twenty-five years of ass-busting for the utility company. But among corporate dynamos this amounted to twenty-five years of life. As baptism marks the true birth of a Christian, the hiring date represented the true birthday of a fearless leader in the utilities.

George had had powerful memories of his life before his hiring date. They used to mold all his decisions. But he had knocked Mussolini off his left shoulder and wound up having a forty-seven-year-old biology with a five-month-old inner person and a twenty-five-year-old record at the employment office. Whatever age

George was, he knew that he would never make one hundred and fifty now. This was what counted.

By the standards of Wayne Piper's modest empire, George's twenty-fifth birthday party ranked as a monster bash. The president did not give George a call, the media did not surround him with a wall of light, but George's new fearless leader did pop his responsibility code for a stainless steel container of cafeteria coffee and a plastic tray of rubbery doughnuts and Danishes. An empire-wide collection paid for a large spread of goodies catered by a deli down the street. And there also were cakes and salads and fruit bowls and meatloaves, donated by the troops from the trenches. The food was laid out on a long able in the lounge. Someone had brought in a stereo, so the air was perfumed with beautiful music. Walter was snapping pictures with his Polaroid.

In provisions, George's twenty-fifth birthday party rated division level. In the outpouring of embarrassed and embarrassing emotion, the party surpassed anything George had seen in his twenty-five years of corporate life. George Clifton had never, in his checkered career, been more popular. His clerks and his coworkers not only felt sorry for him these days, they were also responding to the change in George. In his deuce days George had been held in universal contempt. He rarely took his feet off his Kremlin desk, preferred planetary griefs to the sorrows of the small picture, had no conception of what his troops did in the trenches. Then something happened and he started screwing weekenders, cooking purchasing invoices, chasing gremlins that nobody else saw by leaping around the chillers, and commanding respect. Then he got busted. He took his demotion like a man, mastered the beeper just like every other first-level, put in as much effort as his coworkers, and earned the affectionate esteem of the whole modest empire. As a bustee, as a first-level, George was an okay guy. The splendor of his twenty-fifth birthday party represented the people's appraisal of George.

At the stroke of nine, as everyone stood around the spread salivating, Walter grabbed everybody's attention and handed

George a large box wrapped in checkered gift paper with a fancy carmine bow. George was moved. Not only had they thrown a monster bash for him, now they were giving him a personal gift too. It was too much.

The box seemed pretty heavy in his hands.

—What is this? he asked.

—Open it and see, said Walter.

The tense anticipation around the room told George that this was something special. He ripped the checkered paper off the box, pried it open, and found a thermos and another, smaller box. He unscrewed the top of the thermos and the sickening aroma of chamomile tea filled the lounge. All his former underlings and clerks were laughing wildly now.

—You sons of bitches, said George, smiling.

That brought down the house. George knew what the smaller box contained: a stack of graham crackers. His coworkers were now hooting.

—What time is it anyway? George asked.

Walter couldn't get enough oxygen into his lungs to answer him.

—Ni-ine o-clo-ock, he finally pushed out.

—Hold the fort for me, I'll be right back, said George and headed for the washroom. He had never been one to spoil a good joke.

While in the john, for the sake of the old days, George decided to climb up on top of the handicapped crapper. Swinging his feet, he read the familiar poetry off the stall wall, but it was nothing doing. The eternity never showed on his birthday. He finally pulled up his polyester pants. He washed his face, then studied it in the mirror. There were fans of tiny wrinkles at the corners of his eyes, across his forehead, at the sides of his mouth. Strands of silver shone from his thick chestnut mane. Twenty-five fucking years down the drain. He had accomplished nothing in his life. Flashed more smiles than a professional goddam model, and that was the size of it. Twenty-five years of coffee. One hit of turtle soup. A dozen snails. Infinities of meetings. There had been a fine moment or two in his long career when he was sitting in his phenomenal chair, his feet kicked up on the imperial desk, when fits of wakefulness were blending with intercom dreams, but what a waste. What a fucking, goddam waste of life.

Could he have been somebody else, done something worthwhile? He would never know now. Had he had it in him to be an actor or a fighter pilot? It was too late to find out. He had got stuck in the utilities. He hadn't made the big picture. He could ask hard questions, and he did all right squeezing the fair share out of a modest empire. That was about it.

Then he realized that there had been a few things he did not need to ask back for: he had done right by Mary Ellen's inner person. There was his love affair with Tanya, the QWL, the way he had blown away Mussolini, the masterpiece of the infinite appraisal he had composed, the overtime nap on the shrinking planet of Earth, the leap from the last chiller to the higher ground of the 3B20 that he knew full well he would never make. That had been his finest moment. And he hadn't shot his whole wad yet either: there was going to be a bonfire one of these nights; a red Buick was going up in flames in the most capitalistic suburb of Chicago.

He got back into the lounge, where craft and management resumed grinning at him. George felt a little uneasy. He didn't know what to say, so he defaulted to a vintage cigar-store Indian. He sat, smiled, and listened to beautiful strings whine without energy from the stereo.

—That's the time, the plastic voice of a woman whimpered, that's the time, I feeeeeel like maaaaaaking looooooove to youuuuuuuu.

The awkward pause stretched on; the grins grew wider.

—Now, that's what I call music, Wayne said, finally breaking the silence.

Everyone burst out laughing.

Wayne was confused, didn't know what was so funny. He hadn't understood George's weird birthday gift either. He held the highest rank on premises, but the office was getting away from him.

—So, George, yelled Walter, feeling any better?

—Peter Pan, said George, and he flapped his elbows like stunted wings. What can I tell you?

That brought the house down again, and Wayne grabbed his tie with both hands and gave himself six more inches around the neck.

George had a call. The party was getting loud, so he went into the imperial office to field it. He guessed it would be Fat Fred.

—What the hell do you want now, he said, secretly hoping that it was not Fred but the president of the company.

—To congratulate you, you crab, said Tanya.

—Oh, Tanya! shouted George.

—Twenty-five years—you're an old man, George Clifton.

—Try me, Tanya, said George.

—Did you win in the lottery yet, boss?

—Everybody else's been giving me gifts, Tanya.

—Maybe, said Tanya.

By the time George had hung up he was a happy man. He had a notion to linger in the imperial office, but he heard Fat Fred's laughter booming from the lounge.

The district man's coming to George's twenty-fifth birthday party gave the lie to George's demotion once and for all. No ordinary first-level ever drew visitors of this rank. Not in satellite buildings. (At headquarters, on a slow day, a gregarious third-level might hop the elevator and ride to a first-level service anniversary party to show that he was a people person. A people person could put faces on most of his first-levels and took pleasure in demonstrating it. But no big boss went to the trouble of delving into a cab book and traveling to satellite buildings to get these minor leadership kicks. That wasn't being a people person. That was insanity.) So when Fred Foss walked into the lounge, everyone concluded that it was clearly only a matter of time before George got kicked back upstairs.

Fat Fred switched the paper plate into his left hand and pumped George's arm.

—George, you son of a bitch, I never thought you'd make it as far as this party. Congratulations.

—I never was worried about that, said George. I got big friends in high places.

—Smart ass, said Fred.

For another two hours Fred and George puttered around the spread. Fred had roast beef and sweet peppers, meatloaf and potato salad, punch, cheese and vegetables, salami, a bowl of fruit, sweets and coffee, and nuts. He was resurrecting his favorite part of himself. When most of the good food was gone Fred and George made a clean getaway; Fred told Wayne that he was taking George to a QWL special.

—Better him than me, said Wayne, grinning.

QWL VI

Waiting for the elevator, George and Fred discussed their toughest decision of the day. Decisions were what they did for a living in the utility company, but they could not agree on where to kick off today's QWL quorum.

Fred wanted to comb the working-people's gin mills on the periphery of downtown. They had to find their special conference room where Morose Marty put the pitcher to the tap. Great institutions, he argued, were not plastic daisies or jukeboxes or dusty cacti. Great institutions were bartenders with a personality.

George, however, wanted a pussy rock Reuben. He had his sentimental reasons. He knew this one big-picture greenhouse that he wanted Fred to see. And today was his twenty-fifth birthday, which he wasn't above exploiting for leverage at all.

Fred lifted his hands high above his head and surrendered. They headed for the aquarium with the frantic foreground. Chicago was soaking up the last rays of the Indian summer. There had not been a lid on the clear azure sky in days. After the dog days of August and the allergy season, the city looked its fresh breezy best. The air was warm, the El trains short and empty.

Fred didn't take to George's ferns-and-aquarium joint immediately, but he cheered up after George pulled five crisp hundred-dollar bills out of his wallet. This memory-debt installment was going to make for fine blueberry seed money. Fred was thinking big and planning an expansion of the blueberry farm already. Then he was going to build a summer house on the back of the property. First, though, he had to give up fifty pounds of fat. No, first he had to sample the fab Reubens this place made.

He ordered one.

Somehow today George didn't like the trendy goddam big-picture joint any more than Fred did. He felt stuffed, couldn't imagine swallowing a grain of rice after nibbling on the party spread all morning, much less a Reuben. Still, the bar situated them on the shores of Lake Michelob, and Fred had his Reuben on order now. So George resigned himself to watching the fish that floated above the bar like psychedelic bits of utility wisdom while waiting to see what developed.

The place slowly grew on them. In part this was a matter of timing. They had finished their pitcher before Fred got his Reuben, so they had to order one more. Then Fred pronounced his Reuben good and asked for pitcher number three, whereupon George remembered how snugly their shot glasses fit into your palm here and got a couple of whiskeys.

It was fated to be one of those days: George saw it coming. He resolved to match Fred's bladder beer for beer and shot for shot. And this time he was going to get it right, so today's QWL quorum was shaping up as, hands down, the best birthday of his life.

The QWL specialists drank, celebrated, laughed loudly, splashed whiskeys in their beer, and in due time forgot about the big-picture airs of the joint. The only thing that suffered as their celebration progressed was the QWL itself, because Fred kept on talking blueberries: planting blueberries, growing blueberries, debugging blueberries, selling the goddam blueberries, eating the fucking blueberries, and the blue shit they gave you. Then there was blueberry gear, blueberry weather, blueberry cake, blueberry jam, and blueberry pancakes. Hell, there was even blueberry wine. Blueberries were a fine fruit, but they didn't take you down to the depths of the inner person. George wanted to talk about Tanya and Mary Ellen and Gwen and about the Orchard Mental Health Clinic. So he decided to try to knock Fred off his Blueberry Hill the best way he knew how.

—Fred, he said, we haven't talked about your Buick in a while now.

—Fuck the Buick, said Fred. You know the single most fascinating thing about a goddam blueberry?

—Well, are we still torching it or what?

—Forget the goddam piece of shit.

—You're backing out, you mean?

—George, that's the past. You gotta know when to cut your losses and move on to something positive—like blueberries. Now, blueberries—

—Fuck the blueberries, Fred, said George. I'm talking justice. That alien son of a bitch thinks he's getting one over on us.

—Fuck the fucker, said Fred.

—Hold it, said George. Don't go nowhere.

He got up and staggered to the door.

—Wrong way, buddy, said Fred.

—Don't go nowhere, I'll be right back, said George.

—Damn, said Fred.

George opened the door of the big-picture greenhouse and fell out onto the sidewalk. Fred called the frantic lady bartender over.

—We're ready for another round here, he reported. D'you know what the most entrancing thing about blueberries was for me blueberry is the only berry to grow on trees so I don't have to bend down to pick'em so I won't ruin my back at harvest time harvest time jesus that's poetry isn't it harvest time I think my friend's looking outside for a place to relieve himself—

—Sir, I'm afraid that this is going to have to be your last pitcher, said the lady bartender.

—Blueberries are very good for you you know that zero cholesterol no fat at all, said Fred.

JUSTICE

George was having a hell of a time getting the coupe out of the bowels of headquarters. The driveway rose steeply the height of two floors to reach the street level. George got the usual stick shift. He managed to put the coupe into motion with a lurch in front of the motor pool attendant, but when he shifted into second gear, the engine died. He restarted it and promptly popped the clutch again. The attendant started running after him. George was not interested in the guy's wisecracks, so he lead-footed the gas pedal and concentrated on slowly releasing the clutch. This time he laid rubber right into the attendant's face. The guy was screaming now, but George gunned the coupe up the ramp and out into the sun. He roared across the sidewalk and swerved into the traffic. It was a miracle that he did not run over anybody or hit a car. But George wasn't stopping. He had justice to implement on his twenty-fifth birthday, and if he stopped, he wasn't sure if he could get the damn piece of junk moving again.

Jumping and lurching from light to light, his nostrils full of the stink of the burning clutch, George made it back to the greenhouse, where he double-parked and saved the maudlin Fred. The joint refused to serve Fred anymore. He was out of beer, out of whiskey, out of blueberry poetry. He figured that George had probably been busted for pissing in public and was gone for the day. So all Fred had to look forward to now was shrinking by fifty pounds and losing his favorite part of himself. Depression was setting in. Then George appeared in the door and it was party time again.

George was so drunk now that he operated strictly on the inner-person level. So he took one look at Fat Fred and understood how Fred felt about the place. The big-picture cocksuckers and stockbrokers were staring at them, so George gave them all a solemn finger and led his buddy out to the coupe.

—Is this where you went? asked Fred incredulously when he saw the company car.

—Yup, said George.

Fred pulled two tomes of cab books out of his pocket and flapped them in George's face.

—Look at this, George! And you're wasting time signing out coupes! No wonder you got busted.

—Where we're going, big boss, sir, a cab won't do us a bit of good, said George. Get in.

Puffing and heaving, Fred forced his body into the narrow front seat of the beater. He liked George's idea now. The alien son of a bitch had this coming to him. Yes, justice was all right by Fred. And to get it in Chicago you had to take matters into your own hands.

George burned, then popped the clutch. The engine died. Fred eyeballed him. George restarted the car and released the clutch too soon again. They leaped forward and Fred hit his head on the windshield. He bounced back off the glass, slamming his bad back into the hard seat. The engine died. Before Fred could make any comments, George quickly turned the key and propelled them forward again. The windshield flew within an inch of Fred's nose, stopped coming, fell back, and Fred took another shot on his bad back. The coupe was in motion now. George shifted, the gear box howled, the hair stood up on Fred's chest, George forced the reverse in anyway, the engine died, they halted. Fred gave George a long, hard look.

—Fuck, said George.

—George, when I get ready to hit the First National Bank, you can be my getaway driver, said Fred.

—Fucking stick shift, said George, fucking clutch. Fucking coupe. Fucking company. Fucking life.

George restarted the car, lurched forward, popping the clutch, the engine died. Fred got out and walked around to the driver's side. George climbed into the passenger seat.

—I do strike a mean match, he said petulantly.

Fred set the coupe into smooth motion without any ado. Ever

since Gwen had given away his Buick he had been driving nothing but unfamiliar cars—Rabbits, Cadillacs, fender-bender rent-a-cars, bad-news company coupes. He mastered them all instantly. It made him think that he had missed his calling. Should have been a parking-lot attendant, a valet, or a limo driver. A nice peaceful life in the trenches. Not as good as growing blueberries but definitely better than being a leader of men in utilities.

Driving toward the suburb of greed and capitalism, Fred started doubting again that justice was such a hot idea, so he made George recount his plan of action in detail. George's plan sounded great. Fred had to admit that George had all the angles covered. He had always been a sucker for justice anyway; in the end, against his better judgment, Fred decided that he would go through with it.

They got off the expressway, and George took charge of the situation. He made Fred find a hardware store, where he bought a pair of huge pliers. Their handles measured two feet. Then they cruised down the main street while George looked for a bicycle rack. He finally spotted one in front of the public library. Now George said he was in business. He'd take it from here. Fred was to go and park on the shoulder of the expressway and enjoy his justice.

George stuck the pliers under his jacket, got out of the car, and sauntered to the rack. Fred watched him from the coupe. Paying no attention to a teenage couple standing on the library steps, George slipped the pliers out of his jacket, adroitly clipped off a chain, slid the pliers back under his clothes, backed a bicycle out of the rack and led it into the street, where it took him two tries to mount it. George was not as steady as he seemed, but once he had managed to get on the bicycle and set it in motion, he stopped wavering and pedaled leisurely away. The whole thing took a minute, and nobody noticed George at all.

But Fred's heart was palpitating; his hands were shaking; he peeled off in the opposite direction, thinking this was a big mistake. He swung back on the expressway, then pulled over to a spot that overlooked the street where the DP capitalist rented his basement. He never cut the engine off. He was sorry to see his red

Buick gleaming in the sun among old Chevy and Ford jalopies. He had been hoping his beauty would not be there or that somebody would be watering a lawn in front of it or that kids would be playing in the street. But Murphy was on the side of the birthday boy: the street looked dead, the lawns unkempt; the kids were still in school; the torch was just sitting there, waiting for a match.

After an eternity George appeared at the far end of the block. He was gliding slowly toward the Buick, his feet barely circling through the air, as though he had all the time in the fucking world, as though he were out for the last spin of the season. But when he got beside the Buick his feet suddenly started backpedaling furiously.

Fred's heart kicked into overdrive when he saw this. But there was no way to backpedal out of the deal; the bicycle kept gliding forward. George passed the torch, jumped off the bicycle, stood it up, returned the few paces to the Buick, bent down, and disappeared from Fred's view.

—Thirty-one fucking payments, fourteen goddam thousand dollars, thirty-seven lousy bucks for fourteen thousand goddam fucking dollars, said Fred in the coupe.

He tried to picture all the stubs left in his payment book. The payment book. The thick payment book. The thirty-one checks he still had to mail. But he wasn't able to wrestle his mind off George. His headache first-level had to be crawling around the oil-stained cement striking matches, cupping his hands around them.

—Thirty-one coupons, fourteen grand for thirty-seven fucking lousy bucks, he went.

The street remained dead so far. The FBI wasn't leaping out of the potholes, jumping from the bushes, diving off the roofs just yet, but it was all a capital mistake anyway. He should never have let George do this. He had to speak louder to grab ahold of himself or else he was stomping on the gas, peeling off, never seeing the Buick or George again in his life.

—Thirty-one lousy goddam fucking piss coupons, he went as cold sweat slithered down his back.

He had the brains of a virus. How could he have been such an idiot? What had possessed him? How could he ever have conceived of this? Why would anybody who had so much going for himself— five great kids, fifty lanes of blueberries—put it all up for this tiny jolt of justice? They weren't going to get away with this. He knew it for a fact. Both their careers were over. He didn't need to worry about parting with the favorite fifty pounds of himself anymore. In Cook County jail they were going to fix him in no time. He was an addled scatterbrain, a moronic bonehead, a goofy imbecilic asinine whacky loony harebrained fool.

—Thirty-seven fucking lousy bucks, thirty-seven fucking lousy bucks, shit, thirty-seven lousy fucking bucks.

Finally George popped back up. He moved unbelievably casually. He moseyed over to the bicycle, kicked the stand up, got on, and wobbled away as if time wasn't money. Fred watched him with bated breath while his Buick kept on gleaming in the sun.

An immense relief loosened up Fred's contracted stomach muscles.

—Yeah, yeah, yeah, he said.

Something had gone wrong. Or else George had had a last-minute change of heart. But he had not gone through with it.

—Yeah! Yeah! Yeah!

George was a genius. What judgment. What cool too. God-dam. George was a real hit man, bless him. Fred loved the guy.

—YEAH!

All of a sudden three long tongues of yellow-red flame stuck out from under the chassis of the Buick. They flickered, contracted, licked the side of the car again. A second later justice was rendered; the Buick was a ball of fire; flames were lashing up ten feet into the air.

The air wave of the explosion rocked the coupe; Fred's heart stopped, then cranked over again. At the far end of the deserted street, lazily, George was rounding the corner. His sluggish feet drew the same size circle in the air over and over again; the mode was utility-company; the mood was of a piece with the sunny afternoon at the close of the Indian summer.

THE GRAND LIFE IV

The Schwinn ten-speed purred under George. It rode so much lighter and smoother than his ancient workhorse that there was no reason to rip it off; he wouldn't get any exercise out of it at all. He stroked its pedals for five more blocks. When he saw the light-blue company coupe parked two blocks away, near the entrance ramp of the expressway, he jumped off the bicycle and leaned it against a shaggy hedge fence. The ten-speed sank into the branches, and George ambled toward the getaway car. In his ears he heard the dumb plastic-voiced ditty of this morning—I feel like maaaaaaaking looooooove to youuuuuuuu. He was whistling softly; life was grand.

George found he got off on breaking the law. It struck him as so much easier than making himself invisible behind a smile at a meeting in the utilities. His mind had been lucid from the moment he had bought the pliers. The booze had burned itself out in his head, and he knew that there was no way for anything to go wrong. Not a chance. Never. He owned this place, should have been doing this for a living, would have been sitting pretty by now. But as a fearless leader had said to him once, them were the kinks in the wood.

George got into the coupe, slid the pliers up from his pants and down out of his jacket, threw them on the backseat, composed his best cigar-store Indian smile on his face, and turned to Fat Fred. But Fred went on staring straight ahead. His face was white, his hands shaking; beads of sweat covered his forehead like a rash.

—Yup, said George.

—Jesus Christ, gasped Fred.

—Hope you remember this at appraisal time, boss, boasted George.

—Shit, said Fred.

—What's the matter? You don't look so hot.

—I don't know if I'll be able to drive, George.

—I'll drive.

They switched seats, and George lurched into the traffic. The car died. George's lucidity still did not extend to the stick shift. Behind them cars were honking. Fred sat slumped over in the passenger seat. George restarted the engine, popped the clutch, turned the key off and on again, the motor cut back on, and with three jerky leaps, the clutch burning, George resumed their getaway.

—Fucking stick shift, he said.

—I'm such an unbelievable asshole, replied Fred after a while, such a jerk idiot imbecile moron dumbass stupid brainless shit-head—

While George leaped and lurched back to the pile of high-rises Fred's breathless litany went on and on. George let Fred talk it out of his system. It was EOJ justice, and there was a plastic voice singing in his head, I feeeeeeel like maaaaaaking looooooove, I feeeeeeel like maaaaaaking looooooove—end of job and the same words repeating themselves over and over again.

By the time they pulled up to headquarters Fred had revived enough to chauffeur the coupe down into the motor pool. He knew the fearless leader in charge of company beaters pretty well. Nevertheless he preferred that George should wait for him outside. George paced the sidewalk for a few minutes. Then Fred emerged from the bowels of the building, and he was the old fat dynamo, waving a hundred-dollar bill in his hand.

—I don't wanna hear another word about blueberries, said George.

—What the hell's the matter with this moribund party? said Fred and flagged down a cab.

He commanded the cabbie to head for the QWL part of downtown. He was going to find Morose Marty and buy him a drink, and that was that, and not a goddam thing else mattered.

On the edge of the Loop they found several gin mills and climbed out of the cab. Six-car happy-hour El trains were roaring overhead full of sober dynamos, tired secretaries, and fearless

followers. They were giving Fred a headache, so they ducked into
a bar. There was no trace of Morose Marty there, but they ordered
a beer and a shot anyway. The gruff bartender couldn't break
Fred's hundred-dollar bill, so George got the drinks, and Fred
broke the hundred next door. They were taking their search
assignment seriously, and, crossing the street, moved down the
block, entering each and every watering hole and getting a beer
and a shot at every bar they located.

Given their conscientious attitude, finding Marty seemed only a
matter of time, because all these places had the makings of fine
QWL quorums: lonely drinkers, cacti, jukeboxes, ancient pay
phones, mismatched tables, working-men's specials, baseball caps,
morose bartenders—but there was no Marty.

George kept dumping his shots in his beer, while Fat Fred
preferred his substances separate. Pinkish beige started to seep back
into Fred's cheeks.

—Oh, by the way, said Fred in watering hole number five, I'm
on a diet.

—No shit, said George.

—Lost ten so far, going for sixty, said Fred. And this time I'm
having my apron cut off.

—Oh, by the way, said Fred as they were stepping out of
watering hole number six, I'd pay a lot of money to see that
asshole's face right now.

—You're talking baboon's ass for sure, said George.

Twisting the top off a golden-papered bottle of beer in watering
hole number eight, Fred developed his thought further.

—We did it, didn't we, he said. Goddam, we did it, George.

—Yup, said George, struggling with his twist-off cap.

—Oh, by the way, said Fred in a gin mill down the street, we
got an airtight alibi too—air fucking right, buddy. Don't worry
about a thing.

—I ain't, said George.

—I'm serious, said Fred, I mean it.

—Me too, said George.

In the next bar Fred threw his shot in his beer, so George now kept his poisons separate. He was losing count of how many places they had searched; he ripped off a fistful of checker pieces from a table near the washrooms. He was on a crime binge tonight, felt great, half the people in the place had seen him pocket the checkers too.

The street ahead of them looked promising.

—You want my shot, buddy? asked George.

They were somewhere anyway.

—Still no fucking Marty, said Fred, downing George's shot.

—Maybe today's his day off, speculated George.

—That motherfucker, said Fred.

They were back out on some street, where the evening was turning chilly. Their arms were pretzeled around each other's shoulders; Fred was holding George up. George was holding on for dear life as they staggered from one end of the sidewalk to the other. On Fred's side they slammed into an El column. It didn't hurt, gave them a location: they were still in El country. They ran into a wall on George's side, squashing George like a bug, which didn't hurt, gave them more coordinates: the wall rose up way above the clouds, so they were still downtown anyway.

—I ripped off a bunch of checkers somewhere, said George. Let's go play checkers.

—This is bullshit, said Fred, burping.

George planted his back squarely against the wall and went through his pockets. He had millions of them. This fucking army jacket was fabulous, one of a kind, the best goddam thing that had ever happened to him. He found a handful of plastic jetons in his breast pocket. Goddam, life was great. He showed them to Fred.

—Goddam, said Fred.

—Yup, said George.

—You need a board, birthday boy, said Fred.

—Gotcha, said George.

He attempted to flag down a cab. There were billions of cabs. They were all empty too. But it was the survival game, the natural selection of the fittest fare, and they had a problem. No one would select them. An eternity of hailing later, one Yellow Cab finally stopped. Fred commanded it to a liquor store; no problem breaking a hundred there. George waited in the car, thinking about Mary Ellen. She was quite a gal. Too bad she wasn't with them. She was a champ in checkers anyway. You looked at her blouse and lost. Fred came back, brought a bottle of Rémy Martin, a sixpack of Michelob, a fistful of beef jerkies, beer nuts, cigarettes for the cabbie. Fred worked hard, thought big.

The cabbie said something. Fred ripped the cigarettes out of his hands and pitched them out the window. The cabbie said no more. He let them off at Oak Street Beach. Fred gave him both cab books.

—I'll have 'em print some more, he said.

—Would you, gentlemen, like me to wait for you? asked the cabbie.

—Why don't you, said George.

—Ten-four, said the cabbie.

George needed hardware, software, you-name-it support. He knew where he was headed, though—wasn't going to be sick yet, couldn't move. As a consequence he couldn't get there. Fred was a good friend. He dragged him to the stone gazebo on the lakefront. The sun was setting right behind the city; nothing escaped them.

—That a silhouette or what? asked Fred, burping.

Sure was, tar black. You couldn't see Chicago's billion windows. There were just acres and acres of dark walls and the bright-red sunlight bleeding through the street cracks. Thick shadows of buildings stretched way into the lake. You could cut them with a buzz saw. In the steps of the limestone gazebo, there were granite checkerboards. Several red-nosed chess players were staring at them.

—Who farted? yelled Fred.

They looked away. It was cold too. The funny thing was, the evening seemed plenty warm to George and Fred. They counted their pieces. they came up with thirteen jetons. George grabbed six and won. Fred claimed nine and won. The colors did not matter: you just had to remember who had what. Something had happened. They were down to eleven checkers, but good distribution: five black, five white. What the hell—they played on, George killed Fred. Fred was sick of checkers, games, Americans. They wandered on, leaving the jetons on the board, taking swigs out of the bottle, munching on jerkies, sipping beer. George remembered the checker pieces. They were his, everybody in that bar had seen him rip them off. He staggered back and tossed them into the waves. From up close the lake was no hill, wasn't indigo. It was khaki as far as the shadows reached, spinach beyond, white seams everywhere. They stumbled on a bench. They agreed to sit down, didn't have to call a meeting on it. The waves splashed, broke, licked the cement incline that rose up to them. Before them bicyclists were weaving through joggers and roller skaters. Many were sweaty young women, nothing else wrong with them.

—Oh, maximizers, yelled George.

Fred was embarrassed, had a bigger voice, could outyell George anytime.

—NICE ASS, he hollered.

Fred was a people person.

THE BIG PICTURE

On a bench overlooking a busy jogging path sit an elephantine man in an open-necked shirt and a thin guy in an unzipped army jacket. The thin guy has a red-and-gold silk tie thrown over his shoulder. The fat man is holding a fancy frosted-green bottle and he is conducting with it. They are both crooning their lungs out.

—Goddam, life is grand, gasps the thin man into their breathing pause.

—I feeeeeeeel like maaaaaaaaking loooooooooooove, they roar in two-part harmony.

—Yup, answers the fat conductor as they inhale again.

—I feeeeeeeel like maaaaaaaking loooooooooooooove, they go.

There are many women passing below them on bicycles, roller skates, in jogging shoes, in pumps, on high heels. They do not linger near the beach. The white tongues of khaki waves keep on licking the salt-and-pepper cement; they are the active ingredient. They guarantee that silicone cups are going to get safer, acres and acres of walls are going to be thrown up, meetings shall go on peaking with the arrival of a coffee cart, blueberry trees shall go on blooming, and life will yield doses of grandeur.

ABOUT THE AUTHOR

JAN NOVAK emigrated from Czechoslovakia at the age of 16, in 1969, and received his B.A. and M.A. from the University of Chicago. The author of *The Willys Dream Kit*, a novel, and *Striptease Chicago*, a collection of short stories in Czech, Novak lives in Chicago with his wife and children. He works, as he has for the last eight years, as a computer operations supervisor.